Bolan cocked an eyebrow. "The Company asked for help?"

Brognola shrugged. "Their best operatives are running in Pakistan and Iraq these days."

"So I'm supposed to enter a section of the city of Split that is a law unto itself. A place where everyone is pretending to be something they aren't. Then I start following up leads to find two people who have disappeared, but whose disappearances may or may not be linked."

Brognola nodded. "Yeah. That about sums it up. But don't forget, if anyone suspects you're an American agent, there are about one hundred intelligence and terrorist cells who'll try to kill you."

Bolan leaned back. "When do I leave?"

Don Pendleton's Mack Bolan®

Interception

A GOLD EAGLE BOOK FROM
WORLDWIDE®

TORONTO • NEW YORK • LONDON
AMSTERDAM • PARIS • SYDNEY • HAMBURG
STOCKHOLM • ATHENS • TOKYO • MILAN
MADRID • WARSAW • BUDAPEST • AUCKLAND

First edition May 2009

ISBN-13: 978-0-373-61529-2
ISBN-10: 0-373-61529-9

Special thanks and acknowledgment to
Nathan Meyer for his contribution to this work.

INTERCEPTION

It is not the critic who counts, nor the man who points out how the strong man stumbled, or where the doer of deeds could have done them better. The credit belongs to the man who is actually in the arena, whose face is marred by dust and sweat and blood; who strives valiantly; …who knows great enthusiasms, great devotions; who spends himself in a worthy cause; who, at the best, knows in the end the triumph of high achievement, and who, at the worst, if he fails, at least fails while daring greatly.

—Theodore Roosevelt,
(1858–1919)

I'm not one to stand idly by while the bullies of the world intimidate the weak. It's not in my nature—nor will it ever be. I'll take my last breath defending America.

—Mack Bolan

To the men and women who defend our nation

PROLOGUE

In Croat the name of the suburb was Trg Brace Radic, which meant Old Town. It was underpopulated, filled with ancient structures and isolated from the more urban areas of modern Split and in the shadow of the venerate Milesi Palace.

At that time of night it was a place where people minded their own business and kept to themselves. Inside an abandoned, rundown house Mack Bolan stood facing two men. One of the men was Andrew Vasili, a Croat intelligence official turned mercenary information broker, and the second was his bodyguard.

Vasili opened the envelope Mack Bolan had just handed him. The man ran a thick thumb over the neatly bundled packets of euros. He grunted to himself and nodded, satisfied with what he saw. He turned to his bodyguard and nodded again in a single, sharp motion.

The bodyguard removed his hand from the pistol grip of his silenced H&K MP-5 and reached into his coat pocket, withdrawing a silver flash drive that he handed to Bolan, who made it disappear like a stage magician.

Suddenly the glass shattered with a sound like ice in a whiskey tumbler. The shards flew through the air, then fell to the floor as the bodyguard stiffened. The man's back arched and his eyes grew wide as the heavy-caliber round struck the flesh of his back with a wet, thick slap that was impossible to mistake.

A second later the report of the rifle rolled like thunder through the broken window and Bolan was on the move. The bodyguard turned as he fell, twisting with the force of the round and tumbling like a drunk on the deck of a pitching ship. Blood burst from his mouth in a violent cough as Bolan was dropping and going for his weapon.

Vasili, the informant, shouted as his bodyguard died, letting an expensive black attaché case drop like a stone to the filthy floor. Then he reacted with the honed reflexes of a man primarily concerned with his own survival.

The blood splashed Bolan's face, warm and sticky and smelling of copper. He heard car tires crunch across gravel and the race of a vehicle engine. Crossing quickly to a second window beside the room's front door, he parted the limp curtains. Outside a dented and grimy Stobart pickup with its lights off pulled to a stop in a short slide, raising a cloud of dust beside a long figure holding an SKS automatic rifle.

Asian men wearing green headbands and street

clothes leaped from the back of the truck. Bolan counted four men, plus a driver and passenger in the front seat. That made seven with the first shooter. Time sped by like frames on a film reel. He saw a RPG-7 and a RPK machine gun standing out among the thicket of AKM barrels.

Of course, he thought to himself, turning. The exchange couldn't have gone smoothly. It hardly ever did.

Bolan realized he and Vasili would never make it to the back door in time to save themselves if the hit squad was allowed to execute its plan unchallenged. He wasn't sure who the team of assassins answered to, but it was obvious they had come loaded for bear.

Bolan would need to put a monkey wrench in their well-oiled machinery if he wanted to live.

The Executioner drew his Beretta 93-R and shoved the pistol through the cheap glass of the narrow window of the dilapidated and abandoned house the confidential informant had demanded as a rendezvous point. He cut loose, the 9 mm Parabellum slugs ripping out hard one after the other.

The Asian with the RPG-7 went down on one knee as a double tap struck him center mass. The hit squad responded instinctively to the ambush fire and scattered, their singled-minded purpose having been disrupted by Bolan's aggressive action.

He kept pulling the trigger as he swept the belching muzzle of the machine pistol toward a hooded killer trying to bring the big RPK machine gun to bear. Bolan hit him in the shoulder, then skipped two more rounds past him and into the hood of the Stobart pickup.

An AKM assault rifle opened up from the squad, and 7.62 mm rounds burned through the stamped metal-and-plastic reinforced faux wood of the house's battered door. Slugs whizzed into the tight living room, and then the RPK opened up. Bolan dived to the floor and scrambled down the short, narrow hallway that ran from the living area-kitchen to the single back bedroom.

Just ahead of him the Croat information broker crawled along the floor, as well, heading for the back door, which Bolan had jimmied to enter when he'd first arrived on the uncertain scene. A fusillade of metal-jacketed bullets tore through the fragile structure. Glass shattered as wood and plastic housing materials were shredded under the onslaught. Vasili's black attaché case was ripped apart, and papers exploded into the air like ragged confetti. The furniture disintegrated as more heavy-caliber main battle rifles joined the barrage.

The RPK cut loose in long, distinct *braps* of fire as the machine gunner dragged the weapon along the length of the one-story house. A mildew-stained refrigerator was blown apart as rounds punched through the outside wall and bored into it like lead-jacketed sledgehammers. Bolan's own carry-all, still resting on the kitchen table, was ravaged in a relentless cross fire, and his expensive electronics were pounded into useless, unrecognizable pieces. The machine gun severed the door from its hinges and the perforated structure blew inward.

A green tracer round struck a cushion, igniting a small fire on the ratty couch. A cheap clay vase, empty of flowers, was shattered and another ComBloc tracer round sliced through the flimsy window curtains and set them on fire.

In the hall Bolan scrambled to his knees as Vasili reached up and opened the back door. The big American's ears were ringing from the furious din, and he knew it would only be moments before another gunman in the death squad retrieved the fallen RPG-7 antitank weapon and turned it on the single-story home.

Vasili pushed open the back door and jumped out of the house over the short porch steps and onto the ground. Bolan leaped up after the man and followed him out the door. What happened next unfolded too quickly for Bolan to consider; he merely reacted on instincts so finely honed by continuous exposure to violence that they were evolved to nearly preternatural levels of capability.

The leader of the death squad had placed a security gunner on the rear door in a textbook setup. Bolan spotted the muzzle-flash from the weapon of an Asian killer lying in a shallow depression beside an old metal trash barrel. The man's bare arms were alive with brightly colored tattoos, indicating his affiliation with either the Japanese Yakuza or one of the Hong Kong triads. Bolan had an impression of a burst hitting Vasili and the Croatian criminal shuddering under the impact. As he heard the sound of the gunfire, the Executioner was already twisting in midair. His feet hit the ground, and he sank into a crouch to absorb the impact, his pistol firing a triburst on the fly.

The sniper's head jerked back and his green headband lifted off with a Frisbee-like section of skull and went spinning away into the bushes by a low stone wall. The man's ruined head slumped into the dirt, and Bolan sprang forward out of his crouch. His feet pounded hard against the brown grass of the tiny back lawn as he sprinted the fifteen yards to the downed enemy gunner.

Bolan slid into place beside the corpse and from behind him the house rocked on its ancient foundations as the RPG-7 warhead exploded inside. Jets of flame erupted from shattered windows and the open door. Within seconds, oily smoke poured into the night sky, and a wash of heat rolled into Bolan like a furnace blast. He felt a sting of piercing impact on the big muscles of his shoulder and a distant part of his mind cataloged the shrapnel wound.

Reaching down with his left hand, he grabbed the bloody hit man's limp arm. He rolled the dead man over as he slid the still smoking Beretta 93-R into the waistband at the small of his back. The barrel was warm on his skin. He snatched the AKM used to gun down Vasili and then pulled a Croatian army grenade from the ammo pouch on the fanny pack belt cinched around the dead man's waist. The canister-shaped device was an RG-42 antipersonnel hand grenade, 4.6 inches long and it weighed 436 gms. The deadly little bomb had a blast radius of 75 feet and had come from Soviet stocks when

Split had still been Yugoslavia. Bolan thought it felt damn good in his hand.

The Executioner rested the AKM assault rifle across his knee and jerked the pin from the hand grenade. He grabbed the Kalashnikov and rose, the fingers on his left hand holding down the safety lever on the grenade. He felt the blood from his shoulder wound roll down his back, sticking his shirt to his skin.

Bolan realized speed and aggression were his only allies now. He jogged toward the corner of the smoldering house. As he reached the front of the structure, he released the lever on the hand grenade and the tightly depressed spring shot the metal strip out into the air away from him. Bolan slowed to a walk and peered around the final corner, the grenade cooking off in his fist.

He saw the death squad approaching the door of the smoke-filled house, arrayed in an inverted V formation like geese flying south for the winter. The driver of the Stobart pickup remained behind the wheel of the running vehicle. Bolan tossed the grenade underarm toward the mysterious Asian death squad. It bounced once and rolled toward the team like a can of soda spinning off a desk and across the floor. One of the gunmen caught the motion and turned, his AKM coming up.

Bolan snapped his hand onto the front stock of his own AKM as he pulled the weapon's trigger. He scythed the man to the ground, then peeled back around the corner of the little house, feeling the heat from the fire burning inside against his back. He heard men scream in warning then the grenade blast silenced them.

Angry hornets of shrapnel rattled into the ruined building and buzzed through the smoky air. Bolan rolled back around the corner of the house, snuggling the AKM into the crook of his shoulder like a man hugging an old friend.

The hit team lay on the ground. Some men tried to sit up while others reached frantically for weapons knocked clear by the blast. Bolan raced forward and opened up with controlled sweeps of the AKM muzzle, hosing them down. Spent shell casings arced out of his weapon until it ran dry.

Bolan threw aside the hot, smoking assault rifle and reached for the Beretta 93-R secured behind his back. He spun toward the pickup, falling into a modified, two-fisted Weaver stance with the machine pistol.

The driver had already thrown open his door and jumped from behind the wheel. But, like the rest of the hit squad, the man had brought an AKM assault rifle for the attack and the long weapon banged against the steering wheel and the side of the cab as he tried to yank it free and bring it into play.

Bolan put four rounds through the gap of open vehicle door and windshield in less than a second. All four 9 mm Parabellum rounds found their mark and the man staggered back, dropping the rifle so that it clattered off the truck and onto the ground. Blood rushed in a river from the gunner's ruined throat and jaw as he spun. His feet tangled up in themselves and he went down without a word to bounce hard off the blood-splattered cobblestone.

Senses amped to a peak level by adrenaline, Bolan heard a moan at his feet, turned, dropped his pistol muzzle and put a bullet in the man lying there. Then he started toward the still running Stobart pickup. He dropped the 93-R pistol's magazine from the butt grip and slammed home one of his two backups. His finger found the catch release and the handgun shuddered in his hand as the bolt slid home and chambered a round.

Bolan climbed into the pickup and slammed the door closed. He stood on the gas and cranked the wheel hard, turning the vehicle in a tight circle and leaving rubber skid marks across the pavement. As he straightened the nose of the European pickup back toward the road, his front tire rolled over the body of the driver he'd killed with the 9 mm pistol.

The steering wheel shuddered in his grip as first his front and then his rear tires rolled over the body. Without a backward glance, Bolan sped away into the night.

JACK GRIMALDI had the sleek Saber jet running flat-out over the Atlantic Ocean.

In the back of the private, executive-class plane Mack Bolan had dressed his wounds, then cleaned up and changed clothes. Immediately upon takeoff he'd dumped the contents of the flash drive he'd purchased from Vasili into an Epsilon Protocol Encryption laptop provided to him by Stony Man Farm's mission controller, Barbara Price.

The powerful little computer had downloaded, security checked, encrypted and sent the information contents of the flash drive to Stony Man's mainframes via Keyhole satellite. Now, an hour later, Bolan had just popped the top on a cold beer to wash down a fistful of ibuprofen tablets when the call came in.

"It's Barb at the Farm," Grimaldi called through the open cockpit door. "There's been an update from that Croatian information you passed on."

Bolan placed his beer on a nearby table after swallowing his antiinflammatory pills, then picked up the secure satellite phone lying next to him.

"Go ahead," he said.

"Striker," Barbara Price said. "I've already given Jack new coordinates. We learned something urgent from that file you gave us. Something new has come up."

"When doesn't it?"

He felt the plane shift course as Jack Grimaldi cut the Saber jet onto new coordinates.

And so it began.

CHAPTER ONE

Mack Bolan jumped from the jet at forty-five thousand feet, opened the canopy high and sailed miles in from out over international waters. He wore a thermal suit and used supplemental oxygen to help him withstand the rigors of high altitude.

Over time the Executioner had come to excel in such airborne insertion operations. The nature of the deployment was such that stealth was an even higher priority than the lightning-quick speed of heliborne and fast-boat delivery methods. Often it was by high altitude low opening—HALO—jumps. He'd leave the jump plane at up to thirty thousand feet then free fall down to a height of fifteen hundred to a thousand feet, waiting until the last possible minute to deploy for short exposure over the target.

In the HALO jumps, as in this instance, Bolan's insertion relied not only on the extreme altitude of the plane, but on great, even vast topographical distance, as well.

THE COUNTRY WAS an armed camp. North Korea contained a civilian population motivated and conditioned to a degree of loyalty not seen since the Spartans. To help ensure Mack Bolan's probability in remaining uncompromised by a chance encounter, Stony Man Farm, under mission controller Barbara Price's direction, had picked a landing zone in a remote section of very rugged terrain in the mountains above the objective. After being outfitted at a Joint Special Operations Command forward operating base in Djibouti on the way in, Bolan was now dressed in complete tree/cliff landing gear: padded suit, football-style helmet with full face mask, reinforced ankle guards. The Farm's planning called on him to make a tree landing in an isolated valley, rappel from the canopy, then make his way down a steep crevice and into the Yellow River tributary.

He carried nearly two hundred pounds of mission-essential equipment, weaponry and survival gear for the operation. The mission plan called for infiltration into the site by means of the river, so he jumped with a Draeger Rebreather scuba system. Such an ops plan was horribly "Hollywood" in execution as such a plethora of skills and independent stages greatly increased the operative's exposure to the double threats of military SNAFUs, including the omnipresent threat of a mission-ending injury.

Given the choice, Bolan would have preferred walking in, cutting through the DMZ to the south by means of routes already secured and verified by Special Forces teams assigned full-time to covert LRRP/SU ops in the no-man's land between the north and south of the Asian peninsula.

But as happened so often when Stony Man Farm and the Executioner were called into play, the operation depended on complete invisibility while at the same time remained hamstrung by timing. The train Bolan intended to intercept was going to be on target on time, and only for that time. The Oval Office wanted a surgical strike with no collateral damage.

The land was arrayed below the plummeting commando in an uneven checkerboard of blacks and grays. He flared his canopy hard at the last moment, attempting to curtail his momentum as the ground rushed up. He heard then felt his rucksack crash into the copse of trees, then two heartbeats later his feet, tightly clamped together, broke through the mesh of interwoven branches at the top of the canopy. He kept his legs pressed together as gravity yanked him down through branches and tree trunks. He took several bone-jarring impacts before his parachute caught and his neck whiplashed hard into the special support collars leaving him sore but unharmed.

Taking stock of his surroundings, he looked down and saw he was about forty feet from the ground, caught halfway up a good-size evergreen. His chute seemed securely trapped above him, but he was too far out from the main trunk for the branches to have enough girth to support him.

Hitting his quick-release clip, Bolan let his rucksack fall, then pulled himself along the branches of the pine tree until he was on a more stable support. He disengaged the jump harness and secured his nylon ribbon of a rappel cord from a pocket in the lower leg of his padded suit.

He slipped the strong, flat cord through a D-ring carabiner positioned at his waist and kicked away from the tree, dropping to the ground in a smooth arc. On the forest floor he quickly removed his jumpsuit, helmet and supplemental oxygen along with the rest of his rappel harness. He made no effort to retrieve his chute and paid only cursory attention to camouflaging the gear he was leaving behind. If there was anyone close enough to stumble onto it in the dark, then the mission was probably blown in any case.

From his pack Bolan secured first his primary weapon, a Chinese model AKM with folding paratrooper stock, and a night-vision-goggle headset. Like a modern-day version of the childhood boogeyman, he hunted at night, could see in the dark and was armed with fearsome claws. Straining against the weight, Bolan slipped into the shoulder straps of his rucksack then took first a GPS reading before double-checking his position with a compass to verify his start point. Satisfied, he set off down the steep, narrow valley toward the dull gleam of the wide river below.

In many ways his cross-country navigation was almost more dangerous than the HAHO jump, or even than the potential difficulties he faced in his coming swim. Every model of night-vision device available offered depth perception difficulties. The scree-covered terrain was rocky and steep, making his footing uncertain, and he was cutting down not an actual path but rather a rain wash gully. With two hundred pounds on his back each step downhill sent a biting jar through his knees and lower back, threatening to turn his ankles constantly as his heels came down on loose gravel and powdered dirt. The topography was so steep and uncertain Bolan spent half the two-kilometer descent sliding on his backside as opposed to on his feet.

By the time Bolan reached the floor of the wash he was drenched in sweat and breathing hard. He squatted among the cover of some weeds and cheat grass behind a row of dense shrubs well back from the two-lane blacktop that ran parallel to the river, resting long enough for his heart rate to recover and his breathing to even out. He washed down a couple of the "Go" pills the military gave their pilots on long flights with a full canteen of water. He then opened his rucksack and broke out the dive gear. By his watch he noted he was seven and a half minutes ahead of his pre-op planned time schedule.

With such a strenuous overland hike and steep descent he had been unable to don his wet suit until just prior to submersion or risk heat fatigue and dangerous dehydration. He quickly stripped and donned the neoprene wet suit. Once he was dressed, he pulled on North Korean army fatigues over the insulated swim gear and retied his combat boots.

He was stripped down to the essentials for his swim, and other than his primary weapon everything he needed was tightly fitted inside an oversize butt pack or secured across his body in the numerous pockets of his fatigues or pouches on his H-harness web gear.

Working quickly he fit the poncho-style vest of the rebreather system over his head and shrugged it across his shoulders before pulling the neoprene hood of his wetsuit into place. He fit the mouthpiece and tested the oxygen circuit. Designed for short, shallow dives, the rebreather offered scuba capabilities while eliminating the telltale trail of bubbles of other commercial diving rigs.

Holding his facemask and swim fins in one hand, Bolan cradled his primary weapon in the crook of his arms and crawled out from his place of concealment and into the mouth of the metal culvert running under the North Korean highway.

Coming out the other side, he slid into the cold, sluggish water of the Yellow River with all the deadly, fluid agility of motion as a hunting crocodile. Once in the water he spit into his mask and rinsed the faceplate before putting it on and then tucked his swim fins into place around his boots.

Submerging into the frigid and inky black he began kicking steadily into the middle of the deep river where the current was strongest. Staying about two yards below the surface, he used the luminous dials of his dive watch to judge the approximate distance of travel.

Bolan surfaced after fifteen minutes and stopped kicking, letting the current carry him in among the heavy beams of the crossed pillars supporting a railroad bridge across the river. Working quickly, he stripped his dive gear and let it float down into the cold gray appetite of the water. Reaching up, he grabbed hold of a wide crossbeam and began to climb.

He pulled himself up, hand over hand, twisting around the cross beams and climbing higher and higher. Above him the horizontal beams housing the tracks grew closer and closer and the wind picked up the nearer he drew to the lip of the canyon. He climbed with his Kalashnikov hung muzzle down across his back, and by the time he reached the top the water had stopped dripping behind him. He double-checked his watch and crawled into position, fitting himself tight into the trestle joist.

Intelligence stated that the protocol for all military rail transports leaving the Yellow River Restricted Military Zone stopped on the other side of the bridge to allow for routine security inspections of transport documents. There were schedules to be kept, protocols to be followed, routines to be adhered to. He would have the three-minute window it took for the brakeman to change the tracks to get out from under the bridge and onboard the train without being seen by the armed sentries of the Army of the Democratic People's Republic of Korea, the DPRK.

The time frame itself was ludicrous enough, as any delay along the way could have thrown the whole operation into jeopardy, but such a tight schedule hadn't dissuaded Bolan, and Stony Man hadn't apologized during his initial briefing.

The Executioner focused wholly on the task ahead of him and with the patience of a trapdoor spider as he lay in wait as the North Korean freight train approached then skidded to a stop in a shower of sparks and the harsh squeal of steel-on-steel. Spotlights glared down the length of the track as the military checkpoint on the far side of the bridge followed their established practice. This night the institutionalized paranoia of the DPRK would prove well founded.

Bolan scrambled up through the girders and pulled himself onto the train track. He looked down the serpentine length of the transport train toward the lead engine and saw two men in heavy military overcoats climbing into the engineer's compartment. The searchlight mounted at the top of the checkpoint shack began to rotate and play along the length of the train.

Bolan began to move fast.

He scrambled up next to the coupling housing between two railroad boxcars and out of the path of the advancing searchlight. The powerful beam of illumination ran down the train, and Bolan shrank back into the protective enclosure of the railcar's shadow. Once it was past, he scrambled upward, climbing smoothly until he reached the apex of the boxcar.

At the summit he slid over the end of the train and quickly scanned in both directions. Five cars down there was a gap between the roofs of the olive-green boxcars, indicating a flatbed railcar. Beneath him the train began to sway as the brakes were kicked off and the engineer let go with a whistle blast to signal the imminent movement of the long train.

The industrial locomotive lurched to a start and

began to gather speed, slowly at first but then with greater and greater momentum as the train began to push forward. Bolan hugged the roof as the train moved past the checkpoint and plunged into the sharply mountainous countryside beyond the river. He clung precariously for several minutes as the train finished gathering speed and began placing more and more distance behind it from the access station out of the restricted area.

Finally ready, Bolan lifted up off the roof of the boxcar and began to navigate his way down the line of cars.

THE MISSILE COMPONENTS were housed in wooden crates, but there was no disguising them if a person knew what to look for. The main crates were thirty-two feet long, holding the medium-range intercontinental rockets while additional storage boxes housed the powerful engines and the advanced computer guidance systems inside the conical tips. Stony Man intelligence had them en route to Pyongyang and from there to Iran by freighter.

The Executioner had been deployed to send a message about the traffic of such advanced and powerful weapon systems, and he carried enough Semtex explosives in his kit to guarantee there would be no misunderstanding.

From his position on the boxcar overlooking the flatbed where the pyramid stack of rockets had been secured, Bolan was able to count four guards. The train was traveling at full speed now and the mountain winds were bitter and harsh, driving the sentries into sheltered alcoves. Bolan felt confident he could place his demolition charges unobserved.

He moved quickly, sliding down the iron ladder built into the boxcar. He landed on the access platform just as a fifth soldier, with NCO markings on his uniform, came around the edge of the car on the signalman's catwalk.

The man was shorter than Bolan by half a foot, stockily built with high, flat cheekbones and dark brown eyes that widened almost comically in surprise at the sudden apparition of a dark-clothed Occidental. The man clawed for a 9 mm Tokarev TT30 pistol as Bolan, hands empty, leaped forward.

The man managed a short bark of surprise before Bolan struck. Lunging forward, the Executioner lifted his left knee to his chest and kicked explosively, driving the heel of his combat boot in the man's chest and driving him backward over the railing of the catwalk.

The North Korean soldier flipped and struck the basalt-and-gravel dike running next to the tracks in a spinning tumble before bouncing away. Then the racing train was gone and sparks flew as a burst of AKM fire slammed into the railcar next to Bolan's head.

Spinning, the big American dropped to one knee even as he cleared his silenced pistol from its shoulder holster. From the walkway next to the rockets on the flatbed a North Korean soldier leveled a Chinese AKM at him, aiming for a second burst.

Bolan's pistol chugged softly and spent brass tumbled out of its breech and off over the edge of the train, as lost in the night as the noncommissioned officer had been. The Korean sentry jerked under the impact of the 3-round burst, his head snapping and blood splashing off to the side. As he tumbled to the floor of the railcar, his partner suddenly appeared directly behind him.

For a heartbeat the two men looked at each other, then Bolan's rounds found the other man's chest and he pitched forward, victim of a lead coronary. The man struck the floor of the flatbed, then rolled and was sucked away in a flash.

Bolan leaped forward, grasped the cold metal railing in one hand and vaulted the barrier onto the railcar. The wind cutting across the exposed carriage was hard and cold. He had to move quickly. The burst of weapons fire had to have alerted the other pair of armed guards, but Bolan could only hope that the noise of the train had deafened the reports for any reinforcements positioned inside the railcars.

The Executioner landed hard on his rubber-soled boots, which absorbed some of the shock of his impact. He went down to one knee, then came back up. His right hand tucked his pistol away as his left reached around and swung the silenced Kalashnikov from behind his back on its sling. He took up the assault rifle just as a third North Korean soldier rounded the corner at the far end of the platform, his weapon up and hunting for a target.

Bolan squeezed the Kalashnikov's trigger and felt the recoil of the long rifle thump into his shoulder. The heavy-caliber rounds burned across the space between the two combatants and ripped the other man apart, then Bolan caught a flash of motion out of the corner of his eye and instinctively pivoted to face the new threat.

CHAPTER TWO

The final guard had circled and climbed over the secured crates housing the disconnected rockets. The muzzle of the man's weapon blazed a star pattern, but green tracer fire buzzed harmlessly past Bolan as he drew down and punched the man from his perch with a short burst.

Bolan did not hesitate. He sprinted forward, hurtled across the body of the second man he'd killed, and charged down the length of the flatbed. As he ran, he let the silenced AKM drop to his side and pulled his ready-prepped satchel charges from their web belt carriers and rushed to put them into position.

He moved back and forth in a huddled crouch around the ends of the rockets, working with feverish efficiency. The Semtex was such a powerful compound and he had packed so much into his satchels that the procedure wasn't difficult. Proximity with the engines was enough, and he slapped down the charges and primed their radio receivers for his signal.

He wasn't interrupted though he knew that with so many of the sentries missing it was only a matter of moments before he was discovered; the law of averages demanded it. He worked coolly, planting the satchel charges as efficiently as he could, then standing and sprinting for the next boxcar. Only one more flatbed to go and he would have ensured the destruction of the rocket housing, guidance systems and engines.

He turned and scrambled to the edge of the flatbed. The train swayed and rolled beneath his feet as he circumnavigated the heavy chain tie-downs and sharp-edged corners of the crates housing the rocket components. Looking back the way he had come, Bolan turned and jumped lightly across the distance between the two railcars, letting his primary weapon dangle off its sling against his torso. He caught hold of the hard steel rungs of the ladder set into the freight car and quickly climbed upward.

As soon as his head cleared the edge of the carriage, wind tore into him. He scuttled over the side, got to his feet, caught his balance and began to move forward. He ran steadily, scanning ahead and hunting for the second flatbed containing the unmarked crates and their deadly payloads. The second hand on his watch continued cutting off segments of time with irrevocable consistency.

Finally he saw the break in the row of boxcars that indicated the second flatbed. On one side of the train the mountainside, thick with evergreens and heavy bushes, rose like a retaining wall while on the other side the drop into the valley was sheer and unforgiving.

Bolan's luck had held mainly due to the relaxed posture of an army long used to a subjugated population and one too technologically and financially challenged to provide its ground units with radio communications.

Bolan stopped running and dropped to one knee, the AKM up and ready. He cursed under his breath. A curve in the track allowed him to see the boxcar directly in front of the second flatbed from more than just one angle, and the news was not good.

The final railcar was a club carriage designed to carry passengers, and on a military train that could only mean more soldiers. To reach the second rocket storage area he was going to have to cross a railroad car filled with armed men. Just that quickly the factors working against his success had multiplied exponentially. Bolan worked the pistol grip of his assault rifle as he shrugged against the weight of the modified rucksack on his back. He rose and approached the sleeper car.

THE CURVE OF THE RAILROAD track continued along an inward spiral against the side of the mountain, exposing the inside surface of the train to Bolan from his position on the boxcar roof. He saw the dark face of the passenger car suddenly split open and a rectangle of yellow light spill out. Bolan dropped flat on his belly as a dark figure stepped out onto the train platform.

Immediately, Bolan noticed that the figure was dressed in civilian clothes, a leather overcoat draped across his fireplug frame. The man was talking animatedly into a cell phone. From less than twenty yards away Bolan was immediately struck by how compact, and thus how new, the communication device was. Cutting-edge cellular phones were not available to the average Korean, or even the average military officer. By default Bolan realized he was seeing someone very important. In his other hand the man carried a black leather briefcase Bolan recognized as a laptop carrier.

Moving surreptitiously Bolan raised his night-vision goggles. He had taken off the apparatus before his swim and kept it secured while he moved along the train to avoid the depth perception problems inherent to their use. Now he moved carefully to bring it up over his eyes and then zero in with the zoom function.

The North Korean on the cell phone jumped into abrupt focus. There was plenty of ambient light coming from the passenger car for the advanced-technology glasses to bring every stark line of detail into view. Bolan played the image-enhancement lens across the man's face and knew from accessing his mental mug shots that he was looking at a major player in the North Korean government. He dredged the name from the recesses of his memory—he was looking at Kim Su-Kweon, department chief of the Research Department for External Intelligence—RDEI. The RDEI was a nefarious and sinister organization linked to activities as diverse as creating infiltration tunnels under the DMZ and selling methamphetamines to Yakuza interests in Japan.

If the RDEI was a web, then Kim Su-Kweon was the fat spider at its center. The man turned his back to the wind, his leather satchel swinging in his other hand. Bolan knew instantly he had to acquire that laptop. If he could secure it and then blow the train, there would be every reason for the North Korean command and control to believe the device had been lost in the explosion. It would be an intelligence coup of significant proportions.

Bolan pulled his NVDs clear of his face as Kim Su-Kweon shut his cell phone and turned toward the door leading into the passenger railcar. Bolan pushed up off his stomach and raised his silenced AKM up to cover the man.

Catching the motion out of the corner of his eye, Kim turned in surprise. He gaped in shock as he saw the black-clad apparition of the Executioner above him. He barked out a warning and dropped his cell phone, which clattered to the platform and skittered away to be pulled under the thundering wheels of the train. His hand clawed inside his overcoat as Bolan moved lightly to the edge of the boxcar roof. The North Korean intelligence agent pulled his pistol free and tried to bring it to bear.

Bolan loosed a 3-round burst into the man's face from under six yards and splashed his brains across the steel bulkhead of the railcar behind him. The intelligence agent was thrown backward by the inertia of the heavy-caliber rounds, and his laptop case fell from slack hands as he pitched forward, then crumpled to his knees on the steel mesh of the platform. Bolan rushed forward and leaped across the distance between the two cars.

He landed hard and folded up but fought to keep his

feet in the sticky pool of Kim's spilling blood. The door opened and a uniformed soldier with an AKM in his hands appeared in the entranceway. Bolan didn't hesitate to knock him back into the passenger car with a quick burst that clawed out his throat and blasted the back of his head off.

The man fell backward, and Bolan caught a glimpse of more soldiers rushing forward as the dead man tumbled into the car. The Executioner threw his weapon to his shoulder and poured a long, ragged burst into the tight kill zone of the passenger car hallway, chewing men apart with his bluntly scything rounds. Still firing one-handed he scooped up the fallen laptop case and raced for the metal access ladder set into the side of the railcar superstructure.

He shoved the case through a suspender on his H-harness web gear and let the silenced AKM hang from its cross body sling. He pushed himself hard, felt the laptop start to slip and stopped to shove it back into place.

Below him a burst of gunfire tore through the open train door and bullets rattled and ricocheted off the boxcar behind him. Bolan heard a man screaming in anger and more than one in pain as he lunged over the top of the car and onto the roof. Below him a North Korean soldier rushed onto the grille of the landing and swung around, bringing his weapon to bear. Bolan flipped over onto his back in a smooth shoulder roll and snatched up the pistol grip of his weapon. He thrust the weapon forward against the brace of the sling and angled it downward.

He pulled the trigger and held it back, letting the assault rifle rock and roll through half a magazine before easing up and rolling to his feet. He took two steps and the laptop case fell. He dropped with it and caught it before it bounced away. He used his left hand to unsnap the carabiner hook between his web gear belt and suspender. Quickly he hooked that through the handle of the black leather case and reconnected it to his belt.

He was almost too late.

He saw the muzzle of the Chinese AKM thrust over the edge of the railcar roof and he dived forward. He tumbled haphazardly across the roof as the soldier on the ladder let loose with his weapon. Bolan's chin struck the metal of the carriage structure and he bit his tongue, filling his mouth with the copper tang of his own blood.

Green ComBloc tracers and 7.62 mm slugs tore past him as he slid toward the edge of the roof and the long, steep drop below. He reached out with his left hand and grabbed hold of the metal lip running along the top of the railcar, spreading his legs wide to slow his momentum. From just a few feet away he thrust the muzzle of his AKM forward and triggered a burst.

His rounds roared into the exposed weapon firing at him and ripped it from the soldier's hands as the hardball slugs tore through the stock and receiver, shattering it beyond use. The soldier's hand disappeared in an explosion of red mist, and his scream was ripped away by the rushing wind.

Bolan spun on the slick metal of the roof and gained his feet. He pushed himself up, fired a second burst of harassing fire, then turned and sprinted in the opposite direction. As he neared the edge of the car and the flat-bed containing the second shipment of missile components came into view, he saw a North Korean soldier scramble into position while trying to bring his assault rifle to bear.

Bolan fired and knocked him spinning off the rail-car. The man screamed horrifically as he tumbled over the edge like a pinwheel, bounced off the basalt lip of the track and plunged down the mountainside below like a stone skipping across the surface of a lake. Bolan leaped into the air and landed on top of the flatbed car. He ducked and slid over the side of the pile just as a North Korean soldier sidled around the end of the flat-bed freight car. The soldier fired as Bolan was freeing the last of his satchel charges. The Executioner thrust his own assault rifle forward by the pistol grip, using the sling like a second hand and pulled the trigger.

The shots were hasty and he was off balance as he fired, but he hosed the area in a spray-and-pray maneuver designed to force the man backward. He rolled over, feeling the hard edge of the wooden crate bite into his hip, and squeezed the trigger again, then broke off, re-centered and fired once again.

The bullets caught the North Korean soldier center mass and he staggered under their impact, his weapon tumbling from useless hands as Bolan let the muzzle recoil climb so that bullets chewed the man apart, drilling him from sternum to skull in a staccato hail of slugs.

Bolan turned and slid the last satchel into place, key-

ing up the transponder for his electronic signal. Soldiers
rushed to the edge of the roof of the boxcar next to him
and started firing down at him. Wood splinters flew in
the air as a fire team of North Korean soldiers shot at
him. He ducked behind the end of the crates and threw
his rifle to one side. Green tracer fire burned past his
position as he recentered the shoulder straps of his specially outfitted rucksack.

He pulled the transmitter out of its pocket as more
and more rifle fire drew down on his position. Grabbing
hold of the electronic device, he turned toward the edge
of the train overlooking the open valley. He sucked in
two quick breaths and sprinted out from cover. Three
hard steps and he was on the edge, then he kicked off
and threw himself out into space. Behind him the withering fire petered off as the uniformed men on the train
watched him fall, hypnotized into stunned amazement.

Bolan felt the air rushing up into his face with surpris-
ing force. He saw the snakelike twisting of the Yellow
River five hundred feet below him, then turned and hit
the button on his detonator. There was a pause half a
heartbeat long, then the train was blown off the mountain at the two flatbed points containing the rocket bodies and engines. A yellow ball of fire rolled out from the
mountain and a wave of heat descended on Bolan as he
fell.

His fist came up to his left breast just beside the suspender of his H-harness web gear and jerked the D-ring
handle. There was a pause that lasted for entirely too
long in his racing thoughts as he plunged below three

hundred feet and the dark water of the river came into sharper focus.

The minichute, also called a stunt chute—of the kind used by BASE jumpers—rushed out and caught. Bolan was jerked to a stop for a moment, then gravity reclaimed him and he began to fall toward the river again, his descent slowing modestly. At fifteen feet above the surface, when the dark water of the river filled his vision beyond his dangling feet, Bolan hit the cut-away and dropped out of his harness to fall like a stone.

He struck the cold water for the second time that night and felt it rush in over his head. Letting the current take him, his hand went to his waist where he shrugged out of his web gear and let it float away, keeping only the laptop carry case. He kicked for the surface and deployed his final piece of gear, a life vest designed to keep him buoyant in the water.

Above his head the side of the mountain burned. Working quickly, he swam to the shore and pushed the black leather case out of the water. Putting one knee down on the gravel against the current, Bolan opened the case to make sure it had kept the water out and then resealed it. Moving quickly, he used the air-tight pouches that he had used to transport his satchel charges to insulate the carry case then, after securing it to himself, he swam back out into the fast-moving current.

Forty minutes later he activated his emergency beacon and let the river carry him out toward the Sea of Japan.

When Jack Grimaldi got the signal, he flew the seaplane in low under the radar and put the pods down on the choppy water beyond the breakers fronting the rocky shoreline. He knew North Korean naval units were responding as he pulled Bolan out of the situation, but aggressive electronic jamming by units of the U.S. Air Force based out of the Japanese mainland easily outclassed their counterparts in the DPRK.

SIX HOURS LATER the Stony Man cybercrew cracked the encryption security on the laptop and things really began to roll.

The first of the hijacked information was the most important.

Under Kim Su-Kweon's control, his intelligence agency had forged an alliance with the Hong Kong triad known as the Mountain and Snake Society. Mostly the deal had involved the laundering of forged American money and as a secondary outlet for North Korea's prodigious methamphetamine production operation. But Stony Man had discovered that the use of the triad cut-outs extended far beyond that.

The Mountain and Snake Society had aggressively expanded its influence, most commonly by brute force, into any area on the global stage where there was a Chinese population presence or criminal activity already in existence on an international scale. The waterfront areas of Split, Croatia, had certainly qualified on the latter if not always on the former, and North Korean intelligence had entered into an arms trafficking enterprise with Russian oligarch Victor

Bout through intermediaries of the Mountain and Snake Society triad.

The triad subsidiary had then taken it upon itself to expand its own business interests and began performing mercenary criminal functions for Chechen, Russian and Azerbaijani mafia-style organizations. Most significantly to Stony Man had been the triad's agreement to provide a safehouse for and act as intermediaries to, the kidnapping of the daughter of an American official in Split.

The disappearance of Karen Rasmussen had baffled American security services who had focused their resources on known terror organizations in the area, leading them up one blind alley after another. Kim had known exactly where the young woman was being held and what was to become of her.

Now the Executioner did, as well.

CHAPTER THREE

The long-range helicopter dropped out of the Eastern European night and hugged the ocean surf. Bolan looked out through his door on the copilot side and eyed the waters of the Adriatic Sea. It was even darker than the night, its water black and disturbingly deep. On the horizon in front of them a mile or so out, the brilliant lights of Split flared with near blinding intensity.

Bolan looked over at the helicopter pilot, his old friend Jack Grimaldi. The man, dressed in aviator flightsuit and helmet offered him a thumbs-up and pointed at the GPS display on the helicopter dashboard.

"One mile out," Grimaldi said.

The pilot's face was cast in the greenish reflection of his dome lights, making his features stark and slightly surreal. Bolan reached down between them, then secured his dive bag across his body, which was sheathed in a black dry suit of quarter-inch neoprene against the chilly water below them.

Grimaldi banked the helicopter and lowered into a hover above the rough sea. A sudden gust of wind hammered into the side of the aircraft and threatened to send it spinning into the waves. Reacting smoothly, the Stony Man pilot fought the struggling helicopter back into a level hover. The wind gust carved a sudden trough in the ocean beneath them, turning a three-yard drop to nearly ten in the blink of an eye. If Bolan had leaped when that gust had hit, his amphibious insertion would have shattered bones and left him crippled and helpless in rough seas.

"I don't like this, Sarge!" Grimaldi yelled.

Looking up from the increasingly violent water, Bolan nodded his agreement. "We've been over this before," he shouted back, pulling the hood of his dry suit into place. "It's the most expedient manner to infiltrate Azerbaijani custom controls on such short notice."

"Ten to one Karen is already dead and buried so deep in a hidden grave we'll never see her again!" Grimaldi argued. "There's too much about this we don't know. We should pull back now before we lose track of *two* Americans," he said pointedly. But he also said it like a man who didn't quite believe the story he was pushing.

Bolan tugged his snorkel and facemask into place. "If there's even one chance of getting her out, I've got to try." He snapped his swim fins onto his belt and reached for the handle of the copilot door. He grinned at the frowning Grimaldi. "Try not to splatter me all over the Adriatic."

"No promises, Sarge," Grimaldi answered. But he nodded and worked his controls, fighting the helicopter into position.

Bolan opened the door and stepped onto the landing skid. Instantly sharp wind and needles of sea spray slapped into him. His dry suit kept him warm, but the exposed flesh of his face felt raw and brutalized. Though technically Mediterranean, the water still held a bite this time of year. He squinted hard against the spray and slammed the door of the helicopter shut.

Despite his joke about splattering on the water, Bolan knew he had to move as efficiently as possible to minimize the hovering helicopter's exposure to the variables of the weather and sea. He looked down, saw a swell rise up to greet him and pushed away from the aircraft. He stepped off with one foot to clear the helicopter.

His grip in his clumsy dry suit mitten slipped on the rain-slick handle of the door as an erratic blast of air slammed into him like a subway car. His feet were knocked clear of the landing skid as Grimaldi frantically fought the helicopter back under control and Bolan tumbled out into space.

Cursing to himself, he tried to twist as he dropped as below him the path of the wind cupped out a depression in the churning sea and ten feet became fifteen and then twenty. He got one hand up in time to secure his mask and snorkel, then hit the water hard along one side with enough force to drive the wind from his lungs like a gut punch.

He plunged through the waves and into the deep,

cold embrace of the water. The ocean closed like a black hole around him, sucking him into chilly brine and foam. He turned in the water, briefly disorientated by the fall, and he could no longer discern the surface.

His hands went to his chest and he fumbled for a moment, slapping himself, searching for the release. Just as his lungs felt as if they were going to burn to a cinder with the pain of his asphyxiation, he found and jerked the activation handle.

The compartments in his life vest popped open and jerked him chest-first toward the surface. He rose through the cold black like a buoy and broke the surface, gasping for breath, and began to kick. Above him he heard the sound of the helicopter hovering overhead. He kicked hard and waved a hand to show that he was fine.

Grimaldi pulled up and away, taking the helicopter out of danger. A wave broke over Bolan's head, pushing him down, and when he got to the surface again he was alone.

ESCHEWING THE MASK and snorkel, Bolan cut through the water using the sidestroke, the preferred movement for combat swimmers on endurance insertions. He kept himself oriented toward the brilliant beacon of Split, and after some time the rolling of the surf began to push him in that direction.

The swimming was hard work. He found a rhythm, pulling down with his arm while drawing back his leg and scissor-kicking. The taste of the ocean was in his mouth, the water stinging his eyes.

He kicked to the top of one rolling wave and slid down the trough on the other side. The sea and the sky were black, but the easy landmark of the glowing city light of Split drew him on. His working body was warm inside his suit and he began to perspire lightly. Gradually the lights grew closer.

IN DARKNESS there was death.

The Executioner watched from the shadows, his eyes tracking every movement of the rooftop sentry like the targeting system of a surface-to-air missile. As the guard strolled along the edge of the warehouse, Mack Bolan slid in closer, step by step, with murderous intent.

The Asian gunslinger was a triggerman for the Mountain and Snake Society triad. Compared to more common criminals, the sentry moved around his area of operations with purpose and discipline, hands on the pistol grip of his submachine gun.

The Croat-based triad had carved out a niche serving as underworld enforcers for hire, providing security to drug and weapons shipments as well as occasionally providing shooters for criminal acts throughout the region. Its primary income came from the kidnapping and trafficking of underage girls to fill the prison brothels of India. They were child-rapists and slavers, and the Executioner had come for them.

Bolan crept out of a deep shadow. The guard stood with his back unprotected, facing the lights of the city across the bay. His hands were filled and busy as he worked a lighter to light a cigarette, leaving the submachine gun dangling loose.

The Executioner moved smoothly in a choreographed ballet of violence. His hands were parallel to each other, the knuckles of his middle fingers almost touching as he gripped the wooden dowels of the garrote. The length of piano wire between them formed an oblong loop, and he slipped it like a noose over the man's head. He jerked his hands back and apart, snapping the loop closed, and the wire bit into his quarry's neck with merciless efficiency.

The man gagged as his larynx was crushed. Blood rushed out as the thin wire bit deep. The blunt hammer of Bolan's knee connected hard with the man's kidney and he folded like a lawn chair, dropping to his knees. As the man went down, Bolan's jerked back on the garrote like a tourist hauling in a Marlin into a fishing boat off Mazatlán. Blood spilled out like water from a cracked-open fire hydrant and the man blacked out.

His arms fell limply, and Bolan put the knobby tread of his boot against the sentry's back and pushed against the tension of the wire, finishing the job. He dropped the handles and let the body slump over. The blood was obsidian in the faint moonlight, and it stained the man's cigarette then snuffed it out with a slight hiss.

Pulling a sturdy diver knife from his combat harness, Bolan crossed the roof to where a skylight broke the surface in a Plexiglas bubble. He knelt and began working, as expertly as any cat burglar.

TWO MEN were in the room. One was almost naked, and both looked at Karen Rasmussen with a vulture's bleak appetite. She was tied to a straight-backed chair by a white hemp rope in intricate and stylized knotting and patterns of bonding, clothed in only her underwear. She was unaware of it, but Rasmussen had been bound according to ancient Hojojutsu techniques. The binding was considered an erotic S&M art form in Japan, and when this episode was done that was where Philippine national Abdullah Sungkar hoped to unload at least a hundred thousand U.S. dollars' worth of the DVD.

The teenage girl stared at him with terror in her eyes, and Sungkar looked to his camcorder to make sure it was on. The look was worth cash when the pedophile online network began their critiques and reviews. His tongue, pink and small, quickly darted out to moisten his lips.

Behind him the actor named Sulu was zipping his leather mask into place. Karen Rasmussen was the daughter of the American embassy official in charge of development of agriculture and commerce projects. Sungkar, a field captain in the Mountain and Snake Society, had been paid by a representative of Russian syndicates to kidnap the young woman then rape and torture her. And to film it, so copies could be sent out to the press as an example of America's powerlessness. It was not a request that made sense to Sungkar, as it didn't seem to advance the business interests of the Russian.

Indeed such brutal tactics had already been tried and

rejected by the umbrella terror organization al-Qaeda, but the money spent the same as far as Sungkar was concerned. Whatever plan Victor Bout had, that was up to him. Sungkar took pay for his play, and that was all that mattered to him.

Sulu stepped into the camcorder's picture, already aroused. The sight of the man caused the girl to try to scream around her ball-gag. Spittle flew. Sungkar felt a tightening in his own crotch.

Karen Rasmussen threw herself against her restraints, but the triad captain had learned his knots from a master, and escape was hopeless. Giggling like a little girl from behind a black leather mask, Sulu stalked toward the teenager.

MACK BOLAN UNFOLDED from the skylight like a great malignant spider. He hung for a moment, poised as the twisted scene below him played out. He was dressed head to toe in black from his customary combat black-suit to his balaclava hood. He held the diver knife in his left hand and rappelled easily with his right.

The distance was ten feet, maybe eleven. He laid the blade flat against his leg and let go. He dropped, as silent as a stone falling down a well. He hit the floor-boards of the warehouse's second story and rolled along his right side like a paratrooper on an airborne drop. He came smoothly to his feet out of the shadow cast by the harsh commercial production filming lights used to illuminate the scene.

The mask-wearing rapist with the swirling, full-body

tattoos screamed out loud and tried to swing a clumsy overhand blow at the intruding shadow. Bolan came up out of his roll inside the man's reach and the diver knife flashed in the wattage of the film lamps. Three times it plunged into the rapist's body, and blood thudded like rain drops on the dusty wooden slats of the floor.

The first stab punched through Sulu's solar plexus and pierced his diaphragm, stealing the porn star's air before he could draw breath for another scream. The second thrust took him under the rib cage and sliced up to bury an inch of stainless steel into the thudding drum of the man's pounding heart. The third strike punched through the cartilage of his throat and cracked his C-3 vertebrae.

Bolan yanked his knife free as Sulu's corpse tumbled backward like an animal in a slaughterhouse kill-chute. He sprang forward after Sungkar, who had managed to raise a half shout as he scrambled for a silver .40-caliber pistol lying under his folded jacket on an extra chair.

The Executioner slapped at his chest with his right hand, his palm finding the custom handle of his silenced machine pistol. Sungkar threw back his jacket to dig for his weapon, not bothering to scream because he knew his bodyguards would never reach him in time anyway. His fingers found the cold, comforting weight of the handgun and wrapped around the handle.

The big American's sound suppressor hacked out a triple pneumatic cough.

Sungkar straightened like a man electrocuted as the 9 mm Parabellum rounds slammed into his body just under his right shoulder blade. His body shuddered with the impact, and he arched backward at an unnatural angle not unlike a reverse comma. Bolan's second triburst lifted the top of the hired killer's skull up off his face and splashed his brains across the warehouse. The man stumbled forward and struck the floor.

The Executioner rose from his crouch.

KAREN RASMUSSEN looked over at the long table next to the camcorder. There was a power drill, dental instruments and some bloodstained carpenter tools. In the middle of the implements a black candle burned next to a bottle of Ouzo. Abdullah Sungkar had told her in loving detail exactly what he was going to do with each and every single item, speaking slowly so that each word was captured in perfect clarity by the continuously running camera.

The killing shadow moved toward her, gun in one hand and bloody knife in the other. She recoiled in terror from the gore-stained apparition. Seeing her reaction, Bolan stopped and returned his silenced pistol to its shoulder holster before pulling down the balaclava and revealing his face.

"Easy," he whispered. "I'm here to get you out."

He cut her hands free just as he heard the first thundering of footsteps on the stairs outside the room door. He pulled the blade toward him in one smooth motion and sliced the bonds binding her hands, then pressed the knife hilt into her shaking grip.

"Cut yourself free," he ordered.

She took the knife automatically but when she looked up, the night fighter was gone, swallowed by shadows. The door to the room was kicked inward, the frame splintering along one hinge, and a handful of men armed with utilitarian machine pistols burst into the room. They wore dirty jeans and expensive shirts with gold gleaming in the form of watches and bracelets on their wrists, in their teeth, at their ears and across their knuckles. They looked every bit the part of modern-age pirates.

The leader's eyes had grown wide in surprise at the bloody corpses, his jaw dropping to his chest in a reaction so exaggerated it was nearly comical. His head jerked left then right as he tried to peer into the thick shadows filling the edges of the long room. He saw the bloody knife in the American girl's hands but saw also that she was still bound to the chair at the neck, waist, knees and ankles. She looked at him, her expression blank in her fear. Behind him the rest of the crew tried to press forward.

The man, a lieutenant named Kis, barked something in his own language and waved the stubby barrel of his machine pistol. Karen Rasmussen just looked at him. He switched to a broken, almost pidgin English.

"What happened!" he demanded. "You kill boss?"

The girl tried to shake her head, her mouth locked into an "O" shape by the red rubber ball of her gag. She could barely turn her head against the stylized wrappings of the knots. But she held a dripping knife in her hand.

Cursing, Kis charged forward.

Growling, the crew of triad hitters surged after him. There was a heavy thud on the old floorboards as something metal struck the camcorder and knocked it over. Every head turned in that direction. Kis blinked as it looked as if a pale green can of soda pop was rolling across the floor toward them.

A white light like a sun going nova flashed, followed by a sharp, overwhelming bang that filled his ears with disorienting pain. From behind the milling, confused gang of rapists and kidnappers a black figure detached itself from the shadows and moved among them.

The silenced pistol fired from near point-blank range, putting 3-round bursts into the skulls of confused men. Hot blood and chunks of brain splashed terrified, uncomprehending faces, and bodies started to hit the floor.

CHAPTER FOUR

In her chair Karen Rasmussen watched the Executioner at work.

He moved like a supranatural force coldly dispatching the slavers from the very middle of their milling cluster. He spun and twisted, and his gun hand pointed, lifted and pressed and his trigger finger worked repeatedly. The weapon's slide kicked back, spilling gleaming, smoking brass cartridges out of the oversize ejection port.

Her head whirled and spun from the flash-bang grenade concussion, and her vision was obstructed by blurred spots. She blinked, catching disjointed images like still pictures clipped from a movie reel. She blinked again, seeing those shells tumbling with surrealistic clarity but still seeing the faces of the falling men as blurs. She blinked again, and her vision snapped into focus. There was only the night fighter, his gun still raised, in the middle of a pile of leaking corpses.

The man turned toward her, and she could see smoke curling out the end of the weapon in dark gray ribbons. The stench of cordite cut through her nostrils, burning like smelling salts, and snapping her back into the sharp reality of the moment.

"There's more downstairs," Bolan said. "I've got to take them out if we're going to get out of here. Hurry! Cut yourself free and get a weapon." He indicated the black metal machine pistols scattered around the floor at his feet. Rasmussen looked down. It seemed like the weapons were floating in a lake of blood.

"Get under the table and watch the door," Bolan continued. "Do *not* shoot me when I come back in. Hurry!"

Then he turned and made for the door to the triad snuff film studio. Karen Rasmussen began to free herself.

CHIN HO MEDINA stood at the bottom of the stairs looking up, a Kalashnikov assault in his sweating hands. He called again, confused by the commotion and then the lack of commotion as the first team of bodyguards had rushed up the stairs that ran like scaffolding to the second-story office space. How much trouble could a teenage girl be? Then a black apparition appeared quickly in the doorway and he barked out a single word before opening fire.

He saw a black-clad, balaclava-wearing man and screamed, "BSD!" referring to the Croatian commando group, part hostage rescue team, part death squad that served as a special operations force.

The triad gunmen's assault rifle blazed in his hands as behind him the rest of the criminal cell, already poised and on edge, exploded into action. Bolan pulled back from the edge of the doorway as he saw him level his weapon and the child pornographer began to blast away, the muzzle-flash obscuring the gunmen's own vision as he poured lead into the shadows above him.

He didn't see the deadly black sphere as it dropped toward him.

It arched in a gentle lob over his head and struck the hard, oil-stained concrete floor. The impact detonation grenade immediately exploded. Shrapnel fanned out, riding the edge of the concussive blast, and tore into Chin's flesh seconds before the explosion sent him spinning like a rag doll over the safety railing of the stairs, his weapon spinning away.

Behind the mutilated corpse, razor-sharp shards of metal buzzed into unprotected flesh and a ball of billowing fire mushroomed out behind it. Men were screaming as they were thrown or swept aside. Clothes burst into flame and blood ran in rivers across the filthy floor.

Bolan stepped out of the doorway and rushed down the stairs, his pistol up and ready. He caught a flash of motion and pivoted smoothly at the waist, putting a 3-round burst into one stumbling kidnapper, then a second into another man fighting to stand.

A screaming man staggered about, clutching at a torn and bleeding stump where his arm had been: no threat. Bolan turned away, racing down four more steps, and saw a child-rapist crawling along the ground, his guts strung out behind him, and screaming in agonizing pain. The man was reaching for the blood-smeared grip of a machine pistol: threat. The Executioner used a Parabellum burst to hollow the man's skull.

He thundered down another half flight of stairs and saw movement beyond the edge of the blast radius. He vaulted the smoking railing as heavy-caliber slugs chewed into the wood steps where he'd been standing. He landed in the middle of his grenade kills. He tried to spin and drop but his foot came down in a puddled smear of intestines and he slipped.

The gunner who had fired on him rushed out from behind a stack of fifty-five-gallon industrial barrels, weapon blazing. Bolan shot him with a burst low in the stomach and the man doubled over, firing a second burst into the ground, causing ricochets to whistle and whine madly around the room.

Riding out the recoil of the last burst, Bolan pushed himself up. His blacksuit was soaked with blood along the right side and his ribs felt bruised from the tumble but his adrenaline was running through him in currents of electricity.

He sensed movement and turned his head, the muzzle of his pistol shifting in tandem and steel-steady in his grip. His finger lay welded on the smooth metal curve of the trigger taking up the slack. He saw a shape crouched under an old metal office desk and his arm straightened, his finger tightening on the trigger.

The girl's lips quivered with fear, and her thin cheeks

were smeared with dirt. Her lower lip was split and swollen so that a trickle of blood had run down her chin and dried like a string of chocolate syrup.

Narrowing his eyes, Bolan lowered the pistol. He got to his feet and looked around. Off to his left on the edge of a pile of corpses strung out like toys by the grenade blast, a triad hardman climbed to his feet and staggered away. Bolan shifted, seeing only the motion at first. Then his eyes went to the hands. In hostage rescue situations the shoot teams always looked to the hands in their split-second decisions. Empty hands: no shoot. Full hands: shoot.

The shuffling figure grasped one of the utilitarian machine pistols. The handgun in Bolan's fist spit a triburst, the soft-nosed bullets burrowing into the gunman, cracking his wing-shaped shoulder blade like hammers on a plate.

The man spasmed, his back arching and the machine pistol clattered and bounced off the concrete. The gunner staggered toward a line of fifty-five-gallon oil barrels. He screamed once in pain and staggered, close to going down. His arm came out, and Bolan figured it was a last desperate attempt to stop his fall before he died. The hand came down. Too late Bolan saw the apparatus attached to the industrial barrels by twisted lines of thick coaxial cable.

There was a sharp, dry metallic click and suddenly glowing red LED numerals blinked on in the swatch of gloom as Bolan put a second burst into the man and dropped him dead. The numbers glowed dark red and stood out starkly against the gloom: 00:00:30.

Bolan leaped forward. The demolitions a group like this seemed capable of couldn't be that complex. He wasn't a Gary Manning or a Hermann Schwarz, but he could defuse most simple trigger explosives.

He had almost reached the charges—the number display read, 00:00:28. His eyes fairly danced across the apparatus, taking in the details of the construction, hunting for connection points, trailing wires.

Then the girl shot him in the back.

He grunted hard at the impact and spun even as the echo of the shot was still bouncing through the cavernous warehouse. He felt a sting like a razor slice along his left arm, and the middle of his back felt as if he'd been blindsided by a sledgehammer.

He didn't have time to question why it had happened. He was a man with a gun and men with guns didn't often solve problems in Croatia. The only men with guns the girl had seen, he understood intuitively, had been the ones intent on using her up and throwing her away.

He spun and dropped and fired quickly. His bullets found the floor in front of her and there was a risk of ricochets but he was an expert with his weapons and had no choice but to take the risk. Concrete chips sprang up and slapped the girl with granite shards. She screamed but stubbornly held on to the machine pistol.

Bolan shifted the muzzle and punched a burst through the frame of the desk beside her head, already starting to surge forward. The rounds flattened as they punched through the cheap metal, and the girl screamed again.

From the top of the stairs Karen Rasmussen answered that scream with one of her own.

Bolan felt relief like a punch in the gut when the girl finally panicked enough to drop the machine pistol. He leaped forward and kicked the weapon across the room and snatched her up by the arm.

"American!" he growled.

The girl looked at him and more tears came, but he could feel her tense in his grip as her fear and confusion overtook her. Then she clung to him for a moment and he felt hope. She let out a sudden, sharp piercing scream and her fists began to windmill as she fought him with desperate energy. He looked to the digital timer.

00:00:22.

He wanted to yank the girl free as the clock slid to 00:00:21, but she was glued to him like a wildcat, scratching and clawing and trying to bite. He forced himself to hold on despite the hurt in his back where the Second Chance ballistic vest had stopped the slug. He yelled for Karen Rasmussen to run, and turned away, scanning the big room for the way out he had seen on his initial reconnaissance.

He saw the door and the padlock hanging off the chain from the inside in the same instant. He'd shot the man charged with manning the entry post on his own way down the stairs and saw that body sprawled on the floor, outflung hand inches from an assault rifle.

00:00:21.

"Karen!" Bolan barked for a second time.

"I'm coming!" The teenager answered, and he could hear her running down the stairs.

He tucked the wildly flailing girl under his arm and moved toward the door. He brought up his handgun as he did so, approaching the lock at an angle. He was stunned by the ferocity with which the triad clique had been prepared to defend its base of operations. With the death penalty so frequently employed, maybe they felt they had nothing left to lose.

He saw more clusters of fifty-five-gallon drums connected by television cables designed to carry electronic impulses and digital signals. The triad team had cobbled together a devastating mixture of low- and high-tech. What it lacked in complexity Bolan felt sure it would make up for in raw, explosive power.

00:00:20.

Squeezing the girl tightly, Bolan lifted the pistol and fired into the big padlock holding the thick links of chain together. The metal padlock jumped at the impact like a fish on the end of a line and split apart. Bolan stepped forward and struck out with the tread of his boot, catching the mechanism and ripping it down.

Karen Rasmussen joined him as the thick chain dropped to the floor. The girl was almost epileptic in her spasm now as she kept shrieking a word over and over again, the same liquid syllables in screaming repetition, but Bolan didn't know the word, didn't think he even recognized the language. He stuffed his pistol into its shoulder holster to better control the twisting girl and reached out to pull the warehouse door open.

00:00:19.

Karen Rasmussen threw herself against the handle and heaved her weight against the sliding structure. It came open easily and she stumbled through, Bolan rushed out after, running hard. The little girl bucked in his arms.

He heard a car door open and saw the flash of a dome light out of his left eye even as he was turning. He saw an Asian man in a leather coat with a long pony-tail hopping out of a sleek black Lexus, one of the team's ubiquitous machine pistols filling his hands.

Bolan dropped the twisting girl as he brought up his handgun. Rasmussen was screaming, her voice raw now, hands up around her face and standing directly in his way. He struck her with a heel-of-the-palm blow to her shoulder blade as the gunman lifted his machine pistol, and she spun away from him.

The Executioner leveled his silenced weapon, just catching a sense of the girl darting away from him. His finger found the trigger a split second before the other man's and a 3-round burst struck the Asian in the chest. The man staggered under the triple impact and came up against the edge of the car. Bolan pulled down and stroked his trigger again. The man's face was ripped off his skull, and he hit the broken pavement of the parking lot.

Bolan turned, reaching out for the girl, but he just missed her as she darted back into the building. His fingertips grazed her, coming close enough to feel the feather brush of her hair as he grasped nothing and she slipped past him.

"Sister!" Rasmussen suddenly shouted. "I just remembered the word, I was too scared to translate before!" the daughter of the American diplomat said. "Her sister's in there."

But Bolan was already running.

HE HIT THE DOORS of the warehouse three steps behind the frantic girl. His eyes were drawn to the LED display and what he saw flooded his system with fresh jolts of adrenaline.

00:00:09.

He sprang forward, growling with the exertion and caught the girl as he dived toward the hiding spot he had first pulled her out from. She turned like a ferret and sank her teeth into his palm.

00:00:08.

He swore and let go instinctively as blood pooled up out of the cuts. The girl was under the desk and with incredulity he saw that her "sister" was a little rag doll as filthy as its owner with bright black eyes. He reached out with his unwounded hand and caught the girl by her shirt. Doll firmly in her grip, she came away easy now and he pulled her tightly to him.

00:00:05.

He saw the readout and knew he couldn't make it. His feet hit the ground as he drove with his legs against the concrete like a running back breaking for open field after a hand off. He cut around an overturned barrel and cursed the half second it caused him.

The girl was babbling now at him in some dialect he

was too keyed up to catch, but she was also hugging him tightly. He saw the door standing open and put on the last burst of speed left in his body. His heart was thumping hard in his chest, banging against his ribs with the exertion and his breath was coming fast and hard.

00:00:02.

He hit the door at a dead sprint just as he felt the air around him suddenly draw backward in a vacuum rush that stung his eyeballs. He drew the girl closer against him as he felt the flash of sudden heat come rolling up behind him like a fast-running locomotive.

Cowering on the pavement, Karen Rasmussen watched him dive through the doorway. He seemed to hang for a moment in the air and she could see the ball of fire rushing up behind like a film image on fast forward.

Bolan was hurtling through the air, twisting as he flew to catch the angle out of the doorway and the orange freight train of a fireball rushed past him. The concussive force sent the doors flying like tumbling dice.

She couldn't stop screaming as she watched, and Bolan twisted as he fell to protect the girl, landing hard along one arm and shoulder. He grunted with the impact and recoiled slightly off the pavement before sprawling wide to cover as much of the girl's flesh with his own body as he could.

Behind them jets of flame shot out windows and air vents and punched holes through the roof. Black smoke appeared instantly, and debris began to rain down. The teenager felt her throat choke up with sudden, sharp pain and she realized she had been screaming but that the blast had deafened her.

She stopped, coughing, and then looked up at the savage bonfire lighting up the dockside neighborhood. She felt tears filling her eyes as she realized the bastards were dead.

Just like that, it was over.

CHAPTER FIVE

Bolan eased himself into a chair in the war room at Stony Man Farm. "What's up, Bear?" he said to Aaron Kurtzman.

Kurtzman, head of the Stony Man cybernetics team, turned his wheelchair toward Bolan. "What's up, Mack? Got you some coffee. Barb and Hal will be here in just a second."

Bolan took a seat at the long hardwood table. In front of him was a steaming mug of black coffee and a plain manila folder marked with a single red stripe over a bar code and the word "Classified."

He had always preferred this place in the old farmhouse to the newer Annex. He had taken a lot of mission briefings here, formed innumerable strategies, argued tactics and made life and death decisions. He shrugged the thought away and reached for his cup of coffee as Barbara Price and Hal Brognola entered the room. Bolan nodded in greeting and took a drink.

He frowned at the bitter taste. "That's a nice batch you brewed there, Bear," he said wryly. The thickset man grinned like a Viking from behind his black beard and hit a button on his console panel. "Good for what ails ya," he agreed. A section of the wall slid down, revealing a huge screen.

"Nice work in Split," Brognola said. He sat in a chair and dropped a thick attaché case on the table in front of him. "The State Department is very grateful." He paused and smiled. "If they knew who exactly to be grateful to, that is."

"The girl?" Bolan asked.

"She's fine," Price said. The honey-blond mission controller took her own seat. "We channeled her into an American relief organization. She'll be safe until she can be returned to her family in Jakarta."

Bolan nodded. His face was impassive, but he felt pleased. "What's that leave us with now?" he asked.

Price snorted and Bolan turned to her in surprise. "A ghost hunt," she answered.

Brognola turned to Kurtzman and nodded. "Show him," he said.

The cyberwizard typed briefly on his keyboard and hit his roller mouse with a thumb. Instantly the big screen recessed into the wall came alive. Bolan turned in his seat and regarded the digital image.

First what was obviously an official military portrait appeared in HD quality. Bolan narrowed his eyes and scrutinized the picture. The uniform was Russian, Soviet era, and the rank general or colonel-general, the equivalent of a three-star general in the U.S. Army. The man himself had brutal, peasant stock features.

"That's Victor Bout," Brognola said. "The man himself." Bolan saw a square-faced Caucasian with short, almost bristling salt-and-pepper hair, and narrow-set eyes over a thick nose. The man had a lantern jaw, and he wasn't smiling. "He used to command his own internal security division in the GRU, the Soviet Military Intelligence."

Bolan grunted. He had tangled with more than one GRU and former GRU agent in his day. They tended to be even more brutal and direct-action prone than their KGB counterparts. "Let me guess," Bolan offered. "He turned to criminal enterprise when the Communists lost power?"

"The more things change, the more they stay the same," Kurtzman stated.

"He's more than that, though," Price interrupted. It was her turn to nod at Kurtzman. Instantly the picture on the screen was replaced by four. Victor Bout was in a slick dark blue power suit instead of an olive-drab uniform, his military haircut and regulation mustache replaced by a modest ponytail and a full but well-groomed beard. In another picture the barrel-chested man was standing in swimming trunks on the bridge of a private yacht. Two beautiful women with perfect bodies and eyes so vapid they came out clear as diamonds in the pixilated image, lounged behind him, drinks in hand. In the third, Bout was sitting at the table of some obviously expensive restaurant talking to a mahogany-skinned man in his twenties.

"Who's Bout talking to?" Bolan asked.

"That is the son of the head of the financial projects committee of the United Nations," Kurtzman answered.

"Oil-for-food?"

"Oil-for-food," Brognola acknowledged.

The second man in the fourth picture needed no identification. It was the president of Venezuela.

"Well, that's no problem," Bolan said dryly. "I just saw on the international news how the guy isn't a rogue leader at all. He's just someone who disagrees with the U.S. on oil policy."

"Sure," Price said. "Suspend the constitution, muffle the press, jail dissidents, start a war with Colombia…whatever."

"I do get the point," Bolan stated, turning away from the screen. "Our good Mr. Bout is a very powerful, very well-connected gentleman."

"And he's only third in command of his syndicate," Brognola said, leaning forward. "He *is* the principal adviser to one of the premier oligarchs in Russia today, a man in control of Siberian oil fields, Moscow central banking and Black Sea shipping. Colonel-General Bout's last-known location, Split, Croatia. Status, currently missing."

"Okay, he's missing. But he didn't just pop up because he's next on some hit list," Bolan pointed out.

"Bear," Price said.

Kurtzman hit the space bar then the Ctrl and Tab buttons on his keypad with a practiced motion. The screen changed. Now there was an image of a lanky, disheveled man of some obvious height.

In the picture he stood next to a red Mini-Cooper on a European or Mediterranean city cobblestone street. He had to have been close to seven feet tall.

"Akhilesh Pandey," Brognola announced.

"Mr. Pandey," Price continued, "is the premier researcher of cloning technology in India today."

"Current status, also missing. Last-known location, Split, Croatia," Kurtzman stated.

"Ah," Bolan said. "I'm sensing a perfect storm."

"Sort of. Well," Price allowed, "if you factor in the location, then you're exactly right. This a perfect storm. Bear, let's talk Prisni Prijatelji."

The cyberwizard again worked his keyboard. First a map of the world appeared in greens and blues on the screen, overlaid with lines of latitude and longitude. Then the perspective of the screen shifted smoothly. Bolan watched as it zeroed in on the Mediterranean, then slid past the boot of Italy to tighten focus on the Adriatic Sea. It shifted to the Croatian coastline, played south and settled on the city of Split.

Once in place, the screen's software put a white box around the city and began cycling its resolution, pulling it into focus. A street map from satellite imagery stamped with the discreet logo of the National Reconnaissance Office appeared. From an overview of the entire city Kurtzman quickly clicked down the area of observation into tighter and tighter resolution until an area of five square urban blocks filled the screen.

"I was less than three blocks away when I hit the triad in that warehouse," Bolan commented.

Frowning as the others murmured their agreement, Bolan leaned forward. The western edge of the built-up area consisted of wharfs and industrial piers as well as several large, squared-off jetties. Beyond that, to the north, south and west the area bordered the other streets of the city of Split. Inside the designated area there was a mixture of buildings from commercial to hospitality to warehouses.

Bolan turned and cocked an eyebrow in question to the leadership cadre of Stony Man Farm. "Prisni Prijatelji?" he asked.

"Prisni Prijatelji," Price confirmed.

Settling back in his chair Bolan took another drink of his coffee. "Explain."

"Split has taken over from Berlin as ground zero where east means west. Hell, what East means now is something a lot different from what it meant in the bad old days of the Soviet Empire," Brognola began. "But, for purposes of the War on Terror to our intelligence services, Split is a very important place. As important as Islamabad and more important than Damascus, Beirut or Amman. European and Middle Eastern businessmen mix there in prolific numbers, forming a smoke screen of legitimacy for the thriving black markets beneath the surface."

"Oil money meets former Soviet stockpiles of weapons?" Bolan offered.

"Sure," Price broke in. "Plenty of that going on. But Asian and South American drug pipelines into Europe intersect there. Terrorist cells and fugitives purchase papers and forged documents. Mercenaries cavort. International banking uses Croatian cutout companies to laundry money. As you discovered, there are thriving white slavery rings running girls from Asia into Eastern Europe and girls the other way back out again. It's a flipping strip mall of international criminal activity from the pettiest to the largest."

"Which is why Bout was there," Bolan observed. "He was serving as an intermediary for his banker boss?"

"That's what we think," Brognola agreed. "But as bad as Split is, in general that area along the waterfront—" he indicated the neighborhood with a blunt fingertip "—is the epicenter. Ground zero, part criminal-free fire zone and part intelligence DMZ."

"What do you mean?" Bolan asked.

"That neighborhood is one massive front. Fronts for criminals, fronts for intelligence operatives keeping an eye on the international syndicates...and each other. Success begets success. Once the big players realized how much information there was to be gleaned from this little neighborhood in Split, the services of half a dozen countries began to lean on their governments to look the other way. Let the snakes play in a nest all together so that we could get them in other places."

Price spoke up. "Once word of the hand-off approach leaked out of the tier one agencies to their second tier allies, on both sides, it really began to heat up as every two-bit station chief from any third world country saw opportunities to get their own cut with the geopolitical immunity. Bribes and payoffs began pouring out of the sector. Enough to ensure the local and Croatian federal police keep their noses clear."

"UN peacekeepers?" Bolan asked.

"Some," Price admitted. Then she shrugged. "They're positioned closer to the main industrial docks and the rail lines. They're mostly just symbolic now in Split anyway. Besides all it would take is a word from the intelligence community to the OIC of whatever detachment has Prisni Prijatelji as their district to get them to stand down."

"I've seen cities where the local police have been paid enough to steer clear of certain neighborhoods," Bolan said. "Usually it's a mess of a free-fire zone between pushers and street gangs."

"They had some of that," Brognola stated. "But the organized syndicates leaned on the thugs. Can't sell to the eurotrash *touristas* if bullets are flying everywhere and bodies are in the street. The territories are pretty well defined now. You get street violence occasionally and there are so many free-lancers hunting you can't guarantee anything when the sun goes down and night comes. But it's not like Compton in the late 1980s or something."

"Lovely."

"Make no mistake, Mack," Price said. "Nobody but nobody in that section of the city is legitimate, or who they say they are. Your friends, the Mountain and Snake Society, have really solidified their control and the influence of both Chinese and North Korean intelligence with them. Everyone who's not running a scam is a confidential informant. If they're not a CI, then they're an operative. Failing that, they're a petty criminal."

"Well, there are tourists," Kurtzman broke in. "The libertine controls on the local nightclubs make it popular for twenty-something kids from the more prosperous regions of the EU to hang out there. It's replaced Amsterdam as the 'it' city for the disaffected and chic bored."

"Sheep for the wolves," Bolan muttered.

"Exactly," Price said.

"What's Pandey doing there?" Bolan asked. "I get that you can score anything in this place, but doesn't cloning tech seem just a little upscale even for this modern-day version of Casablanca?"

Kurtzman spoke up again. "The international law on bioweapons is very clear. Certain technologies used to regulate such weapons in mass quantities are as tightly controlled and monitored as their nuclear counterparts. Not so the cloning tech. You take a strain of weaponized Anthrax, or Influenza and you replicate them, or modify their DNA helixes to be sturdier *then* replicate them, and you can work in peace from international monitoring agencies until the bureaucrats writing the laws can play catch-up."

"Seems almost too simple." Bolan grunted.

"We're always playing catch-up," Price said.

"Unless we can be proactive," Brognola observed.

"That's where I come in."

"As always, Striker," the big Fed acknowledged. "As always."

"Right now we know both men entered Prisni Prijatelji," Price continued. "Then they disappeared. We want to know why and we want to know where. Two of Bout's bodyguards, ex-GRU naval infantry Spetsnaz, turned up yesterday floating facedown in the ocean outside the neighborhood. Two days before that a call girl named Marlina Dubrovnik disappeared in Prisni Prijatelji's only hotel."

"A hotel where Pandey had a room where she was going to meet him?" Bolan supplied.

Brognola held up a loosely clasped hand and blew on it, spreading his fingers wide as he did so and showing it to be empty. "Just like that. She goes to his room. He lets her in. Then they're gone."

"We have people on them?"

"We did. Team of military spooks out of the Pentagon. The unit Rumsfeld created."

Bolan nodded. "The Strategic Support Branch."

"Right, a SSB team with some electronic and signal intelligence special reconnaissance units, Special Forces commo guys, a DIA electronic intelligence analyst. Solid operators. Code parole is 'Center Spike.' They had a military attaché operations in Zagreb. When the Agency caught Pandey's movement out of New Delhi, they asked for assistance."

"The Company asked for help?" Bolan asked.

Brognola shrugged. "Their best operatives are running Pakistan and Iraq these days. They had a lone tail on Pandey, and Prisni Prijatelji is no place for a single operator."

Bolan lifted a single eyebrow. Brognola laughed. "Unless it's you, Striker."

Bolan turned serious. "The SSB unit know I'm going in?"

"They know something is going on and that they're to provide imagery and surveillance assistance to an American intelligence operator," Price said. "But I've had them replaced in position."

"Replaced?"

"With Jack and Charlie Mott," Price answered. "We're going to keep this in the family."

"Akira and I set up a line of communications to ensure Farm security," Kurtzman broke in. "They constructed boosted relay stations for our Computer Room right here on the Farm. What Jack and Charlie have is real easy 'point and click' stuff, less sophisticated than the controls on the planes they fly. But, by them being live we'll have the electronic equivalent of a field office right in your back pocket."

Bolan turned toward Price. "So I still do my commo through the Farm?"

Price nodded. "You'll have an enhanced cell phone-PDA for urgent visual updates. And direct audio with them. Otherwise the Jack and Charlie team will do its thing completely separate from you and feed us updates every eight hours. They'll go trolling to see what they pick up until you point them in a direction."

"So I'm supposed to enter a section of the city of Split that is a law unto itself. A place where everyone is pretending to be something they aren't. Then I start following up leads to find two people who've disappeared, but whose disappearances may or may not be linked."

Brognola nodded. "Yeah. That about sums it up. But don't forget, if anyone suspects you of being an American agent, there are half a hundred intelligence and criminal cells who'll try to kill you."

Kurtzman leaned in. "And there's so much going on that the potential that you could stumble onto something nefarious is high. Almost guaranteed. It just won't be guaranteed that it'll be the exact nefarious activity we want."

Bolan leaned back. "When do I leave?"

CHAPTER SIX

The underground railcar came to a stop and Bolan climbed out, went through the requirements of the security checkpoint and entered the Annex. He found Akira Tokaido sitting in front of three separate computer screens at a desk with the music from his MP-3 player so loud it bled out of his earbuds. When the lean Japanese American saw Bolan approaching, he lifted his chin in greeting and killed the volume on his digital player.

"'Sup, boss," Tokaido said.

"Barb told me you have something I could use."

Tokaido grinned. "I got something good cooked up for you." He swung around in his chair and pulled open a desk drawer. Bolan watched as the cybersorcerer removed two electronic devices and placed them on the desktop.

Bolan nodded then pointed at the pot of coffee brewing over on the wall across the room. "Bear make that?"

"Yep. Oh yeah," Tokaido bobbed his head. "You want some?"

"No. I don't think my stomach could take two cups in the same day. What you got for me?"

"This is a BlackBerry. Common model, the latest but nothing that screams 'spook.' Inside however, under the hood, I've created a system of incredible power. So incredible that I prefer to think of it as magic.

"This will let Jack and Charlie give you a head's up on anything they find using our advanced placed relays. Your laptop will display any of the TEMPEST info they pick up, as well as parabolic and laser microphone readings. Video surveillance, still shots digital relay, whatever. All passive and all linked to them through our cutouts here on the Farm. Very secure."

Bolan knew TEMPEST technology allowed individuals in physical proximity to read the energy emitted from computer screens and translate it. There were commercial programs available to thwart the program, but nothing existed to defeat the version of the TEMPEST equipment used by the NSA.

"Excellent."

"Look, I put an interactive layer over the tech. Reduced it to point-and-click shortcuts so you don't need to be an MIT grad to use it and defend it—same thing I did for the gear Jack and Charlie will be using. But that was a risk, so if you don't put in the passive code indicator that I'm going to show you, within six seconds of initiating use, it'll scramble and dump everything. A prompt screen will not appear—just your desktop icons, but the software will be monitoring your keystrokes. Miss the window and the thing shuts down and buttons up." Tokaido leaned forward, his face intent. "Then the weaponized laser on our Keyhole satellite fires."

Bolan looked at him, one eyebrow cocked.

The young man chuckled, obviously amused at his own super-secret agent joke. "Just so you know, *if* we did want to, I could hook that up."

"I know, you're a mad scientist of binary process."

Tokaido grinned. "You know, boss, it's nice to be appreciated."

FIFTEEN MINUTES LATER Bolan left the Computer Room and carried his new items to John "Cowboy" Kissenger's workshop.

The gunsmith sat at a desk filled with a multitude of firearm parts. Barrels, receivers, springs and trigger mechanisms were spread out in seemingly random patterns next to a laptop showing diagnostic images of various handguns. He looked up as Bolan entered the room and waved him toward the only uncluttered seat.

"Put some nasty little surprises together for you," Kissenger said by way of opening.

"I'm not going to have to tell you what a wizard you are in order to get anything in a timely fashion, am I?" Bolan asked.

"Been working with Akira, huh?"

Bolan smiled and shrugged. "He works some funky magic."

"Yeah, if I could just get his mind off putting a damn

death ray on Barb's Keyhole I'd be happy." He laughed. "But hell, I just put a submachine gun in a briefcase for you, so if anyone could write code for a space-based laser it's our boy Akira."

"You use a H&K MP-5?"

"No, that's standard, but I figured accuracy in a briefcase configuration isn't really what you're after. I went with an Ingram MAC-10 so you could have .45-caliber rounds. With the squat body and stub barrel I was able to thread it for the same silencer we use on the M-11 and it all fit nicely with a 32-round magazine."

Kissenger picked up an expensive leather briefcase from behind his chair beside the desk. He set it on the table. "Someone's gonna think I'm a lawyer," Bolan commented.

"Right up until you depress the button on the handle," Kissenger stated.

PRISNI PRIJATELJI, in Split, had been deemed a national historic landmark by the Croatian government some years before, after cessation of hostilities. That designation had done little to relieve the crushing weight of brutal poverty and squalor that marked the labyrinth of twisting, narrow lanes and haphazardly stacked buildings.

Life was cheap in Split, and nowhere was it cheaper than in that hypercriminalized section that ran along the waterfront. Every manner of vice was bartered here and violence was a common salutation. The commodities of criminal enterprise flowed through the area, washing dirty money and camouflaging the activities of terror merchants among the masses of impoverished but hard-working families.

Jack Grimaldi flew the Little Bird helicopter low over the ocean, racing toward the shoreline of Split's Prisni Prijatelji. Bolan looked down through the bubble windshield of the agile helicopter and once again watched the whitecaps breaking on a dark sea.

Grimaldi cut and drifted, navigating the mass of ships and boats that dotted the ocean on his insertion into one of the busiest seaports in the world. Among the teeming masses of humanity engaged in the game of survival there one man sat as an information node with intelligence Bolan required about Victor Bout.

For now he would dispense blood and thunder in a hell storm of retribution for what had been done to Karen Rasmussen. Grimaldi popped up to a slightly higher elevation to jump a pleasure yacht floating on the swells of the Adriatic and make his final run in on the waterfront industrial property of an Azerbaijani criminal named Dadashbeyli who was ostensibly an import-export entrepreneur with connections to Hong Kong and North Korea in the Orient. In reality he was a pimp who had found his operation strong-armed into servitude to the Hong Kong triad.

According to Kim Su-Kweon's files and the information Karen Rasmussen was able to give, he was the man who had first come to serve as communications facilitator between Victor Bout and the Mountain and Snake Society. DEA and Interpol files had shown intelligence revealing a connection with the property of Dadashbeyli and the fencing of materials gained through criminal activity as far away as Chechnya. Thieves of any stripe never stole what they couldn't sell, and Bolan had learned through long years of experience to follow the flow of the money right to the top, to the very head of the hydra.

Flying low to avoid Croatian military air traffic control, Grimaldi turned sharply left and began flying south, perpendicular to the wharves and docks of the Split waterfront, out just beyond the reach of the floodlights and streetlamps. He flew the blacked-out helicopter by instrument readings and a GPS feed that ticked off the meters as they flew by.

Bolan sat next to him, prepped for a hard probe in his nightfighter black, his face covered with a thin balaclava hood. He was reunited with his .44-caliber pistol, and it rode in its place of honor on his right thigh while his silenced Beretta 93-R was in its customary shoulder holster under his left arm. From the shipboard armory Bolan had taken an H&K MP-5 SD-3, the suppressed version of the famous special operator submachine gun, and a reliable standby.

Grimaldi avoided a series of power lines and cut up an abandoned alley in the narrow space between warehouses and industrial plants. Bolan turned in his seat and put his feet on the helicopter's skid as he prepped for his second heliborne assault into Split.

Grimaldi suddenly cut left, skimming above a parked flatbed truck, and hopped over a chain-link fence to come down in an asphalt parking lot behind a three-story office building set above massive concrete loading docks lined with semi-tractor trailers, sitting quietly and unmanned.

The Stony Man pilot flared the Little Bird into a knap of the earth hover and Bolan dropped the last eight feet off the skid. He hit the ground smoothly, bending at the knees to absorb the impact, then raced toward a small door made of wood, its paint peeling and set some distance away from the loading bays.

Behind the sprinting Bolan the Little Bird helicopter was powered away quickly and had disappeared into the night before the Executioner had covered a dozen yards of his run. He reached into the split pocket of his left pant leg and removed what looked like a bag of a popular brand of European snack chips. Inside was a device about the size of a cigarette pack used to boost localized electronic signals.

Without breaking stride Bolan dropped the camouflaged booster pack among the copious amounts of trash and garbage that littered the place. It was instantly lost in the scattered rubbish strewed about.

Still running in a tight double-time Bolan reached the door, lifted the MP-5 up to his shoulder and triggered a silenced burst. The 9 mm Parabellum rounds struck the door's commercial lock mechanism and blew it apart.

Satellite imagery and downloaded blueprints had provided the information Bolan needed on which side the hinges were located and the material strength of the door structure. Without breaking stride Bolan raised a big boot and kicked the mutilated door open.

It swung inward to reveal a long hall of gleaming linoleum floors under industrial tract lighting. Bolan's rubber soles slapped a hard rhythm as he sprinted down the corridor. He ran with a loose, easy stride that ate up the interior distances, his submachine gun up at a three-quarters port arms that left the muzzle of the silenced weapon oriented toward his front.

Bolan turned a corner, sprinted down the short stretch, then took a left-hand turn, the path he had memorized off the building blueprints. He cut down another hall, then opened a seemingly random door where he found stairs that he immediately ascended.

He looked up and saw a stunned Croatian mobster in a grubby T-shirt and jeans coming down the stairs. The young man's hair had been gelled into a carefully crafted just-rolled-out-of-bed look, and his lower lip was pierced in three places.

The man scratched for the butt of a Beretta 92-F pistol that jutted from the front of his jeans. Bolan squeezed his trigger and the H&K kill box cycled through a tight pattern. A triumvirate of bloody divots appeared over the man's heart and he tumbled. Blood smeared the wall behind him as a crimson mist settled like dew on the floor.

Bolan stepped over the corpse and raced up the stairs to the next landing. He bypassed the landing door and took the next flight of steps, running faster now, taking them two at a time.

He reached the top of the stairs, covering the three flights in under thirty seconds. At the top of the stairs he pulled open the door and entered a less industrial-looking hallway.

The corporate office space was sheathed in laminate flooring and sandalwood paneling. The lighting was soft and intimate. Pictures of shorelines, ocean views and ships were interspersed along the walls. The air smelled of freshener and cleaning products. At the far end of the hallway two Asian men in dark suits lounged in front of a pair of oak double doors.

Bolan hurried down the hallway, a blacksuited terror hurtling straight toward the stunned men, his weapon up and at the ready as he charged forward without uttering a word. The men scrambled to bring P-90 submachine guns out from underneath suit jackets, but Bolan's finger was steady on his trigger.

The German-made weapon coughed and Bolan saw the shirts of the men puff up as the 9-mm slugs sliced into them. The men staggered backward under the impact of the man-killer rounds. Seeing no blood on the bulky-framed bodies, Bolan realized the bodyguards were wearing ballistic vests.

While the two men shuddered under the initial impacts, Bolan shifted his weapon on the run and triggered it twice more. Each man took a round to the head, pulverizing skulls and spraying blood and brains across the sandalwood paneling.

The men dropped like sacks of loose meat and bounced hard off the floor. Bolan raced past them and snapped open the door leading to the inner sanctum of the corporate office.

He snapped open the door and stepped through, holding the H&K MP-5 SD-3 one-handed as he transitioned through the entranceway. He found a reception lobby commanded by a large desk and outfitted with several comfortable chairs.

Three more young Asian men lounged around the room reading magazines and smoking cigarettes. Bolan took the man directly in front of him first. The guy held his P-90 in his lap while he sat on the edge of the desk and looked at a glossy magazine. Bolan's burst punched through the shiny pictures of the periodical and mangled the flesh and cartilage of the man's throat. Blood splattered across the phone and clock and keyboard mounted on the desk.

Bolan came to a stop in the middle of the room. He swiveled to his left, firing at a second gunman. The impact slammed the man against the wall, then he slid lifelessly to the floor.

The Executioner snapped back around to his right, bringing his weapon to bear on the last man. The guy was rising to his feet, smoking cigarette tumbling away as he tried to fire his submachine gun from the hip. Fear caused him to trigger his weapon too soon, and a burst of 5.7 mm armor-piercing ammo burned into the carpet.

Bolan's burst caught him between chin and nose. The man absorbed the rounds and tumbled forward.

A second door to the office was thrown open and a

man in an expensive business suit ran out. Bolan held
his fire for a split second to identify his target, allow-
ing the pistol-wielding gunman to get off a round.

The .40-caliber bullet flew wide and Bolan scythed
the man's feet out from under him, then finished him
off with a tight burst to the top of his head. Bolan angled his weapon up, then fired a burst through the doorway to keep the room's occupants down as he charged
in.

Two men were seated at a desk that made the impressive table in the reception area look insubstantial by
comparison. He identified Dadashbeyli, immediately
from the triad lieutenant sitting across from him. The
man had thrown himself to the carpet while the Asian
man in the room began firing bullets from a Glock 17
at Bolan as soon as he crossed the threshold.

Bolan's initial burst of harassing fire had thrown the
man off balance, his shot winged wild. The big American drew down on him and put three tight bursts into
his body, splashing him across the conference table and
interior decor.

"Dadashbeyli!" Bolan snarled. "Stay down and you
might live. Down!"

He raced forward and shoved the smoking barrel of
his weapon into Dadashbeyli's face. He pressed down
hard into the Azerbaijani crime lord's face, insulting and
intimidating him. His voice was a cold wind to a helpless man.

"Don't talk. Don't breath. You do, and I'll ventilate
your thick skull."

Bolan's hands roamed the corrupt mobster's body. He removed a handgun and slid it behind his own back, jerked the man's wallet out and scattered the contents across the carpet. He took an expensive, sleek black cell phone and smashed it against the edge of the desk. If Dadashbeyli wanted to make a phone call later, he would be forced to use a landline.

He finished scattering the contents of Dadashbeyli's suit pockets and as he did so he managed to slip a tiny microphone and tracking device mounted on a slim straight pin in along the lining of his jacket. Mission accomplished, Bolan struck Dadashbeyli twice along the head with the muzzle of the H&K submachine gun to further confuse and distract the man.

"You're coming with me. Fight and you die."

CHAPTER SEVEN

Bolan raised his weapon and brought the butt down on the pinned man's head, cracking it hard into the floor. Dadashbeyli shuddered under the impact and went limp. The terrified man fought against his sense of vertigo and tried to focus his eyes again.

When he looked up, the Executioner snatched him to his feet by hands now secured behind his back and forced him out the door.

Bolan raced out of the building, driving Dadashbeyli in front of him. He left the office suite and ran down the hall, the soles of his boots slick with spilled blood and his captive stumbling. He hurried down the stairs, hurdled the quickly cooling corpse of his first kill and pushed Dadashbeyli out into the hallway on the ground floor. He sprinted back out the way he had come and kicked his way clear of the access door to jog into the parking lot, pushing the older and bound man ahead of him.

He double-timed it across the parking lot toward the back fence. Suddenly, Jack Grimaldi's helicopter darted around a building and swooped down. Bolan ran forward into the rotor wash and pushed the bound Dadash-beyli into the copilot's seat, then slid into position in the back of the helicopter to cover him.

The engine whined as Grimaldi reversed his pitch and pulled up from the ground, snatching Bolan away to safety.

"How'd it go?" he asked as Bolan slipped on his flight helmet.

"Pretty smooth," Bolan allowed. "Let's get this guy to the black site for interrogation. The sooner he talks, the sooner we move on to the next phase."

THE TAXICAB CAME to a halt and Bolan paid the driver.

He got out of the cab with his suitcase in his hand and looked around. Night was falling and streetlights were clicking on with automated efficiency as twilight thickened. Across the street the Hoteli Croatia marked the northern boundary of Prisni Prijatelji.

He looked to his right and noted the street ran down a few blocks to a dead end overlooking the waters of the Adriatic. He could smell the brine on the breeze. He waited for a break in the traffic then crossed the street toward the hotel.

Prisni Prijatelji was a pedestrian-only section of shops and restaurants up from the waterfront with narrow lanes and short alleys too tight to maneuver any vehicle larger than a Yugo or Mini-Cooper. The sole exception was a wide-access road for delivery vehicles cutting down from the street Bolan was now crossing and running behind the warehouses and fish processing plants that lined the piers on the western edge of the area.

Bolan stepped up onto the curb and regarded the Hoteli Croatia. It was nondescript brick-and-mortar building two stories high, to the west of the hotel was a channel filled with sea water. On either side of it, facing each other across a narrow concrete foot bridge, was a pub named the Vslick and an anonymous building Bolan couldn't determine the purpose of.

Down the alley between the hotel and the two businesses, he heard the sound of running feet. Instinctively he turned toward the noise. Out beyond the edge of the two-story building making up the hotel, where the alley intersected with a narrow cobblestone lane, he thought he caught a flash of movement but then it was gone. He lifted his eyes to the rooftops with the automatic diligence of a trained countersniper. From the pub to his right and down the lane in front of him, where he knew from studying a map of the area that a restaurant with outdoor seating was located, he heard the sound of people in conversation. Hip-hop music began to bleed out through a closed window above his head and he turned and began walking toward the entrance of the hotel.

BOLAN PICKED UP HIS KIT from a bored night manager with a scar running down his left cheek in a thick pink line. There was a skylight over the front desk and some indifferent Monet prints on the gilded wallpaper, but other than that the lobby was clean but unremarkable.

He got out of the elevator and walked along the hall, watching the doors as he did so and noting which of them showed lights underneath or had sounds coming through. According to the intelligence that Stony Man had been given, back channel deals got done in the Hoteli Croatia. The people doing those deals could form the first link in the trail of breadcrumbs that could lead him to Bout or Pandey.

Throwing his gear and luggage on the bed, Bolan pulled out his enhanced cell phone and sent the predestinated code alerting the Stony Man overwatch unit that he was in position and ready to begin.

Immediately the Jack Grimaldi-Charlie Mott support team replied. He felt a slow smile spread across his face as he read the text message on his screen. They'd already discovered a clue on location of Pandey's missing prostitute. As soon as they had double checked a confidential informant's information, they would call.

Settling into a chair by the window, Bolan prepared to catch forty winks. Things were going to get hot in Split very soon, and he needed to be ready.

THE PHONE RANG.

Bolan opened his eyes. The phone rang again. He blinked the room into focus and saw his equipment and arsenal spread across the worn covers of the single mattress bed.

The phone rang again and Bolan reached over to the

table next to his chair and picked up the cellular unit. He didn't bother to turn on a light, and the room remained choked in darkness broken only by the feeble light bleeding in through the window.

He checked the number on the Caller ID and hit the button. His voice was rough as he answered the phone.

"Go ahead."

As he listened to the voice on the other end, he looked around the dimly illuminated room. It was worn and shabby, the cheapness of the fixtures and furniture apparent even in the uncertain light. The value of the guns on the bed was worth more than the contents of the room, perhaps even worth more than the old building that housed it.

"I understand," Bolan said. He mentally repeated the address back to himself with a sniper's acumen for remembering details. "I'll bring the money."

The blunt tip of his thumb found the End button and killed the connection. His thumb then worked the buttons, opening his speed dial menu and hitting the 3. He rose from the tattered easy chair and stood by the window while he waited for his connection.

The curtains were flimsy and reeked of cigarette smoke. Outside on the dirty asphalt the street was quiet. He was a hunter in his hide, alone and preparing for the stalk and kill.

On the other end of the line one of Bolan's oldest comrades and allies answered on the second ring.

"Your source came through," Bolan said without preamble. "The meet is on. She tried to juke me for the price, but it's no matter. Whoever did the interrogation on Dadashbeyli did a bang-up job. This snitch seems to know her business."

He listened to Brognola's admonishment and a grudging smile tugged at the corner of his mouth. The big Fed was quite the mother hen when he wanted to be. It was oxymoronic considering the countless impossible situations the government control sent him into, time and again. Still it was better by far than indifference, with only the cold certainty of his mission to keep him connected to the humanity that he watched over like a vengeful guard dog.

"No. A place called the Hard Glass Club once you translate," Bolan replied to a question.

Brognola gave him an update on the latest developments, but they didn't amount to much. If the trail hadn't been so cold, the clues so elusive, then he wouldn't have been forced into such a dangerous meeting in the first place. "All right, Hal," Bolan said. "I'll let you know how this turns out. No, I'm leaving now. Go ahead and have the cleaners come through, I'll leave the front door unlocked."

Bolan snap closed his phone and turned away from the window. He didn't bother turning on the lights. He crossed the room to the bed and picked up the familiar weight of his Beretta. With deft, practiced motions he secured the four-inch sound suppressor to the specially threaded barrel. He eased back the slide until a greasy gold bullet fed out of the extended magazine, then let the bolt snap forward, seating the round in the chamber. He tucked the little machine pistol with its oversize trigger guard into the small of his back.

He put his right foot on the bed and pulled his pants leg up, revealing thick dark socks over which a nylon ankle holster had been secured. Picking up a compact Detonics .45 caliber Combat Master, he slid it into the sling.

He returned his foot to the floor and in quick order tucked a stunt gun designed to look like a cell phone to his belt, slid a folding clasp knife with thumb-post into his front pocket, then picked up the smallest version of an extendable baton.

He shrugged on his leather jacket and placed the baton in the deep front pocket of the coat. Lastly he picked up a brown manila envelope and shook it. Several rolls of money, in hundred-dollar bill denominations, fell out onto the bed, as fat as bunched-up socks. He was using U.S. dollars rather than euros as part of his cover.

He counted out a few thousand dollars, then returned the rest of the money to the envelope and left it on the bed.

The Executioner was on the move.

BOLAN STEPPED into a doorway a few blocks down the street from the Hard Glass. This section of Split was a meat-packing district bordering Prisni Prijatelji and was devoid of any other businesses. It should have been quiet on a Saturday night past two in the morning. As it was, the parking lot of the abandoned warehouse was filled with expensive cars and the street was as busy as a workday at noon.

Intelligence showed the private after-hours club had been run by the local branch of a crime organization, but six months ago representatives of the Mountain and Snake Society had informed the owner of a change in management. Now the triad provided security. Their motorcycles, expensive and powerful street bikes, were parked in front of the club in territorial splendor. It was rather like a primitive tribe sticking the heads of their enemies on poles as warnings, Bolan mused as he surveyed the building.

According to the CI, the basement had been co-opted for the illegal enterprise with the loading dock area given over to bar and dance floor while the warren of storage rooms running under the building were dedicated to even more nefarious pursuits.

The only lights on the avenue came from the cars cruising by in search of parking spaces as the streetlights along the thoroughfare had mysteriously ceased working on both sides of the street for a distance of a city block in either direction.

That was fine; Bolan preferred the dark.

He crossed the street to where a late-model German SUV had been left by his Stony Man support team. He felt under the lip of the wheel well for the magnetic key hide, found it and unlocked the vehicle. He reached up and pushed the switch controlling the dome light into the off position and then closed the door again, hitting the automatic lock button on his key fob before stuffing it into the pocket opposite the one where he carried his baton.

Bolan checked traffic and crossed the street. He could hear the throb of modern dance music coming from the building, and suddenly a bar of light appeared out of the gloom in the corner of his vision, causing him to turn toward the front door to the Hard Glass Club. A burly European male came hurtling out of the doorway, arms windmilling wildly, sputtering curses. Music poured out the open entrance in deafening crescendos. Bolan stopped walking and watched as the big man struck the concrete hard, his head bouncing cruelly. Three big Asians with bare arms covered in swirling tattoos appeared in the doorway. One held an upside down pool cue. The other held a sawed-off shotgun.

The man who had just been ejected staggered to his feet and the shotgun wielder lifted the weapon. Bolan tensed, prepared to move into action, but the first man held up his hands and spit blood on to the sidewalk.

"I'm leaving," he snarled, his voice slurred and speaking German well enough for Bolan to follow. "You tell Taz I'm through."

The man with the shotgun looked past his victim and his eyes met Bolan's. "Problem?" he asked in heavily accented German across the twenty yards separating them.

Bolan met the man's gaze with a steady look. Slowly he shook his head no. The man seemed satisfied and he turned back to look at the patron they had just thrown out of the club. Bolan took the moment to memorize every detail about the triad thug. He was big, as tall as Bolan, and powerfully built, his arms crawling with multicolored tattoos.

The man handed the sawed-off shotgun to the lanky bouncer standing next to him. The guy retreated into the private after-hours club and the door shut behind him, muting the cacophony. The two remaining bouncers stood like Sphinxes in front of the door, over four hundred pounds of anabolic steroid muscle between the two of them.

Bolan frowned.

This was a meet-and-greet, not even a simple soft probe. Fighting his way past the doormen would do him no good. He couldn't simply kill them, no matter their list of crimes, and hope to continue on with his rendezvous. He had to make his meet, he desperately needed the information the confidential informant could provide. If the clues were correct, then biocloned weapons were about to make their way into circulation on the world market.

Bolan walked closer as the beat-up patron stumbled off. The two bouncers crossed their arms across torsos that seemed to have more in common with lowland gorillas than human beings. Bolan didn't try a friendly smile or to cajole the muscle; it wouldn't work.

"You mind if I get a drink?" he asked, stepping up to the entrance.

He addressed the man who had produced the sawed-off shotgun, assuming he was the leader, or most alpha male in the triad crew providing "security" for the establishment. The man's face remained impassive. This close to the big guy, Bolan could see the red veins standing out against the yellowed tinge of the sclera in his eyes.

"I don't think this is your kind of crowd," the man replied.

"I want a beer." Bolan avoided mentioning the name of the CI he was supposed to make contact with. If things went south getting through the door, it would only put him in danger and offer no advantage to Bolan himself.

"So go to a fucking store," the man replied. "This isn't a place for you."

"Is there a cover?" Bribes made the world turn.

But the triad bouncer just cocked his head to the side and squinted at Bolan. "You a cop?"

"I just got out of the Army," Bolan said, thinking quickly but keeping his voice neutral. "I'm knocking around. I just want a drink and to see some girls dancing."

"Bullshit," the man said, and he said it in English.

Very deliberately he reached out a hand the size of a dinner plate and placed it against the muscular plane of Bolan's chest. The Executioner remained motionless, and it took every ounce of will power he had not to break the man's wrist and kick his teeth in.

Very slowly, but with undeniable strength, the man straightened his arm out, pushing Bolan backward.

"I don't like you," the bouncer said. "I don't believe you. I ever see you in the club, I'm going to bust your ass. Now blow before I break something on you."

Bolan lifted his arms up, showing empty hands. "Sure. Sure, whatever you say," he replied, still speaking German.

"Oh, I *know* that, asshole."

Bolan turned on his heel and stalked back to his vehicle. He was going to have to try another approach.

CHAPTER EIGHT

Twenty minutes later Bolan stood in the alley to the rear of the old warehouse housing the Hard Glass after-hours club. Like muted thunder the music from inside the place pulsed outward through the brick and mortar, bleeding into the night.

He looked around, evaluating the building like a rock climber sizing up a cliff face. Above the first floor the squat building was constructed with five uniform windows running the width of the building along each floor.

Bolan made his decision and zipped up his jacket. It would keep him from getting to his concealed weapons quickly, but it was a necessary risk if he was going to attempt this climb. He reached for the lip of the door-way and put one foot on the knob. He placed his other hand against the edge of the building, using the strength of his legs to support him as he released one handhold on the door frame and reached for a gutter drain set into the wall.

He grabbed hold firmly there and held on before moving his other hand over. The drain was chilly and damp, as he pulled himself up and grasped the vertically running structure with both hands. He moved his right leg and stuck his foot between the drainpipe and the brick wall, jamming it in as tightly as he could to anchor his position.

Once he was braced, Bolan pulled his boot from the doorknob and set it on top of the door frame. It was slick along the top, and he was forced to brace his foot tight against the wall along the narrow lip. Confident with the placement of that foot, Bolan pushed down hard against the lip at the top of the door frame and shimmed himself farther up the drainpipe.

Bolan's muscles bunched and burned, and he forced himself to breathe in through his nose. He squeezed the slick pipe tightly as he inched his way up. He lifted himself until only the toe of the boot on the door frame was in contact with the narrow edge. The muscles of his calf flexed hard under the strain, and he released his left hand from the drainpipe and reached out and grasped the ledge of the second-story window closest to him.

He set himself, then dug his fingers into the wood. He pushed down against the ledge and inched his right hand farther up the drainpipe. One of his legs found a metal bracket securing the gutter drain to the wall, and Bolan wormed his boot toe hard into it. He shoved down with his left arm and lifted his free leg until his knee was resting on the second-story window ledge.

His body stretched into a lopsided X, Bolan carefully

pressed his hands against the windowpane and pushed upward, testing to see if the window was open. He met resistance and realized it was locked. Bolan eased his head back and looked up. A light was on in the window on the floor directly above his position. Above that the fourth floor was as dark as the second. Directly above that was the roof.

Decision made, he shimmed his way up to the third floor despite the toll the physical exertion was taking on him. Bolan was in exceptional physical shape but the task of urban climbing was extremely arduous. Hand over hand and toe hold to toe hold, Bolan ascended the outside of the building. He worked himself into position by the third-floor window where a light burned from behind a thin blind, causing butter-yellow light to seep into the calm of the early morning.

Bolan paused. He could hear the murmur of voices above the music pounding beneath them and sensed shadowed movements beyond the blind, but not enough for him to gather any intelligence. Moving carefully to diminish any sound of his passing, Bolan climbed the rest of the way up the building.

The soldier rolled over the building edge and dropped over the low rampart onto the tar-patched roof. He rose swiftly, unzipping his jacket and freed the Beretta machine pistol. Exhaust conductors for the building's central air formed a low fence of dull aluminum around the freestanding hutch housing the door to the fire stairs.

Bolan crossed the roof to the side opposite his ascent,

old gravel crunching under his boots, and reached the
door. He tried the knob, found it locked and quickly
worked his lock-pick gun on the simple mechanism.

He darted into the building and descended into
darkness.

THE SOUNDS OF THE AFTER-HOURS club was loud through
the walls. He could actually feel the vibration of the
bass humming up through the floors and into his feet.
Bolan entered Suki Bruja's apartment building. The
low-rent facility housed above the after-hours club was
a known drug dive, and the conditions were appalling.

He carried his silenced Beretta 93-R out and ready,
held down by his leg. Enough time had passed that, by
now, Bruja had to know their initial meet was compromised.

Bolan mounted the stairs leading down to Bruja's
fourth-floor apartment. If she was spooked by his being
late, Bruja would have fled, Bolan figured. In which
case he needed to make a careful search of her residence
before moving on to follow other leads. If, for some reason, the woman had failed to run, then Bolan could
take the trail up where he had left off.

Reaching the fourth floor, Bolan stopped at the corner of a wall and reconnoitered the hallway. It was
empty and silent, with soft overhead fixtures providing
a subdued illumination. Spray-painted graffiti stained
the walls and plastic bags of trash lined the hallway.
Bolan looked toward Bruja's doorway where a bar of
dark space separated the edge of the door from the jamb.

Bolan scowled to himself. There was no good reason for Suki Bruja's front door to be standing open in the middle of the night. Bolan ticked off the options. Had she simply run, leaving her door open? Was she there, waiting with a weapon? Had someone been sent to clean up the mess? If so, by whom? Bout? The triad? His list of enemies in Split was growing.

Bolan continued down the hallway. He lifted his pistol and held it at the ready, walking carefully, back to the wall, trailing hand out for support. He moved slowly, crossing one leg over the other. He gambled on hugging the inside wall because he estimated that if someone were covering the hallway from just inside the door, the person would have to shift or even open the door farther to get off an accurate shot, giving him fair warning.

Moving down the corridor, Bolan felt naked and exposed under the overhead lights. Any resident looking out the peephole as he passed would see him clearly, pistol out and ready. The alternative, keeping his pistol hidden and approaching the door openly was too suicidal to even be considered at that point. He also held a deep-rooted suspicion that the occupants of the apartments above the Hard Glass Club tended to mind their own business very studiously.

Reaching the door to Bruja's apartment, Bolan halted. He cocked his head, listening. He could hear nothing from inside the apartment through the open door. Pressing up against the wall for support, Bolan carefully placed the heel of his right foot against the edge of the door.

After a long, tense moment, Bolan pressed firmly with his heel, pushing it down toward the floor. The already ajar door swung wide, creaking in a low moan on unattended and old hinges. Bolan froze for a moment at the sound, poised.

When no reaction was forthcoming, he carefully slid down until he was crouched beside the now fully open door. Bolan put his free hand down and pivoted smoothly around it, pistol up and ready. He leaned over to the side in a base runner's stretch, trailing leg cocked outward to help keep his center of balance, enabling him to shift in either direction quickly.

Bolan shot a brief glance around the door before pulling his head back again. He had seen nothing—no figures, no movement. Slower this time, he peered around the corner and took a longer look. He scanned the interior of the apartment. It was like looking into a dark cave. A breeze stirred the lank curtains of the room's only window, but he detected no other motion.

Standing quickly he stepped through the doorway and into the room, sliding his back against the wall just inside the door, under the light switch. He swept his pistol around in memorized patterns of movements, efficiently clearing his zones.

Finding nothing, Bolan gently closed the door. He left the lights off in case they'd alert any sentries set to survey the building, or on the off chance that someone was still here, hidden deeper in the living quarters. He began methodically moving through the tiny apartment, clearing what rooms there were before moving on.

He moved through the living area into the kitchen. He cleared the cramped bathroom and a hall closet. The final door at the end of the short hall had been pulled shut and no light shone from underneath it.

Bolan held his silenced Beretta close to his head, the bulky cylinder of the sound suppressor even with the rise of his cheekbone. The pad of his fingertip rested confidently on the trigger of the weapon, taking up any slack in the pull. The weapon was close enough that he smelled the mellow scent of the oil he had used to lubricate the slide.

The Beretta's magazine was fed with subsonic hollowpoint rounds designed to flatten and mushroom out upon impact for maximum damage. At such close range the dum-dum ammunition would more than compensate for the light powder charge designed to complement the sound suppressor and medium-caliber 9 mm rounds.

Bolan reached out and grabbed the doorknob to Suki Bruja's bedroom, wrapping his fingers around it. He flexed his grip and slowly twisted the handle.

The door swung easily under his hand, revealing a bedroom cloaked in darkness. Bolan paused in the hall, listening, then entered the room, his pistol tracking. Using a Weaver-stance shuffle, Bolan moved past a dresser and then the large bed, both shadowy silhouettes in the dark. The drawers to the dresser hung open and articles of clothing spilled haphazardly from them. The covers on the bed were thrown back, and a pillow lay forgotten on the floor.

Bolan moved deeper into the room. He checked an open closet, saw only a few ratty coats and sweaters. He closed the closet door and went forward. His shoes made no sound on the thin bedroom carpet. The loudest noise in the place was the sound of his own breathing. He crossed the bedroom to a gloomy corner where he could barely make out the shape of a chair. Two steps forward and he finally was able to make out the figure, dropping the Beretta's muzzle to cover it. Suki Bruja looked up at him.

In the ambient light her eyes were open and glazed with the film of death. Her jaw hung slack and her skin glowed softly, like the alabaster of a statue, in the dim light. Bolan's gaze traveled off her relaxed face and took in her body. Bruja's arms hung loosely by her sides and her knees were splayed open. There was a rubber tubing band around her scrawny bicep, and a hypodermic needle hung from her arm.

She wore a tattered black T-shirt, and her hair hung loose in silken tresses the color of coal. Bolan reached out a hand and touched the dead woman's flesh—it was still warm. It was, in fact, so warm it felt feverish, and Bolan realized the corpse wasn't even minutes old.

He heard the rush of the attacker in the next moment, and spun. The edge of a hand as hard as wood slammed into his wrist and punched the Beretta to the floor. Bolan spun into the attack, saw the long-bladed knife coming up and struck the forearm with his own, stopping the killing stab cold.

When he heard the blackened figure grunt at the impact, he shot a straight punch out, knuckles vertical in an attempt to catch the figure in the solar plexus. The man bobbed and the blow struck along the rib cage instead. The figure staggered backward and Bolan pressed his advantage.

Too late, he realized the stumbling retreat had been a ploy and he only just managed to block the knee to his groin in time, taking the hard strike on his thigh instead. His hands came up and caught the next two arm strikes on the figure's wrist, sending the knife spinning away and stopping a roundhouse punch cold.

They both tried knee strikes at the same time and banged shins. Bolan twisted at the hip and rolled a left-handed elbow strike inside the figure's guard and felt a surge of savage satisfaction as he connected with the man's face. This time the attacker stumbled, and Bolan sprang forward like a big cat on a kill.

His right hand shot forward and the webbing between his finger and thumb caught the stunned attacker under the jaw on the throat right above the Adam's apple. The man made a hacking, gagging sound and stumbled again.

Bolan put his left leg outside of the other man's stance along his left leg at the knee. Moving like quicksilver, Bolan grasped the attacker by his head and twisted and pulled, executing a rolling hip throw. The man made a gurgling sound low in his throat as his body was thrown across the fulcrum of Bolan's leg and his head remained locked in place. The whiplash was as sharp as a man at the end of a gallows rope and the cartilage snapped right before the final, sharp crack that indicated the spine had separated.

The man sagged loose in Bolan's grip. In the confined space the sudden smell of voided bowels wafted up into the Executioner's nose and he knew for certain the man was dead. He let the body fall to the floor.

He crossed the room and found a light switch. It was a risk, but he didn't have a penlight with him and he needed to make a thorough search of both the apartment and his attacker. He blinked against the low wattage of the cheap, naked bulb hanging from a single chain in the center of the water-stained ceiling.

Suki Bruja, his contact, looked ghastly in the sickly yellow light. Her glassy doll's eyes seemed to follow him and the tip of her tongue poked out from her hanging mouth. Bolan let his gaze slide off her toward the man lying dead at her feet.

He was somewhat surprised to see that it wasn't an Asian thug from the triad. The man's coarse features looked brutish and Slavic. Bolan stepped closer to get a better look and then cursed silently to himself as the slamming door reverberated through the apartment.

CHAPTER NINE

Reaching up to his knit cap, Bolan pulled it down over his face so the balaclava obscured his features, then crossed the room toward the door, moving fast. His mind was racing as he ticked off options. Bolan reached out and grabbed the handle of the bedroom door, twisting the knob slowly and then, when it unlatched, lifting up slightly as he swung it open, preventing the hinges from squeaking.

Bolan straightened, shifting his body position. When the door was about halfway open, it suddenly imploded toward him. Despite his vast experience he was surprised. The intruder had moved fast.

Bolan was knocked off stride by the force of the blow, and he staggered back, arms windmilling to catch his balance. A heavy figure burst through the entryway hard on the heels of the swinging door. Unafraid, he charged straight into Bolan, pressing his attack. The man was big and fast for his size. He rushed in, using a shuffling side step but throwing haymakers and pressing his advantage.

Bolan retreated before the onslaught, his hands up and deflecting blows. He got a good look at the face and was hit with another surprise. He was facing Victor Bout himself. The Russian's big fists hammered through his guard, and Bolan rocked from the impact of the big punches, reeling under their force, staggering backward.

He came up against the bed and was bent over backward under Bout's onslaught. The change of position left him vulnerable but also changed his elevation, forcing Bout to reorient himself to continue his attack.

Bout turned to face Bolan fully and thrust himself up and forward, leading with a big right-handed hammer blow.

The expression on Bout's face was oddly detached, like a man performing some slightly odious but necessary task. It was red from his exertion but betrayed no emotion whatsoever. His hair was thick and pulled back in a perfectly coiffed ponytail, his beard had been groomed recently. Shoved up this close to the man's bulk and mammoth power, Bolan realized Bout had to have been pushing over 220 pounds and was heavily muscled under a misleading layer of fat.

Bout leaned in over the awkwardly positioned Bolan and brought his right hand down like a railroad maul toward the Executioner's exposed face. Bolan made no attempt to block the powerful blow. As the arm came down, he turned his head to the side and lifted his left shoulder up toward the strike while wrapping his arms around the descending fist in a hugging maneuver.

Bolan winced as the strike hammered home into his shoulder and neck hard enough to rattle his teeth before he snapped his trap closed. Bolan's right hand captured Bout's arm at the wrist while his left arm snapped up and bent back to grab the same wrist, pressing his elbow and forearm in a parallel position with Bout's own grasping arm.

Joint lock in place, Bolan grasped as hard as he could and twisted like a snake around Bout's grip. His legs came up and wrapped themselves around Bout's upper arm, sinking in a brutally tight lock at the thick man's wrist and elbow. One foot pushed hard into Bout's face while the second foot found position under the bigger man's extended arm.

Bolan threw himself over, holding Bout's entrapped arm tightly to his torso. The Russian grunted with the sudden pain and was thrown off his feet beside the bed. Now on top of the hyperextended arm, Bolan threw himself backward off the bed, as well. This time Bout screamed.

The sound of the elbow popping was sharp, the sound of the shoulder coming out of the socket was sloshy and more muted. Both men sprawled to the floor of the dirty bedroom and Bout screamed again.

He was frantic to shake Bolan loose, but couldn't shift his bulk quickly enough to rise up. Bolan, refusing to let go of Bout's now mangled arm, began to hammer the heel of his foot into the big man's face.

Bout's head rocked with each impact, but Bolan felt as if he were putting his boots to a stone. The flesh of the Russian's right ear tore and blood soaked the side of his face, running freely down into his sporty mustache and beard. Bruises like horse shoes blossomed on the man's cheek and face. The tread of Bolan's boot tore an ugly gash in Bout's forehead above his bushy eyebrows.

The Russian swung his bulk around until he faced Bolan, and with his free hand he began to shove at the legs entangled around his injured arm. Bolan felt the big man's weight shift and rolled sharply with the changing leverage. He spun with the trapped arm in the opposite direction, brutally reversing angles.

Bout screamed again and was driven over Bolan's turning body. He planted his nose hard into the thin, blood-splattered carpet. Now on his belly, facing away from Bout with the man's arm trapped beneath him, Bolan started using his heel stomp again.

His face a bloody mask, Bout managed to grasp hold of Bolan's ankle and slow the force of the kicks. Blind with pain now, and beaten to a mess, the big Russian managed to get his legs underneath him. Bolan was stunned at the amount of damage Bout was able to absorb. The man rose to his feet, threatening to upend Bolan in the process.

The big American quickly changed positions. He released the man's arm just as Bout reared up and sought to lift Bolan from the floor. The man went stumbling backward, his balance completely compromised. He slammed hard into the wall and nearly tripped over the outflung arm of the dead assassin. Bolan leaped to his feet and started toward the other man.

Bout bent and snatched up the first man's knife, sending it hurtling into the rushing Bolan. The Executioner twisted to avoid the projectile, and Bout lunged toward his adversary's dropped pistol. Bolan came around the edge of the bed and leaped toward Bout as the man stooped down. He smashed into Bout, driving him up against the wall beside the chair holding the body of the dead girl. Bout grunted in pain as his mauled shoulder struck the unforgiving wall. They bounced backward and stumbled into the chair, knocking it hard enough to send the girl's corpse sliding to the floor with splayed limbs.

Bolan lifted Bout and then began rocking blows toward the big Russian's head. Bout swept his good arm back, driving the elbow into his opponent's head. Bolan rocked back, staggered. Bout twisted sideways and used the little space he had created to lash out with a side kick.

Bout's foot strike hit Bolan on his thigh as he stumbled and pushed him back. Bolan spun, absorbing the force of the blow, and reset himself. Bout turned back toward the safe, plunging his good hand down to the floor, scrambling for the dropped Beretta 93-R machine pistol.

Even as he moved Bolan knew he was too late.

Bout whirled, gun in hand. His toe caught on the deadweight of the girl's head and he tripped, stumbling.

Snarling, the big man brought up his pistol. His right arm useless, Bout had grabbed the weapon with his left hand, which was what saved Bolan. The pistol exploded as he dived forward.

Bolan felt the impact like a hammer blow low in his gut, just high enough that his vest still took the bullet and stopped the round. Two more rounds spun out, missing as recoil carried Bout's pistol muzzle off target.

Bolan changed tactics instinctively, throwing himself backward, and leaped for the protection of the filthy bed. Shooting with his off-hand, Bout fired another burst at the diving blur Bolan had become. The big American hit the bed and slid across it to the other side. Bout's bullets slapped into the thin wallboard of the apartment.

Bolan found his Detonics Combat Master and pulled the compact .45-caliber pistol free of its ankle holster. Unsure of Bout's tactics, he fired up at an angle in case Bout had followed him over the top of the desk. The crack of the .45 was impressive, intimidating in the confined space. Still firing, Bolan reached up over the edge of the bed and pulled the trigger repeatedly in a longer blast designed to drive the other man back. Finally he popped up behind the firing weapon and pumped several more rounds around the room.

The door to the bedroom hung open and .45-caliber rounds from Bolan's weapon punched into the wall outside the office door. Bolan picked himself up, holding the smoking Combat Master at the ready. Spent shells spilled onto the stained sheets of the bed and bounced to the floor.

Bout's beefy hand came around the edge of the door and he triggered the captured machine pistol. Bolan ducked behind the bed again, then answered with a double tap that chewed up the door's cheap wooden frame.

Rolling out from behind the desk, he came to his feet, bringing up the Detonics pistol. In the hallway Bolan heard an empty magazine strike the floor followed by the metallic click of a round being chambered. Then he heard nothing else.

Despite his ability to hear what was happening across the short space, Bolan's ears still rang from the deafening gunfire in such an enclosed room. He rolled over one shoulder behind the bed in the other direction, coming up against the wall on the same side of the room as the door. This angle gave him a drop of seconds should Bout choose to rush the room.

Weapon up, Bolan padded to the door. He heard nothing. Now was not the time for half measures.

Bolan burst into action. He thrust the Detonics pistol around the corner and opened fire. Once, twice, a third time. Still firing, Bolan pivoted around the fulcrum of his weapon and threw his back against the wall on the opposite side of the door, giving himself a narrow view of the short hallway.

He saw a corner of the living room down the hall and could make out a piece of the dark couch pushed against the wall in the center of the room. Bolan ducked back from the opening and dropped the spent magazine from his Combat Master. He slammed home his only fresh replacement and released the bolt on the pistol, priming the weapon for use.

Bolan swept the barrel up and stepped into the hallway, keeping to a tight crouch. His finger was taut on the trigger as he moved along the hall. Three steps down from the bedroom door more of the living room revealed itself. Tensed, Bolan pushed forward.

Bout popped up from behind the couch, triggering his stolen Beretta machine pistol. He fired a triburst of 9 mm rounds and Bolan threw himself backward. A ragged fusillade of slugs tore down the hallway. Bolan dropped to one knee and triggered the Detonics .45, answering Bout's vicious burst with two tight shots.

Sparks flew from a tiny TV set on a rickety table. Glass shattered in the window behind Bout, and the wallboard was reduced to splinters. Stuffing flew from the couch as Bolan pulled the trigger twice more.

Bout came around the side of the couch, triggering double 3-round bursts under Bolan's arc of fire. The Executioner threw himself up against the inner wall of the hallway to avoid the furious spray of bullets. A third burst cut the air through the hall, pinning him back.

Bolan slid down to one knee, still pressed against the wall. Once he changed elevation he dived forward, thrusting the Detonics .45 out and up in front of him. He fired a double tap as he dived, taking the force of his landing on his elbows and recentering his aim as he absorbed the shock of impact.

He heard the reverberation of the slam as Bout threw open the front door and struck the wall next to it. Instantly he realized the man had fled and he crawled forward and peered quickly around the corner of the hall. He saw the door standing open and knew Bout was making for his vehicle, or to alert any allies he might have with the triad bouncers down below. As the ringing in his ears faded, Bolan could hear the club music pushing up from the basement below and knew it had covered the sound of their brief, intense battle.

He hopped up, pistol at the ready, orienting himself, then rushed forward, chasing Bout. As Bolan entered the living room proper, he could see into the hallway and he caught a dark flash as Bout threw himself through the single access door leading to the building stairs. Firing through the open door, Bolan tossed off a double tap to chase the fleeing Russian mobster. More wood splintered, but his rounds were late and the wall absorbed the bullets.

Bolan moved quickly back out through the apartment. If time had permitted, he would have tossed the place but stopping Bout was his immediate concern. He broke into a jog and, leaving the back hallway, he cut through Bruja's living room and headed for the front door to her apartment.

Throwing the door open, Bolan raced outside and pursued Bout. Sprinting to the other end of the landing, Bolan threw open the door to the fire stairs and plunged down them.

He'd risk a lot to catch up with Bout but if push

came to shove, he wouldn't risk a firefight in a crowded club. Bolan's footsteps were loud in the narrow passage as he quick timed down the stairs.

Reaching the bottom landing, Bolan threw open the door and stepped through it. He cursed. The back stairs let out onto the entrance hall of the second floor of the building where the apartments began. The music from the Hard Glass Club was even louder here. The back door to the building was almost immediately on his right, but was in full view of the opposite door at the other end of the hall. Bolan turned and began to cross the short stretch of space between the stairs and the back entrance to the apartment building.

He heard the first doorway to the floor fly open and knew he was in trouble even before he heard angry shouts in German commanding him to stop. As he ran, Bolan risked a look back over his shoulder and saw two triad gunmen, one with a cell phone to his ear, weapons already drawn.

He reached out and grabbed hold of the doorknob as the bouncer from before barked at him for a second time. Without thinking of the consequences Bolan simply hurtled himself through the doorway and outside.

The gunfire from the sawed-off shotgun boomed loud in the sound tunnel of a hallway, and pellets cracked into the wood of the door as Bolan leaped past and down a narrow staircase. He shouldered a door open and ran down the back stairs. He spotted a chain-link fence across a tiny square of asphalt where the garbage containers were housed and made for it, icy squirts of adrenaline fuelling his flight.

He moved fast, images coming at him like flashes in a viewfinder, incongruous, juxtaposed and overwhelmingly rapid. Bolan's awareness swelled with each burst of adrenaline. He saw the fence and raced toward it, avoiding random obstacles in the courtyard that threatened to bring him down—trash cans, empty bottles, bits of refuse. At the same time he was keenly aware of the geography and any movements beyond his own line of sight.

Bolan could hear the shouting of the triad gunners as they sprinted behind him, and he caught the flashes of lights turning on inside buildings. He heard and sensed more vehicles racing onto the scene and moved instinctively, not bothering to identify each threat before avoiding it, like a running back breaking free from the line of scrimmage.

This night was turning into a real hell ride, Bolan thought as he threw himself into the air. He caught the top of the fence and heaved himself up and over. His belly scraped painfully across the horizontal metal pole at the top of the high fence. He kept one hand in a solid grip on the pinnacle of the fence and slapped the other one down at arm's length so that he could push away from the fence as he fell.

His legs swung over and he somersaulted to the ground. He landed on both feet, dropping at the knees to absorb the shock. He pivoted first left and then right. He was in an alley between the lines of warehouses and meat-packing buildings. It was wide and relatively clean but not particularly well lit. One end of the alley let out to his right and was closest to the direction where he had parked his car.

Bolan dug his heels into the ground, exploding into a sprint like a racer out of the blocks. His hands cut in perfect time to his steps, increasing his speed. He sucked in a huge lungful of energy-giving oxygen and expelled it forcefully. His legs drove down into the ground and propelled him forward.

Time stretched for him, reaching out from the center of his perception. Out of sight on the main street he heard men shouting then heard the squealing of brakes locking up, tires screaming in protest. A low-slung sedan shot into the mouth of the alley, directly into Bolan's path, headlights pinning him in midstride. It was an expensive black Lexus, and Victor Bout was behind the wheel.

Bolan didn't think, he simply reacted, moving automatically and trusting his instincts. He spun sideways and threw himself nearly prone backward into the direction he had just come. He dug in and erupted back down the alley. As he ran, Bolan heard a car door thrown open and the chatter of keyed-up triad gang members.

Ahead of him Bolan saw the first of the bouncers from inside Bruja's building clear the fence and land on the other side. The man leaped out of his crouch and reached for the gun he'd holstered while scaling the fence. His eyes went wide as he saw Bolan hurtling toward him.

Bolan raced in close, jumping into the air at the last moment as the thug abandoned his gun and attempted to fall back into a defensive martial-arts stance. Bolan drove his knee straight into the man's side, mauling the wind from his lungs and throwing the smaller man back against the fence.

The bouncer stumbled and Bolan moved in, relentless as a jackhammer. He clasped his adversary with both his hands around the back of his head, using his body weight to push the man's face down. Like triphammers, Bolan's knees fired up, cracking hard into the line of the man's jaw down near the point of his chin.

CHAPTER TEN

It was finished in three moves and Bolan dropped the unconscious bouncer, leaving him in a heap on the ground like a discarded rag doll. Not missing a beat, the Executioner reached up and caught the second hired gun as the man rolled over the top of the fence to back up his partner. Bolan jerked him from the top of the fence and hurled him to the unforgiving pavement. The man gasped for air and moaned before Bolan's foot pummeled him into darkness.

He ran for it then. A shot rang out, but the shooter was still running as he fired and the round flew wide. Not wanting to sacrifice raw speed, Bolan made no attempt to cut back and forth as he sprinted. He simply lowered his head and charged forward. Reaching the end of the alley he turned sharply to the left, putting a wall between him and the growing number of men gunning for him.

Behind him more shots rang out and a distant, disassociated part of Bolan registered the angry whine of pistol rounds as they cut through the air. Windows in a car parked across the street from the open mouth of the alley shattered, scattering glass onto the street.

Out on the avenue Bolan cut back to his right and sprinted across the street. He ducked between two buildings and scaled a second fence. Cutting across the little courtyard, Bolan skirted the edge of the building in the narrow space between the fence wall and the side of the structure.

He burst out onto another street and crossed it at a dead run. A red two-door Peugeot locked its brakes as Bolan cut across its trajectory. Without breaking stride he leaped up and slid across the hood of the vehicle. The driver, a middle-aged woman wearing a scarf over her hair, screamed and threw her hands up to cover her face.

Bolan hit the ground on the other side of the vehicle and finished sprinting across the street. The woman slammed her hand down on her horn in outrage. Bolan pulled his keys out of his pocket as he ran, hit the electronic key chain and unlocked the SUV. Reaching it, he opened the door and slid behind the wheel, chest heaving.

Starting the vehicle, Bolan turned to look out his rear window. He hammered the SUV into reverse and punched the accelerator.

The SUV responded smoothly despite its size and Bolan shot out into the street and roared past the stalled sedan in reverse, so close to it he almost swiped the woman's car. Once the front of his vehicle had cleared the trunk of the other car he whipped the steering wheel to the side and turned in a tight bootlegger maneuver around the European auto.

Now pointed in the direction he'd reversed in, Bolan again worked his clutch and put the SUV into gear. The tires on the big vehicle gripped the pavement and the vehicle surged forward.

Within seconds Bolan disappeared into the labyrinth of narrow streets. He snapped the wheel back and forth, cutting straight back toward the scene he had just escaped from. Victor Bout had been driving the first car that had tried to stop him in the alley and Bolan planned on paying him a surprise visit.

In two hard turns he was back on the street in front of the Hard Glass after-hours club. He cut toward the alley running behind it, looking for the black Lexus. He popped the middle console open and pulled out a compact H&K submachine gun chambered in 10 mm.

Running hot and angry, Bolan locked the brakes and turned the car sideways. He threw it out of gear and leaped from the vehicle. If the enemy wanted to go head-to-head, then he was willing to play. He ran forward a few steps to the corner of the chain link he'd vaulted earlier.

Bout, jabbing his finger in anger at a handful of tattooed Asian gunslingers, looked up at the sound of Bolan's screaming brakes. As the Executioner leaped forward the men scattered, going for weapons, and Bout jumped back behind the wheel of his car.

"Surprise," Bolan muttered.

He didn't hesitate as he opened up with the H&K submachine gun. He knew from long experience that Bout's vehicle would have bullet-resistant glass and reinforced bodywork, but he refused to make even one second of Bout's escape easy. The stutter gun erupted in his hand as the car shot forward. Spent shell casings rained out in an arc from the bucking machine pistol, bouncing wildly off the pavement at Bolan's feet as he brought the weapon to bear.

Dimples appeared on the side of the vehicle and ricocheting bullets shot sparks in the air. Bolan walked his line of fire along the line of Bout's car, up the front fender, into the door and up into the passenger-side window. The car continued to gain speed as it raced past Bolan, and he stubbornly held down the trigger.

Rounds hammered mercilessly into Bout's Lexus, knocking the hubcap on the rear wheel spinning into the street of the quiet residential neighborhood.

Bout sped away, then cut the big car into a power slide as he turned hard at the first corner. Bolan felt the vibration of his weapon cease and the sound of gunfire died as the bolt snapped back into the locked position. Looping the empty Heckler & Koch from a strap around his shoulder, Bolan pulled his Detonic Combat Master from behind his back.

He stepped backward, raised the .45-caliber weapon and sprinted out into the street. The Lexus's red brake lights flashed as Bout made the corner, then Bolan heard only the sound of that powerful upgraded engine as Bout raced toward safety.

Bolan started running toward his own vehicle but saw more of the triad gunners sprinting around the corner at the end of the alley. The Detonics pistol boomed in his hand as he fired a quick series of double-taps toward the men.

One of the triad gunmen caught the heavy-caliber slugs in his chest and was punched backward, his Russian M-4 submachine gun discharging into the street. The man next to him lost his face in an explosion of red gore and the other two gunmen turned and ran.

Gripping his smoking pistol tightly Bolan turned and ran back down the short stretch of alley toward his waiting vehicle. He had Bout on the run, but this was home territory for the Russian mobster, and Bolan suspected he could disappear if he chose. He had to stop the man now while he had the chance and try to pick up loose ends at a later time.

Bolan had a single lead left after the debacle that had just occurred, the Indian scientist Pandey, and he was afraid it was a lead Bout might already be on to. If Bout caught up with the man, presuming he didn't already have him, before Bolan did, then he could ensure that his investment, whatever that might be, in Split and the cloning technology was safe.

Off in the distance Bolan heard the sound of police sirens as he reached his SUV, and swore. He'd assumed that this close to the border of Prisni Prijatelji he could expect delayed response, but he'd been wrong. He jerked open the door and threw both the H&K machine pistol and the Detonic Combat Master onto the passenger seat as he slid in behind the wheel. Bolan revved the engine and left a stretch of rubber to rival Bout's as he shot out of his parking spot and into the street.

Bolan whipped around a battered black Polish sport wagon stopped dead in the middle of the street. The young man behind the wheel had both his hands raised in horror to his mouth, and his eyes were big as saucers as Bolan gunned his vehicle past him and after the fleeing Bout.

Every second counted now because Bout knew Split like the back of his hand after all this time, it was *his* town. Grimly, Bolan shifted from first gear until he had the vehicle moving flat-out. He had no intention of making things easy for Bout.

He raced the SUV, driving it hard as he chased the Russian through the streets. He was thrown against the restraints of his seat belt as he took his corners sharp and floored the gas through the straight stretches. He darted in and out of slower traffic as if the other vehicles were stationary cones on an engineering track. Horns blared in his wake, and his tires wailed in protest as he leapfrogged through the growing traffic.

Keeping his gaze fixed to the road, Bolan reached down and rooted briefly in the open top of the console set between the SUV's front seats. He secured his extra magazines for the H&K and tossed them onto the passenger seat. He jerked around a construction truck and then squeezed in between two passenger vehicles and a battered old civic transit bus. Bolan picked up the H&K and hit the clip release, ejecting the spent magazine.

He tucked the still warm barrel of the weapon between his legs and inserted a fresh 30-round magazine into the well of the buttstock. He picked up the weapon and jammed the bolt handle up against the underside of the dash and shoved sharply, cocking the weapon one-handed.

Bolan jerked his car back into line, saw Bout ahead of him and gunned his vehicle forward. Bout had to be on his phone by now, alerting his support system to the situation, perhaps calling in reinforcements.

Like a bloodhound on the scent, the soldier had followed the trail of clues and blood across the city. As always, the closer he got to the lair of the monster, the more dangerous the quest became. The trail Bolan had picked up in Split would go as cold as Bruja's corpse if Bout wasn't stopped.

Bolan gained on the fleeing Bout at every turn and at every ebb and flow of traffic that forced the racing vehicles to alter their speeds.

Bolan was racing not only against Bout, but also against the arrival of Croatian authorities. So far there were only angry drivers and panicked pedestrians to witness their reckless cat-and-mouse competition, but the stakes had grown serious enough that, when he pulled close enough, Bolan held every intention of continuing the gun battle if that was what it took to shake Bout down.

They hit a red light and Bout ran it without hesitation. Bolan sped out around the intervening vehicles and shot into the street. He laid on his horn and burst out into traffic. Cars racing from either side locked up their brakes and slid sideways as Bolan shot the eye of the needle. A battered old blue Yugo swerved around a stalled four-door family sedan and tried to apply its brakes too late when the driver realized Bolan was speeding past in front of him.

The nose of the braking compact struck Bolan's larger vehicle in the rear fender. The concussion jarred Bolan hard and his rear end swerved out of control. The top of his vehicle's fender crumpled from the abrupt impact, causing the rear access hatch to warp.

Bolan turned his wheel away from the skid his rear end was taking, trying to prevent the vehicle from spinning around completely under the impact. The four-wheel-drive caught and the powerful engine churned as Bolan downshifted to a lower gear. The tires gripped the pavement and Bolan felt the vehicle surge forward. He snapped the wheel to the side, avoiding a head-on collision with the line of traffic piled up on the other side of the light.

Behind him Bolan heard another automobile lock up its brakes and their immediate protesting screech as the attempt failed. There was a loud, flat bang and the sound of metal crumpling as another driver slammed into the back of the blue Yugo. Bolan instinctively glanced in his mirror and caught a brief image of an airbag deploying through a cracked windshield, to his relief.

The steering wheel was rock steady under his grip and Bolan figured the rear suspension and heavy axle had been undamaged by the glancing blow. He shifted up out of third gear and laid the car open. Setting the H&K in his lap, Bolan used his left hand to power down the windows on both the driver and passenger sides of his vehicle.

Driving smoothly with one hand, Bolan grasped the H&K tightly and lifted the weapon. He straight-armed the machine pistol out the driver's window and swerved out from behind a preceding vehicle, putting himself directly behind Bout. Bolan triggered a 3-round burst, striking the back windshield of Bout's car. The rounds slapped onto target, scratching the glass.

The vehicle between Bolan and Bout slammed on its brakes as the driver responded to the sound of rattling gunfire. Unfettered, Bolan shot past the stalled vehicle, tight on Bout's tail. He lowered the H&K again and triggered another tight burst. The 10 mm rounds struck the windshield inches from the first burst, scarring the reinforced glass again.

Bout twisted hard on his steering wheel, leaping his vehicle into the next lane of traffic. Bolan swerved around another slower moving car and locked onto Bout like the rear jet in a dogfight. He rested his forearm against the door frame, steadying his aim. Bolan lined up the muzzle of his machine pistol and triggered a third burst from the weapon.

His rounds struck the rear windshield of Bout's vehicle in the same tight pattern as the first two bursts. The safety glass spiderwebbed in protest under the repeated assaults. Bout turned his car sideways at a street corner, using his emergency brake to freeze his rear wheels as he attempted the maneuver. Bolan's foot cut to his brakes and he cranked his wheel at the last moment to avoid losing Bout as the man initiated a ninety-degree turn on smoking, screaming tires.

A group of civilians threw themselves backward and up onto the sidewalk as Bout slid around the corner. They scrambled onto the hoods of parked cars, shouting and screaming. A motorcycle rider parked at the light jumped clear, leaving his motor bike overturned on the street, the wheels still spinning. Bout rolled over it, flattening the frame and spinning it off to curbside.

Bolan revved his engine and his vehicle raced forward, ramming Bout's automobile in the trunk. Rebounding sharply from the impact, the Executioner gritted his teeth and brought his vehicle back on line. Bout swerved sharply, fighting to keep his car under control. Bolan thrust his weapon out of his open window and tore loose with another burst at close range.

The rounds hammered into Bout's trunk, which absorbed the damage. Bout swerved his car again, forcing Bolan to follow him. Sweat soaked Bolan despite the temperate weather and he squinted in concentration. He was bruised and raw where he'd been thrown repeatedly against his seat restraint.

Bolan fought his vehicle in behind Bout's again. He lowered his weapon and took aim at the other vehicle.

He stiffened his arm to hold the machine pistol steady, bracing his grip and wrist against the recoil. With cool deliberation Bolan squeezed the trigger.

CHAPTER ELEVEN

This time the rounds struck the weakened, spider-webbed glass and punched through, leaving fist-size holes in the rear windshield. Through the opening Bolan saw Bout frantically twisting his steering wheel with one hand while shouting into a cell phone. The soldier triggered another burst but it hit Bout's vehicle low, ricocheting off the reinforced materials of the trunk.

Reflexively, Bout jerked his wheel to the side and Bolan shot forward into the gap, the nose of his vehicle just past Bout's passenger side door. The Russian saw him in his sideview mirror and snapped his vehicle back over, slamming hard into the front of Bolan's SUV. Bolan predicted the maneuver and cut his own wheel sharply in toward his adversary's car.

The two vehicles clashed hard, rocking the drivers. Bolan jerked his wheel around, turning his tires into Bout's vehicle. The Russian slammed on his brakes and spun his vehicle away from Bolan's press in response.

The front of Bout's fender tagged another car in the back tire and sent the smaller vehicle spinning. It struck another motorcycle just ahead of it and the rider was tossed over the handlebars and up onto the back of a parked car. The motorcycle went spinning end over end into the plate-glass window of a storefront, sending pedestrians scattering for cover.

Strung out perpendicular to the flow of traffic, Bout panicked, killing his engine. Leaving his car running, Bolan popped his engine out of gear and engaged his emergency brake. He heard Bout try to turn his ignition over, heard the attempt fail.

Bolan got out of his car in a fast, fluid motion. He leaped up into the air and slid over Bout's trunk where his own left front fender was locked in tight with the car. As he came down, Bolan heard the other man's engine roar back to life.

The big American landed on his feet directly behind Bout's vehicle. He raised his H&K and triggered a blast through the blown-out back window as the Russian kicked his vehicle into reverse.

Bolan put his burst directly into the back of Bout's seat and saw the big man shudder with the impact of the rounds. Then the car lurched backward and Bolan was forced to dive up onto his own vehicle to avoid being run down.

Bout's Lexus missed Bolan by inches and struck the back bumper of Bolan's SUV, knocking it aside and spilling him onto the pavement. Bolan struck the ground hard, tearing the flesh of his left hand, but he stubbornly refused to release his Heckler & Koch machine pistol. He stood as Bout straightened his car. Bolan didn't have a clear angle into his adversary's automobile, but fired anyway, cracking the rear passenger window with his burst.

Bullets from Bolan's gun streamed through the back of Bout's car as the man swung it around. They flew wide of the driver's seat and burrowed into the dash. Bolan caught a glimpse of the housing from Bout's steering wheel flying apart under the impact of Bolan's rounds.

Pieces of the steering column housing flew up and Bout released the wheel, instinctively covering his face with his hands. The Lexus swerved out of control and rammed a parked car on the side of the street. Bout's car rebounded from the impact and stalled dead, the hood crumpled upward under the impact.

Bolan staggered to his feet and lifted his weapon as Bout threw open his car door and struggled out of his vehicle. Twisting, the Russian lifted his pistol and pulled the trigger.

Bolan dived out of the way and the bullets burrowed into the back of his SUV. Bolan rolled over his shoulder and came up with his weapon ready. Bout darted around the front of his car while pedestrians cowered on the sidewalks or fled into shops.

The Russian jerked open the door of a vehicle stopped in the middle of the street. A dowdy, middle-aged woman in a bright pink track suit shouted something at Bout who clubbed her with the butt of his pistol.

The woman sagged under the impact and Bout pulled her out of the car and into the street.

From behind the cover of the vehicle door, Bout turned and fired on the maneuvering Bolan, forcing him to scramble back toward his own vehicle. The mobster jumped behind the wheel of the injured woman's vehicle, a white BMW sedan.

Bout accelerated forward, the undamaged vehicle responding well under his hand. Bolan fired another burst at the retreating vehicle, saw a spark fly off the back frame and then twin shatter marks burst on the rear windshield.

All around him people screamed on the street in abject terror. The civilians around the combatants had no idea of what to make of the gun battle. Bout was more than a block away and moving fast by the time Bolan made it back into his vehicle.

Bolan shoved his battered and bullet-riddled SUV into gear and cranked it around so that it was pointing in the right direction once again. He stomped the gas pedal to the floor and drove the big auto away from the scene. In Bout he had found a dangerous opponent as committed as himself and it whetted his appetite for the kill, made his hate and anger sharper.

With Bout escaped he needed to regroup and reevaluate his situation. He had managed to salvage nothing from Suki Bruja's rat hole apartment, and there appeared to be no lead in all of this mess. As he heard the distant sound of sirens fast approaching, he tried to drive away only to have the much abused vehicle suddenly die on him.

He reacted instantly and without hesitation jumping out of the SUV and crossing the street while ignoring the gawking faces of the strangers who had witnessed the violent clash and its immediate aftermath. Moving nonchalantly to avoid panicking innocent bystanders any more, he strolled over to a two-door coupe and tried the handle. The door came open and he slid behind the wheel. He pulled the lock-blade knife from his pocket, clicked it open and jammed the narrow blade of the stiletto into the ignition housing. He turned the skeletonized handle and the smooth German engine roared to life.

Bolan heard the shriek of sirens and looked up in his rearview mirror. Red lights spun on the top of the compact police car that was arriving first on the chaotic scene. Slower moving, but more heavily armored troop carriers would be following behind the lead cars. If the first officer on the scene decided the situation warranted it, UN gunships could be mobilized almost immediately from military bases around Split.

Bolan tensed then relaxed as the police car shot past him and turned onto the street littered with the detritus of the gun battle. Bolan stepped on the accelerator and turned his vehicle in a tight semicircle. Straightening, he smoothly powered his stolen car down the street. He checked his mirror. An overweight woman in a loud housedress had run out from a business with a bullet-shattered window. She rushed up to the police car and began frantically pointing in Bolan's direction.

"Damn," he snarled.

Bolan pushed the accelerator to the floor. He had to make his escape before the police behind him got a good look at his vehicle or its license plate. Once he had procured the Hard Glass Club's address from the CI, Bolan had taken city maps and planned both his approach and a successive series of escape routes depending on likely variables. He hadn't had time to drive any of the routes, but he had worked to memorize them. Under pursuit now, Bolan immediately launched into one of his preset blueprints for evasive action.

He locked up his rear wheels and spun the car in another tight circle, keeping his transmission in a lower gear. Straightening, Bolan punched the gas pedal and shot down a narrow secondary street. Two city blocks down he repeated the maneuver, shooting into a service alley. His speed was dangerously high as he sought to execute his turns before the following police cruiser could spot his taillights and pursue.

His tires screamed in protest as Bolan attempted the near ninety-degree turn. As soon as the nose of his car was pointed in the right direction Bolan pushed the accelerator pedal down. The tires caught and Bolan speed-shifted up through two successive gears. He blasted out of the alley and onto a dark and narrow secondary street.

Bolan slammed the vehicle into position between other automobiles on the avenue and gunned it forward, ignoring the angry blasts of horns. He wove quickly in and out of the light traffic, keeping to right-hand lanes for the quick turn whenever threatened by stops or intersections.

In the rearview mirror Bolan could see a column of black smoke rising into the night from one of the ruined cars. The silhouette of the city's skyline was backlit by the fire he or Bout had instigated. A yellow fire engine screamed past him in the other lane followed by a security vehicle filled with armed soldiers. On the street, pedestrians emerged from bars and apartment buildings to stare and gossip.

Bolan arranged his features into a grim mask and drove deeper into the city. After several miles he pulled over and got out of the car, walked across the street and slid into a waiting taxi. He managed to nap on his ride down to the Prisni Prijatelji after directing the man toward the Hoteli Croatia.

THE LOBBY OF THE HOTEL was subdued but still populated, mostly by spill over from the lounge, which seemed popular. A few tired-looking travelers, luggage in tow, stood at the marble-topped counter, checking in. Knowing how he looked, Bolan headed straight for the elevator up to his room. He walked down the hall and pulled his key card from his pocket.

He was bone-tired from his hectic pace and exhausted by adrenaline bleed off. He wanted to take a shower, change clothes and get in touch with his support team to see if they still had a lock on Bout's cellular traffic. He didn't blame himself for Suki Bruja's death; he was too pragmatic for that. Bolan put the blame right where it belonged—on the woman's killers.

Still, Bruja had, to an extent, been an innocent in the

game and Bolan mourned the senseless, captious loss of light. The female junkie would never get an opportunity to turn her life around. Given the chance he would move heaven and earth to extract vengeance from her killers. Sometimes the world didn't give second chances.

Bolan inserted the key card into the electronic lock and opened his door. He walked into the hotel room and snapped on the light. The door swung closed behind him and the spring-loaded dead bolt snapped shut. He began to unbutton his shirt as he started toward the grungy little bathroom, his thoughts on a hot shower. His tired, aching body had made him careless.

The waiting assassin stepped out of the shadows behind the door of his hotel room and sprang into action.

Bolan caught the motion at the last possible instant and thrust his left arm up in front of his face. A piano wire garrote looped around his neck and Bolan felt a hard knee shove into the middle of his back as the man yanked the piano wire back in attempt to decapitate him.

Bolan's arm was slammed against his face by the force of the assassin's combination garrote and knee strike. The wire bit deep into the muscles of his forearm and blood splashed out as the white-hot laceration carved through his skin and muscle. He gasped in pain and staggered back.

He shifted his shoulder to the right so that he was at an angle to the attacker. He caught a glimpse of street clothes, a leather jacket and a ski mask. Bolan smashed the heel of his right foot onto the man's toes through his leather boots. The man grunted and snatched his injured foot back.

Bolan used the shift to slam his elbow into the man's gut, pushing outward against the piano wire even as it cut deeper into his arm. Blood poured down the front of his clothes, soaking him further. He struck out with his elbow again and this time caught the man in the solar plexus, which was indefensible by voluntary muscle contraction.

The assassin sagged as his breath was forced from him in a gasp, and Bolan managed to turn fully and shove him backward. The man staggered and Bolan saw that the eyes behind the ski mask were Asian and he knew instantly that Bout had discovered his identity as a Western agent and set his triad hired guns onto him.

The man struck the wall, fighting for position despite the disabling blow. He blocked a roundhouse Bolan aimed at the side of his head but was unable to return a blow in answer. Unable to use his left arm, which continued gushing blood, Bolan fired off a snap kick.

The man used his shin to block the kick and a knife appeared in his fist. Bolan danced back and finished shimmying out of his bloody shirt as the man lunged forward. The big American darted to one side to avoid a hard slash, the man shifted angles smoothly and stabbed out again with the knife.

Bolan caught the blade with a wild flail of his shirt and jerked. The assassin held on to the hilt of his knife and pulled back. Bolan let go of the shirt and suddenly danced forward. He kicked once and struck the man in the wrist, driving it back against his body and knocking the straight-bladed knife from the man's hand, forcing him back up against the wall for a second time. The man blocked one kick and Bolan shot another, breathing hard with the exertion.

The man turned a thigh and absorbed the strike, then came off the wall in a rush. He threw a series of vertical-fist strikes in the whirling, machine-gun motion common to the southern styles of kung fu popular in Hong Kong. Bolan took four blows to the chest and a glancing one off the point of his chin.

He staggered back and the assailant pursued. The angry eyes behind the ski mask narrowed in concentration as the man pressed his advantage. He bore into Bolan, driving him backward and onto the hotel bed. Bolan struck the mattress with the back of his knees and went down on his back. The Asian killer dropped his right arm and brought it around in an overhand hammer strike aimed for the big Westerner's vulnerable throat.

Bolan swept his legs up and locked them around the man's narrow waist like the jaws of a trap snapping close. His ankles locked above the man's buttocks and Bolan twisted hard at the hips, throwing his upper body into the roll and shoving off the mattress with his good arm.

Startled, the overextended killer fell as Bolan rolled off the bed and swept him to the floor. The man thrashed as they struck the ground in front of the nightstand but Bolan hung on like a rodeo rider. The Executioner leaned in and threw two elbows into his attacker's face that shook the man so hard Bolan felt the force shivering down through the assassin's body.

The man launched a heel-of-the-palm blow into Bolan's floating rib and he gasped, but the angle was wrong and the bone did not snap. Bolan snarled at the pain and punched down with his nearly useless arm, striking again and again. The man easily fended off the attacks, causing Bolan more pain with every successful block.

The left-handed attacks were purely diversionary. Bolan snatched the heavy lamp off the nightstand and lifted it with his right hand. He brought it down on the assassin's upturned face. The blunt force trauma crushed the man's nose and knocked several teeth loose so that blood soaked the balaclava instantly.

Stunned, the man went into a seizure, his arms dropping. Bolan used the lamp to finish the job.

Bolan staggered to his feet. Unsteady, he moved to the door and threw the second dead bolt. He put his chain across the door; every minute counted. He was obviously under surveillance and his actions in Prisni Prijatelji had earned him a death warrant from both the Russian mafia and the Mountain and Snake Society.

Despite this he couldn't very well go running out covered in the blood of another man or while bleeding so profusely himself. He slid a chair under the doorknob to his room door. He went to the bed and picked up a pillow, spilling blood across the covers and sheets as he worked. He yanked off a linen pillowcase then retrieved the adhoc medical supplies included in his general kit supplied by the Farm.

He poured hydrogen oxide from a small travel bottle over the nasty laceration left by the piano-wire garrote. He kept the window curtains drawn and the lights off as he worked in case the Chinese triad had a backup team outside with long weapons in play.

He wrapped the pillowcase around his bleeding wound, holding it in place until blood had seeped through the linen and stuck it to the wound. Bolan let go and began to quickly wind white surgical tape around the makeshift bandage. He used the tape to seal the wound and reduce blood flow to the area, further helping the injury to clot. It was crude but effective. It would have to do until he could get to better supplies.

He moved to his luggage and began to rip out the lining of his suitcase, pulling out the soles on the shoes he had packed as part of his checked luggage.

In four minutes he had put together a Glock 19 compact pistol out of its mostly plastic assembly pieces. He racked the slide and chambered a 9 mm round. Armed with his holdout weapon, Bolan stripped down and turned the shower on full-force.

Holding his bandaged arm clear, Bolan slid under the hot needles of water and quickly washed down, careful to avoid wetting his bandage. His injured arm throbbed with pain, but it kept him alert against his exhaustion. Once he was rinsed clean Bolan dressed quickly and searched the body lying on the floor by his bed.

He found a second knife and about a thousand dollars in local currency as well as a "skeleton" key card the hitter had used to enter Bolan's room, but no identification. The man had dressed in casual clothes and raised no suspicions as he penetrated the hotel. Once in Bolan's room he'd obviously pulled the ski mask from the pocket of his leather jacket and waited for the interfering Westerner's return to unleash his strike with the silent garrote.

Absentmindedly, Bolan touched his crude bandage. Like many before him, the assassin had come damn close.

Bolan prepared to leave. He wouldn't take his luggage to avoid tipping off any surveillance teams as to his intentions. That would give him until noon the following day, checkout time, before maids discovered the mess in the room. Bolan would be long gone by then.

He crossed the room, double-checking the Glock 19. He slid it behind his coat and smoothed the fit. His arm hurt badly, but he kept his expression neutral as he removed the chair, chain and dead bolts before opening the door to his room.

Bolan stepped out into the hallway, every nerve alive as he searched for hidden killers. The hall was quiet, the lighting muted and tasteful. He checked the time on his watch and fixed his cuff against the bulge of surgical tape sealing his wound.

It was time to put the show on the road.

CHAPTER TWELVE

Bolan moved down the hall toward the short flight of stairs leading to the lobby. As he reached the intersection of hallways that converged in front of the elevators, a laughing, drunk couple passed him. The man was a ruddy-faced European with a thick beard over heavy jowls, and longish gray hair. The woman was a quarter of his age and strikingly beautiful, with blond hair and a low-cut dress.

Bolan knew he needed to contact the Farm, but he didn't want to open communications until he was certain he was safe from another attack now that his base had been penetrated and his identity compromised.

The drunk man stumbled past, his eyes never leaving the creamy mounds of the younger woman's cleavage. Bolan returned the woman's smile as they passed. He reached the elevator bank, then turned and continued to the lobby.

If a backup team was waiting, then they'd have all

the exits covered. It was better to minimize his exposure to the public. The triad and Russian gangsters had no qualms about collateral damage. They had already forced Bolan into public altercations, and he would do his absolute best to avoid repeating that if he could help it, even in a place like Prisni Prijatelji. If there was a backup hit squad waiting for him, then his most dangerous time of exposure would be in the taxicab on the way to the secondary safehouse set up by Stony Man.

The elevator to the lobby opened with a ding as Bolan turned toward the stairs. He jogged down the steps quickly, his hands up in a casual manner to put them in closer proximity to his weapons. Coming through the stairwell door, Bolan scanned the lobby carefully before stepping out fully. He was more worried about a surveillance team at the moment, but he was prepared to react to whatever the Chinese might throw at him. He crossed the lobby, carefully scanning for more threats. It was growing late now and the place was close to empty. The front desk was unattended.

Making his decision, Bolan cut down the hallway away from the lobby and toward the back door to the hotel. Once he was in a secure location he needed to contact Grimaldi and Mott and figure out the best way to proceed.

THE HEAD OF THE Snake had to be cut off. Unlike the Russian mobsters, the Mountain and Snake Society had claimed specific geographical territory within Prisni Prijatelji. After Bolan's blatant takedown of one of their subsidiary or franchise properties, cellular traffic had exploded. With their scanners already plugged into powerful NSA AI programs designed to phish certain words and phrases out of traffic, it had been child's play for the Farm's cyberteam to triangulate the signals of the channels discussing the Hard Glass hit and to work its magic.

Within ninety minutes of the failed hit at the Hoteli Croatia the Executioner was locked on to target and fully equipped to begin his blitzkrieg all over again.

BOLAN STOOD IN THE ALLEYWAY behind the Chinese restaurant.

Several streets over the sound of a busy night met his ears. Here along the Prisni Prijatelji waterfront it was quiet. There were few streetlamps, and the only consistent illumination came from bare bulbs set over the back doors of various businesses.

It was quiet enough that he could just make out the gentle lapping of harbor water against the wooden pilings of the piers. The alley stank of urine, rotting vegetables and fish guts. Under a naked bulb casting a weak light, Bolan faced a battered steel door. The paint was peeling and the metal showed through, rusty from the erosion by salty air. A Chinese ideogram had been spray painted in the center of the door.

Bolan recognized the symbol from his research. It was the ideogram of the Mountain and Snake triad. Down the alley three Chinese men in their early twenties crouched and smoked, talking in rapid dialect. One of them watched Bolan, dragging on his cigarette. Bolan knew the youths likely to be security forces. Soldiers in the triads were differentiated by the slang numeric code: 426. The recruitment teams had appealed to the local youths' sense of national identity to swell their numbers of streets soldiers—but most of the qualified muscle had been imported into Split from Hong Kong and other Russian cities.

The head man in Split was named Lau Wing Kui and he made his office in Prisni Prijatelji, right in the middle of the Split underground. If Victor Bout had purchased a lease on triad muscle, then he had gotten it from this man. Lau Wing Kui was Bolan's best lead in finding Bout and perhaps Dr. Pandey.

He did not think Lau would be happy to see him.

Bolan turned the knob on the battered metal door in the alley and let it swing open. A concrete staircase, littered with multicolored stubs of paper and crushed cigarette butts, ran up to a small square landing on the second floor above the restaurant. From this landing a second set of stairs led to another story into the building over the Chinese restaurant.

Bolan walked through the door and began to ascend the stairs. The door swung shut behind him and the gloom on the steps thickened. A naked bulb hung from a cord above the landing below him, and Bolan carefully moved up the stairs toward it.

The smell of the enclosed staircase was dank. He could faintly hear the squeal of rats moving behind the plaster drywall and rotted timbers. The staircase had absorbed decades' worth of body odor, spilled alcohol and cigarette smoke. He was entering the yún, or the Clouds, an internal acropolis of small rooms and low hallways devoted to the greatest money-making vice of the Chinese gangs: gambling, and its twin sisters of prostitution and narcotics.

Bolan turned the corner in the narrow staircase at the landing. Below him the second staircase ran down and halted at a sturdy metal door. A single Chinese male with a bored expression on his face sat on a tall, three-legged stool in front of the door. Bolan slowly descended the stairs toward the entrance to the Clouds and walked toward the sullen sentry.

As he drew closer in the uncertain light, Bolan saw the man had the butt of a Beretta 92-F sticking out of his waistband past his hip and a second one stuck down the front of his pants. On the back of the man's left hand was a tattoo of the same ideogram painted on the door in the alley above them. More ideogram tattoos crawled up the man's thick neck in precise, if sprawling, patterns. Through the cast-iron door Bolan could hear muted but obvious raucous activity.

The triad hitter scrutinized Bolan with narrowed eyes. He barked something in what Bolan took to be Croat. Bolan shrugged helplessly. He lifted out his hand where he held a thick wad of euros. "Lau Wing Kui," he said.

The doorman took the brightly colored euros and thumbed through them suspiciously. He looked back up at Bolan and repeated Lau's name.

"Lau Wing Kui," Bolan said again.

The wad of euros disappeared into a pocket and the hand marked by the triad tattoo rose up and rapped sharply against the metal door. It swung open and a slim, sallow-skinned man with a hand-rolled cigarette clenched between crooked, yellow teeth eyed Bolan up and down. From behind him the noise of the room spilled out.

He said something to the doorman, and the other grunted and repeated Lau's name. The skinny 426 nodded once and stepped out of Bolan's way. The big American ducked his head and stepped through the door into the chamber beyond.

His senses were fully assaulted as he entered. The ceiling was low on the long upstairs room. The haze of cigarette smoke was thick in the air and looked like a gray-blue fog above the heads of the shouting gamblers. The cacophony of chattering, arguing, belligerent voices was punctuated by the sharp clacking of a roulette wheel. He saw numerous tables filled with frantic men, many clutching their own wads of euros.

Bolan's gaze wandered across the room, noting additional exits and the hard-eyed men standing sentry on the edge of the gambling pits. Other than the two guns tucked into the waistband of the first doorman, Bolan so no other weapons on flagrant display, though he was positive they were present. He'd been somewhat surprised not to have been searched at the door, but he assumed most customers here were local and, from the look of it, older.

The sallow-skinned Chinese man repeated Lau's name and indicated a brightly lit hallway leading off the main parlor. Bolan began to make his way across the crowded room, sticking close to the back wall as he did so. More than one pair of suspicious eyes followed his progress.

He crossed the room and ducked into the narrow hallway running at a sharp angle from the parlor. He felt at once exposed and claustrophobic in the hallway. The Clouds was a perfect place for an ambush, and he had a hunch that its proximity to the harbor made the disposal of bodies an uncomplicated matter.

Bolan stepped over the sprawled and unconscious body of a young woman. He looked down to make sure she was breathing, saw the rubber tubing wrapped around her arm. He immediately flashed back to the corpse of Suki Bruja, but the telltale needle had been removed. He felt a bad taste in his mouth. This place was a cesspit.

The female's eyes stared dully, her pupils glassy and out of sync with the gloomy light in the tunnel, and her filthy, short-sleeve T-shirt was stained with vomit. Her breathing was so shallow that Bolan at first thought her a recent corpse.

Bolan walked away and turned a corner in the hallway. Up ahead two heavyset Chinese men stood in front of a door set back in the hallway wall. Both of these 426 grunts openly sported twin Beretta 92-F pistols. Despite the damp, they wore stylish black T-shirts and black slacks with shiny dress shoes. Their arms crawled with tattoos, and their thick black hair was greased into pompadours.

Though the hallway ran past them and split off into an intersection, Bolan felt sure he had found Lau Wing Kui's office. He walked up to the men as they watched him from beneath hooded lids.

"Lau Wing Kui."

One of the guards knocked softly on the door. At a muttered response from within, the man opened the door and stuck his head inside. Bolan was mildly surprised it had been this easy. The hairs on the back of his neck rose as he realized it looked more and more like he was being led to the slaughter.

Bolan heard a rush of what he thought was whispered Cantonese and then a gruff response from deeper within the room. The bodyguard pulled his head out from behind the door and indicated with a curt gesture that Bolan should enter.

The big American stepped forward and crossed the threshold. The interior of the office couldn't have been more at odds with the general atmosphere of the Clouds. Bolan stepped onto thick carpet accented by tasteful lighting. A massive desk of Oriental teak dominated the room. The narrow, vertical paintings popular in Asian cultures hung from walls made of the same teak as the desk.

The desk itself could have belonged to any successful businessman from Taiwan to Kula Lumpur. It was neatly organized and two separate laptops flanked the main PC screen, all done in a lacquered ebony sheen.

One of the screens was turned in such a way that Bolan could see it and he recognized software designed to track up-to-the-second stock market variations.

The man behind the desk regarded Bolan with the eyes of a reptile. He did not rise as Bolan entered. His dark, Western-style suit was immaculate. Bolan knew from Lau Wing Kui's file that the Hong Kong mobster had gotten the Split fiefdom over the corpses of his two main rivals. In the parlance of his kind, Lau Wing Kui was the Red Pole of the Mountain and Snake Society triad.

Behind him a long, low cabinet ran the length of his office wall. Books in stylish and expensive leather binders took up one side. On the other side there were two closed-circuit television monitors. Each of the screens was divided into four squares, each square revealing a different image as captured by Lau's security system.

Bolan noted that one screen showed the alley where he had first entered the Clouds. The three youths he had witnessed loitering there were now gone. Another screen showed the gambling parlor Bolan had cut through. On a third, pale, potbellied and middle-aged European men lounged as young women in skimpy costumes and heavy makeup pampered them. On the other screen one of the picture sets showed the two men standing guard outside of Lau's office door.

Set on the wall above the cabinet was an HD television. The TV was on with the volume turned down. On the screen two men fought it out in an octagon-shaped cage of chain-link fencing. To the left of the screen a single door made of dark wood was set into the wall. Bolan could tell at a glance that the door was very heavy and solid in construction.

"You come without impressive introductions," Lau said. "You also come matching the physical description of a man who has caused me considerable loss of face and property."

When the Red Pole spoke, his English was precise and clipped, grammatically perfect. The man's black eyes glittered like a snake's. Bolan recognized Lau Wing Kui as an accomplished killer.

"An unfortunate coincidence." Bolan inclined his head.

Bolan understood the ways of the East, the excessive manners common in the Orient, and the preoccupation with "face" that was almost stereotypical but still entirely prevalent. However he had a larger agenda than a local kingpin. He had to run down the Russian oligarch, Bout, and in as expedient a manner as possible.

He remained standing until Lau Wing Kui indicated he should sit as a gesture of respect. When the Hong Kong gangster pointed, Bolan took a seat in a comfortable leather winged-back chair set on Lau's right side. Unruffled by the pointed hesitation, Bolan inquired after Lau's health. The Hong Kong killer snorted his laughter.

"I appreciate the effort," he continued in his perfect English. "But I assure you it is unnecessary. I know how important it is for you round eyes to 'get down to business.' So—" Lau pressed his fingers into a temple at his double chin "—let us get down to business."

"Good enough," Bolan said.

He reached into his jacket and pulled out an envelope and a photograph, leaned forward in his chair and casually tossed both onto the top of Lau's desk. The businessman reached out with one hand and pulled the items toward him, his eyes never leaving Bolan.

The Executioner leaned back in his chair and studied the room. Lau opened the envelope and ran a thumb across the tightly packed bundles of U.S. dollars. He opened a drawer in his desk and slid the money into it.

Only after he had securely closed the drawer did Lau look at the picture. His eyebrows furrowed slightly as he inspected the image on the photograph Bolan had given him. Lau looked up and his eyes were quizzical as he regarded Bolan.

"I recognize this man," he grunted. "I am not his keeper."

Thinking he was being held out for more money, Bolan replied, "Bout has a location here in Split. Obviously, I would not have walked into the dragon's den if I did not come with considerable backing. It is time for the Mountain and Snake Society to disavow this Russian."

"His location?" Lau snorted.

"Yes. And that of Pandey's."

"I wouldn't know."

"You know Bout, don't you? My people think you do. I think you do."

Lau Wing Kui regarded Bolan, his face expressionless, but a certain low, animal cunning made his black eyes glisten. He reached out and pushed the photograph back across his desk in Bolan's direction.

"My establishment is a good place to hear rumors, you understand?" Lau said carefully. "I have heard that certain men of…influence sometimes move certain contraband products out of Prisni Prijatelji and around the globe. As I do not engage in such illicit activities, I do not have firsthand knowledge of these things myself, you understand?"

Bolan nodded. If Lau was uninterested in admitting his part in ongoing criminal activities operating out of Croatia and into Europe and points west, then Bolan wasn't going to challenge him. At the moment, anyway. Everything he learned would go into Stony Man files, and Bolan new that sooner or later such a heavy hitter as Lau would screw up and the Executioner would have him.

"Go on," Bolan said.

"I can tell you nothing. My associates know these men. They do not deal with these men. We would have no idea how to find them."

"You are a liar," Bolan replied.

CHAPTER THIRTEEN

In response to Bolan's accusation Lau held up his hands as if to say "who can tell" and smiled. "So they say." His voice was soft. "I am told, and I'm quoting now," he continued, "that the man you seek will find you."

Bolan pondered Lau's words and their implications. He felt deeply dissatisfied. He looked away from Lau's sneering mask of a face and tried to decide on a fresh avenue. His gaze drifted to the CCTV monitors and a flurry of motion caught his attention.

Three men with balaclava hoods burst into the camera view. One wielded a sawed-off Remington 870 pump-action shotgun. He was flanked by a man with a mini-Uzi machine pistol, the sound suppressor nearly as long as the weapon itself. In response to the sudden appearance of the masked gunmen the sentries had pulled their pistols. But they did not appear to be resisting the new group of men. Quite the opposite.

Behind the knot of men another man stepped into

view. He wielded twin Beretta 92-F pistols, and he pointed in an authoritative gesture toward the door. Instantly one of the sentries reached out to swing it open and Bolan knew his gamble had been in vain.

Bolan was going for the Beretta 93-R under his shoulder as behind him 12-gauge slugs slammed into the room, and he heard the booms of the Remington 870.

Mack Bolan had walked into hell one more time.

Time began to unfold for Bolan in slow motion. He spun up out of his wing-backed chair as the door to Lau's office was kicked open. The Beretta was a familiar extension of himself as it filled his palm. Behind the desk Lau Wing Kui had grabbed up a custom-engraved .40-caliber pistol.

Bolan swept the Beretta up in a two-fisted grip. The shotgun-perforated door swung wide and bounced off the inner wall of Lau's office. The hit man wielding the mini-Uzi rushed into the room, his silenced subgun cycling fast and flame spitting from the muzzle.

Bullets sprayed the room. Lau's computer exploded with a shower of sparks. His laptops were torn apart and swept to the floor. The executive phone console burst into pieces and broke apart. The twin CCTV screens caught a single 9 mm slug apiece and went dark as the glass cracked open like eggshells.

The leather-bound volumes were shredded and kicked up into the air. Gouges and pockmarks burst from the walls and finely wrought cabinet. Bullets slammed into the massive teak desk, splintering it under the onslaught. A stray series of bullets caught the huge target of the HDTV screen, generating an avalanche of sparks. The huge television rattled and shook apart under the fusillade until it was knocked off its moorings and plunged toward the carpet in smoking ruins. Splinters of screen rattled like ice across the destroyed cabinet underneath it.

Bolan hunched against the fusillade and turned his muzzle on Lau Wing Kui.

No matter how horrible his crimes, the triad Red Pole showed courage as he died. The Executioner's bullets struck him in rapid-fire torrents. Blossoms of scarlet bloomed on his dark expensive suit, spilling blood in surging fountains across his wide desk. Lau shook under the impact and the smack of lead slugs burning through his torso was clearly audible to Bolan.

Lau was rising as he caught the first burst, swinging around the fancy showpiece of a .40-caliber pistol. The six rounds struck his chest and gut knocked him back into his seat as he leveled the pistol. The Hong Kong crime lord triggered his handgun twice, and the report was like a cannon in the room. The shots flew wide around Bolan as the Executioner put more Parabellum rounds into him.

Lau's face disappeared in a splashing wave of crimson and flying bone chips as a 3-round burst smashed into his head. The force of the 9 mm impacts bounced him off the back of his seat and he pitched forward, a bloody ruined mess sprawled across his desk.

Blood gushed out across the flat expanse of the table-top and spilled over the edges to stain the thick carpet burgundy. As he tumbled forward, Lau's hand jerked on the trigger and the pistol fired a last time.

The .40-caliber round burned across the office wildly and struck the submachine gunner in the thigh, causing the man to crumple and almost fall. Blood spurted bright against the dark material of the hit man's pants. He looked up from behind his balaclava mask and tried to bring the mini-Uzi back under control.

Bolan's single pistol shot from off to the side and just behind the winged-back chair took the assassin in the temple. The man's head snapped sharply on his neck and blood spurted from the wound as a red halo appeared behind his ruined head.

As the first hit man fell, Bolan's perception of time caught up with his adrenaline and everything began to unfold in fast forward. The gunman crumpled, his submachine gun bouncing off the carpet. From behind him the shotgun-wielding killer charged into the room. The man moved in with the Remington 870 pump action held out in front of him, the weapon stock tight in against his shoulder.

The cavernous muzzle of the 12-gauge swept the room for a target as Bolan stepped forward and kicked the heavy chair he had been sitting in across the room at the gunman. The hit man tried to swivel as he caught the motion and the barrel of the shotgun dipped as the shooter instinctively drew down on the object. The chair bounced off the floor and struck him in the shins, causing him to stagger and remove one hand from the shotgun.

Bolan fired three times in rapid succession on semi-automatic. His rounds burrowed through the flesh of the second hit man's throat and pulverized his spine. Bullet holes appeared in the wall behind him as Bolan's 9 mm slugs ripped through him.

The man fell and Bolan dropped to one knee as he shifted aim with the Beretta 93-R. Two more men went down, weapons tumbling, blood flowing. The last hit man was already entering the room, his arms extended straight out and his hands filled with spitting automatic pistols. Bullets passed harmlessly through the space where Bolan had been standing, whizzing over his head.

Bolan's pistol barked and a gaping red gash appeared in the balaclava. The dead man's momentum carried him farther into the room until his feet tangled up with corpses of his crew and he pitched forward. His body slammed to the carpet, his head snapping forward and bouncing off the floor.

Through the ringing in his ears Bolan heard angry shouts from beyond the open office door. He knew there was no way that members of the Mountain and Snake Society triad would stop now that their warlord was dead. They'd follow him into hell to avenge the insult.

Bolan quickly crossed to the desk of the departed Lau Wing Kui and grabbed the man's cell phone off the desk. He stuffed the phone into the pocket of his jacket, then yanked open a desk drawer and plucked the envelope full of cash he'd given Lau for the information. He saw a BlackBerry device and took that, as well. The icons on the screen written in some form of Chinese or

another, so he had no idea of exactly what he was looking for but it seemed a safe bet it would yield something
of value once Grimaldi and Mott used their proxy
equipment to upload it to the Farm's cyberteam.

As he shoved the BlackBerry in his jacket pocket, he
heard a rush of movement outside the door and dropped
behind the desk. The slap of footsteps became muffled
on the carpet, and he bounced back up out of his crouch.
A Chinese gangster with a ponytail and an M-16 A-3
assault rifle held at port arms stood in the doorway,
momentarily stunned by the carnage.

Bolan took him out with a single Parabellum round.
Hearing more shouts from the hall, he spun and tried
the door set in the back of Lau's office. Already the spacious office stank like a slaughterhouse. The door was
locked. Bolan shifted the fire selector switch on the 93-R
to 3-round-burst mode.

He checked to ensure that the hinges were on the
other side of the door and fired several rounds from the
Beretta into the wood around the polished silver handle. The ornate doorknob burst apart, and Bolan lifted
one big boot and kicked the door open before darting
through the opening.

As he passed into a small antechamber at the foot of
a short staircase carpeted as plushy as Lau's office, an
automatic weapon fired from behind him and a storm
of bullets cracked into the door frame.

Bolan twisted around in the cramped space of the
landing and thrust his hand around the corner of the
door, triggering two bursts of blind harassing fire, hop-

ing to drive the triad gunmen back. Bolan pulled his hand back and sprinted down the stairs.

He took them two at a time as he leaped toward the bottom, soaking in his environment as he raced. Lau's private access stairs were plush and well—if softly—lit. The thud of Bolan's pounding footsteps was absorbed almost completely by the thick, luxurious weave of the carpet. He could see the bottom of the stairs just ahead. The landing above him was narrow, and a small, three-legged table on which a blue ceramic dragon, holding fresh cut roses in its open mouth underneath an austere, square-edge mirror, faced the stairs. Directly oriented toward the cabinet to the left was a second interior door, the twin to the one below Bolan.

The door he had shot through to get out of Lau's office had swung shut behind him, and Bolan heard it slam open. He whirled and dropped the Beretta's muzzle, tracking for a target. Below him on the stairs a wild-eyed triad member, shirt off and upper torso wildly swirled with tattoos, leaped through the doorway, a commercial model H&K MP-5 in his fists.

The gunman yelled and lifted the submachine gun. Bolan stroked the trigger on the Beretta 93-R, putting three rounds just to the left of the thug's sternum. The street soldier buckled at the knees and pitched forward, triggering a burst into the carpet on the stairs.

Knowing the Red Pole had to have fielded numerous street soldiers in defense of the Clouds, Bolan spun and continued racing back up the stairs. He bounded to the top and tried the door. It was locked, but this time he could see the lock on his side of the door and he worked the latch and pushed through. His plan was fluid. From the harbor he would make his way into the Prisni Prijatelji, then make his way to his vehicle and the secondary safehouse.

He had gambled that a criminal like Lau Wing Kui would be willing to sell out a nonmember like Bout. He had guessed wrong, but the gun battle at the Clouds, following the Hard Glass Club and the kidnap site, had to have broken the back of the triad franchise in Croatia. There might be low-level gunners left floating around, but the command-and-control had been buried in a bloody blitzkrieg that had decimated the intelligence operational bulkhead of the Chinese and North Koreans.

Now there was only Victor Bout to finish off.

Bolan moved through the door and stepped into a crowded kitchen. The room was big and white and filled with staring Chinese cooks and busboys alerted by the gunfire on the stairs. As one, they shouted and began to scramble over one another in panicked efforts to escape.

Sensing no threat, Bolan cut through the kitchen, heading for a swing door in a far wall. He followed close behind two teenage dishwashers who were running through the exit just steps ahead of him. Bolan burst out into a crowded restaurant of open floor design filled with stunned Asian couples and a smattering of Europeans.

He raced up an aisle between semiprivate booths,

heading for the front door of the restaurant. He caught a flash of motion and tried to turn. A lithe 426 sentry in a heavy leather jacket leaped toward him from behind a decorative support beam adorned with narrow paintings on cloth. A long-bladed knife was naked in the snarling man's fist.

Bolan blocked the wild thrust with the hand holding his Beretta and twisted at the waist, diverting the man's energy. The 426 sentry was tossed around Bolan's center of gravity and crashed into a deserted table, spilling bowls of steamed noodles. The man's blade sliced a six-inch shallow wound along Bolan's arm, splitting the sleeve of his jacket.

The pain was sharp and intense and his clothes were soaked with blood instantly, but the wound was superficial and Bolan was able to bring up the deadly Beretta. The 426 sentry twisted smoothly as he slid across the table, recovering with the agility of a cat.

Bolan caught a flash of steel and instinctively ducked. The well-balanced dagger flew from the thug's hand and tumbled smoothly. Bolan just managed to jerk his head to one side as the knife spun past him and stuck in the support beam, pinning a narrow silk painting to the lacquered wood.

Bolan's finger was already on the trigger as he ducked, and the Beretta coughed across the point-blank range between the two men. Avoiding the knife throw pulled Bolan's aim, and the round meant for the heart punched through the gangster's upper abdomen instead.

The man shrieked at the sudden agony and Bolan put

a second round under his jaw, silencing the knife fighter before turning and running toward the front door of the restaurant. He could see a knot of panicked people blocking the way. Desperate men and women clawed at one another to escape as a tight group of 426s attempted to punch and kick their way into the restaurant. Bolan had a moment to feel grateful that the hour was so late that no children were present, and then a tall 426 gunner fighting through the doorway identified him.

The man's eyes widened in the shock of recognition. His hands came up, and Bolan saw that the 426 killer was wielding a Chinese Type 64 submachine gun in 7.62 mm. The stripped-down design of the simple weapon boasted a cyclic rate of fire at over 400 rounds per minute.

Civilians screamed and parted like the sea as the man unleashed the fury of his weapon. Bolan turned and dived backward over the corpse of the knife fighter as the submachine gun began to chatter.

Bullets cut a path down the aisle Bolan had just cleared and then drifted to the left in pursuit of the American. The 7.62 mm slugs tore into the dangling feet of the dead knife fighter's corpse and chewed them apart. As Bolan rolled over the table and landed in the next aisle, the sentry he'd killed soaked up more submachine gun rounds.

Bolan hit the ground, rolled over a shoulder and came up with the Beretta braced in two hands. He put the sights on the submachine gunner and drilled him across the tables with a neat 3-round burst. The man fell and Bolan shot the man standing directly behind him. The third 426 gunner staggered backward as the weight of his dead brother pitched back into him. He fired a sloppy shot that went wide, and tried to turn and run. Bolan's next 3-round burst struck him twice in the skinny flesh of his shoulder and put a single 9 mm round through his neck, knocking the gangster into the street.

Bolan struggled to his feet and raced for the door. He passed huddle knots of terrified people who watched his rapid progress with wide, unblinking eyes. He stepped over the sprawled corpses of the men he'd shot and left the restaurant to emerge onto a quiet street. No cars moved on the thoroughfare. He could discern no sound of approaching sirens; no other triad soldiers rushed him. The third triad 426 sentry he'd killed lay in the gutter, scarlet leaking steadily from his neck.

Bolan lowered the smoking Beretta to his side and jogged across the street into Prisni Prijatelji. His mind clicked off options, running down possible choices. He needed to get the cell phones to Grimaldi and Mott's proxy servers to upload to the Farm. He needed a line on Bout, a line on Pandey. He needed this raid to pay off, and every minute was a minute Bout could be using to cover his trail.

The scream saved him.

He heard the angry cry and rolled to fling himself flat in the middle of the street. Even as he hit the ground shards of gravel kicked up from the road as lead slammed into the street all around him in a maelstrom of bullets. He heard the high chatter of a submachine gun and caught the muzzle-flash blinking out of the darkness at the mouth of the alley.

He saw the shrieking 426 gunner walking toward him, his eyes narrowed into slits like an angry cat's, the submachine gun bucking wildly as the man fired from the hip. Behind the gangster two more triad soldiers, each armed with twin Beretta 92-Fs, spilled out onto the street.

Bolan rolled up onto his left side and swung his right arm out, triggering the Beretta five times. His rounds cut into the crazy 426 just under the lead man's bucking submachine gun, ripping open his stomach. The man staggered to one side and fired his weapon into the ground. He stumbled then went down, dropping the submachine gun to the street.

The two 426 gangsters behind him stood their ground, side by side, each man blazing away with the 9 mm Beretta pistols they held in either hand. Bolan sighted in on one, moving too fast for anything other than instinct, and drilled the man through his open, screaming mouth.

The street soldier's head jerked and a bloody halo framed his head as he pitched over backward. The triggerman beside him stopped firing as his partner went down. His face registered horror, and he thrust out his arms as he began to run back into the cover of the alley, his pistols belching flame and lead in a sporadic, indiscriminate pattern.

Bolan drew his sights down on the man and put a 9 mm

round into his torso under his waving arms. The man shook with the impact and staggered, his weapons moving out of play as he instinctively wrapped his arms around the spurting wound.

Bolan's second shot hit him just under the collarbone and swept him to the filthy floor of the alley. The man went down like a tree in a high wind and bounced off the ground. When the 426 triggerman's head came to rest, his pistols fell from slack fingers and clattered on the pavement.

CHAPTER FOURTEEN

Bolan pushed himself up from his prone position, weapon
out and ready. He cursed in amazement at the sudden
violent storm he had just weathered. His body shook
from the supercharged adrenaline blasts that had powered him through the encounter.

He dropped the partially empty clip from his weapon
and rammed home a full one. Then he shuffled backward across the street, scanning the restaurant and
alley for even the slightest hint of hostile movement.
Bolan made it across the street and onto the sidewalk,
then he turned and sprinted down a small side street,
putting solid cover between himself and the battlefield.

TWO HOURS LATER he was on the road and in the mountains above Split. The area had been the fallback refuge
of armed brigands and war criminals after the UN inter-
ventions. Even now allied special operations forces

hunted and skirmished among the valleys with determined criminal holdouts.

It was a place that, unlike the city proper, hadn't received much in the way of postconflict rebuilding funds. Outside Split, Jack Grimaldi was forced to slow the SUV to better deal with the increasingly deteriorating roads.

Bolan quizzed him on the trip but was left discontent with the answers the man had gotten from the Farm. He knew only that Bout operated out of a house in the mountains where in addition to his own men, he paid former Serb commandos turned mercenary for both protection and privacy. Because his position gave him access to information that had become Bout's main financial pipeline, the triad Red Pole, Lau Wing Kui had been made privy to the Russian location.

Twilight gathered as Grimaldi took a labyrinthine procession of back roads to avoid military and interior police patrols. After turning off a narrow blacktop road, the SUV made the climb into the mountains above the city with little trouble.

The road to Bout's retreat was as narrow and winding as the area was rough and isolated, giving Bout little in the way of neighbors. By the time darkness had completely fallen, Grimaldi stopped at the edge of a gated compound on what appeared to originally have been a logging road.

Bolan surveyed the sprawling, two-story house behind the wood-and-metal fence. Bout's place made Lau's base of operations in the Clouds look like a second-rate shack. No guards were in evidence. There was an intercom station with a camera set next to the black metal gate at the end of the drive. Bolan took that in and frowned, deep in thought.

He picked up his GPS unit from the middle console of the vehicle, activated the device, then double checked his results. Satisfied, he pulled out his own modified BlackBerry and typed in his GPS coordinates. He sent them through a wireless burst transmission before he returned both items to his knapsack.

"Keying in Charlie?" Grimaldi asked. The second Stony Man pilot had positioned himself with a Little Bird helicopter on the backside of the Split international airport.

Bolan looked up and nodded. "We're about to get down to it, all right."

"Shoot our way in. Take what we want. Shoot our way out," Grimaldi confirmed.

"Bout has to know we're coming. Even if he doesn't know for sure, he knows with Lau dead that he's next on my list. He'll be ready. So let's not beat around the bush. He thinks I'm coming? Then I'll come. Just as soon as Charlie starts putting bombs down."

Grimaldi grinned. "Sounds good to me."

After a couple of minutes Bolan got his signal from his secured cell phone.

He looked up. "Let's roll," he said. Having come to a decision, he unlimbered the weaponry in the SUV, getting ready to bring it straight into the teeth of the Russian mobster.

"The satellite imagery has an old logging road cutting across the terrain to the back of his property. Let's head for that, then when we do our approach we can be rolling downhill."

Grimaldi killed the lights and put on his night-vision goggles. Next to him Bolan mirrored his actions, and the Stony Man pilot put the big vehicle into gear and began to drive.

He pushed the SUV hard and it ate up the miles as blacktop gave way to gravel and gravel to the logging track. The ride was rough, even with the improved suspension, and they were dealing constantly with rain-weakened roads sliding out from beneath their tread.

By the time the first hint of light creased the horizon they crested the final rise in the wooded hill. Bout's estate spread out before them in the uncertain light of their NVDs, set five miles off the main eastern highway behind a sharp defilade of shale stone and sand.

After they had removed the front windshield of the SUV and set up organic weapons placements, Bolan picked up the handset for his base unit. The communication kit interfaced easily with the Single Channel Ground and Airborne Radio System, or SINCGARS, outfitted with a VINSON device for security, and operating in the VHF-FM, 30-88 megahertz range. The VINSON devices utilized by Stony Man had been modified by Aaron Kurtzman to be symbiotic encryption units. Code generated by the sending unit was specific and random to only those VINSON, not generic.

"Hard Light, this is Good Boy. Over."

"Good Boy, this is Hard Light," Charlie Mott answered. "Over."

"We're at the gate," Bolan said. "We have overflight confirmation? Over."

"Affirmative," Mott answered. "Ground vehicles ID match. The 'money is in the account,' Good Boy. Over."

"Copy. T-time two minutes. Over."

"Roger. Two minutes," Mott repeated. "You'll see me. Hard Light out."

"Good Boy out."

Bolan secured the handset into its cradle. He looked down the long slope of the desert hill toward Victor Bout's compound. An hour ago an MQ-9 Reaper, a larger more capable improvement on the older RQ-1 Predator, Unmanned Aerial Vehicle had come on scene, launched by Charlie Mott and controlled by Stony Man tech wizard Akira Tokaido.

After making a reconnaissance overflight, its camera had confirmed the make and license plates of vehicles used by Bout. The information had been immediately relayed to the Stony Man electronic forward operating base in Split. The money had been deposited in the account.

The Reaper UAV then powered up to a holding pattern at its fifteen thousand feet, the Honeywell TP331-10 turboprop engine easily performing as instructed by the operator in the Blue Ridge Mountains half a world away.

Bolan looked down at the sprawling, walled compound and began to prep his Special Operations Forces

Laser Marker, SOFLAM. The handheld Laser Target Designator would put the two 500-pound laser-guided bombs carried by the Reaper directly on Victor Bout's house.

Bout's compound was lavish and the contrast it held to the rugged and remote mountains positioned north of Split only emphasized the ostentatious display of wealth. The main house was a four-story estate with all the hallmarks of traditional Caspian architecture. It held spires, arched windows, open courtyards with fountains and rooftop patios. Lights set just below the surface illuminated a swimming pool that would have seemed at home in Beverly Hills or Monte Carlo.

The landscaping around the main house gave the estate a rustic look, with thick copses of evergreens and heavy shrubs marking flower gardens. Both the driveway and paved footpaths connected the main building to guesthouses, stables, tennis courts and a helicopter pad. One side of the compound had been dedicated to a short runway capable of hosting small jets.

The complex, surrounded by a ten-foot-high, adobe brick wall, was not just a residence. In addition to the runway and helipad there was a line of large warehouses set against the east wall beyond the landing strip, which intelligence had shown doubled as a shooting range. One of the guesthouses was believed to serve as a fully functional clinic for the Croatian-deployed Russian mobsters. Bout had simply taken property formerly held by the Soviet GRU and turned it to his personal use.

Servants' quarters divided the house from the industrial areas where semi-trailers were parked next to garages with service bays designed to accommodate light aircraft and heavy ground vehicles. It was rumored that air traffic controllers from the Russian air force served two-month tours at the mountain compound and that it was a launching point for air force reconnaissance helicopters to monitor UN troop movements along the Bosnian border.

Nothing as obvious as gun towers lined the walls, but Bout's bodyguards were vigilant and a small gate in the rear, on the northern side of the compound, was used for mounted patrols in customized black Range Rovers to conduct security sweeps of the wooded roads outside the perimeter walls. Bolan could see two armored vehicles on opposite sides of the flatland below his position, trundling slowly through the desert like giant, wheeled cockroaches.

The Bout compound was a fully functional, criminal forward operating base in the former Soviet republic.

"You ready?" Bolan asked Grimaldi.

"Ready," the Stony Man pilot replied.

THE EXECUTIONER activated his SOFLAM and "painted" the main house with his laser pointer while Grimaldi, beside him, spoke the activation code into the radio, simultaneously alerting Mott in his Little Bird and Tokaido, the UAS operator in the Annex of Stony Man Farm.

While Bolan held the SOFLAM steady, Grimaldi climbed into the back of the SUV behind the driver's seat where he unlimbered the XM312 .50-caliber heavy machine gun. He slammed open the modified sunroof and secured the weapon on the same weapons mount favored by the CIA's paramilitary units. He racked the charging handle and seated a bullet in the chamber.

Adrenaline began to leak into the veteran pilot's system as he waited for the bombs to fall. The carry racks on the inside of the SUV had been filled with light arms, grenades and rocket launchers. Both he and Bolan were outfitted with a lethal personal arsenal in addition to the weapons systems indigenous to the specially modified SUV, which had both an M-60 and a Squad Automatic Weapon.

The estate housed Serb mercenaries, Russian mobsters and elite bodyguard troops who were formerly GRU commandos, as well as some remnants of the Mountain and Snake triad. With the odds so heavily stacked against them, Grimaldi knew the Stony Man kill box could quickly become a deathtrap for the would-be ambushers.

Up in the stratosphere he saw a streak of fire then a second one. He forced himself to look away from the rain of descending death and to focus in on the two black, hard-shell Range Rovers patrolling the clear-cut ground between their position and the back gate of the Bout compound. They would be his first targets once the hellfire began.

A screaming whistle pierced the night. The twin GBU-12s landed like the fists of an angry god. The explosions shattered the upper stories of the estate in twin balls of fiery retribution. The top floor disintegrated under the impact, and flames blew out the windows and doors on the bottom floors. The concussive force of the blast uprooted trees and bushes in the various yards and gardens. The third and fourth stories collapsed inward, and the structure raged into a screaming inferno.

"Oh baby, *yes*," Grimaldi muttered, his satisfaction almost palpable.

The Reaper UAV began to circle down in altitude. Its camera rolled feeds that ran back through a bounce of the Keyhole satellite to Stony Man Farm, where Hal Brognola and Barbara Price watched the unfolding action along with the Stony Man cybernetics team headed by Aaron "the Bear" Kurtzman.

In the front of the SUV Bolan hurriedly secured the SOFLAM laser designator and slid across the seats and behind the steering wheel. The geography in the two men's NVDs was brightly illuminated by the leaping flames of the raging fire.

Out on the edge of the flames Charlie Mott's AH-J6 Little Bird helicopter swept into view, a deadly metal wasp. Bolan gunned the SUV and it sprang forward and raced down the hill, tearing into the loose, wet turf and spraying gravel wildly. He felt the rear end start to slide and he steered into it so that the four-wheel drive straightened itself and shot forward like a bullet from a gun.

Out ahead of them each of the exterior mounted patrols in the hard-shell Range Rovers skidded to a stop at the sudden explosion from the compound. Top hatches sprang open and gunners took up positions behind swivel-mounted M-60D machine guns. Neither mounted sentry unit had seen the approaching SUV yet, and they foolishly kept their faces pointed toward the burning palace compound.

Blacked out and running hard, the SUV swept down on them like a cheetah cutting a pack animal out from the herd. One of the turret gunners suddenly shouted and pointed, and from behind the wheel of the SUV Bolan saw the vehicle sentry gesture and followed the line of his pointing arm. The man had seen Charlie Mott's Little Bird.

"Take 'em down!" Bolan shouted over the SUV's screaming engine. "They've spotted Charlie!"

The General Dynamic .50-caliber XM312 heavy machine gun had a maximum effective range almost twice that of the M-60D, and Grimaldi exploited his superior firepower with ruthless abandon.

Above the house the Little Bird turned in the air, rotating like the gun turret of a tank. The twin, seven-tube launchers for the 2.75-inch rockets lit up like fireworks and began striking the compound in streaks. Mott moved in a methodical sweep from left to right.

As he pivoted his fire, placing rocket after rocket on target, he launched on grounded aircraft, parked vehicles and the little guest villas running along the short runway. The effect was catastrophic.

Sitting helplessly on the pad a fourteen-passenger Sikorsky S-76 Spirit went up as Mott put a 2.75-inch rocket on target in its fuel tank. The helicopter leaped into the air as fire mushroomed out and cast burning debris across the east half of the compound.

The nose of an expensive and ultra-posh private jet protruded from the open doors of a Quonset hut-style hangar. Mott put a rocket through the sleek, jet-black windows and into the cockpit. The explosion was contained by the hangar, but the open doors served like a chimney and black smoke, clearly visible in the light of the raging fires, roiled out. Mott turned the Little Bird on a dime, smoothly swinging the tail around so that he faced the closest guesthouse. Lights had clicked on in the structure as Bout's "guests" and employees scrambled to respond to the raid.

Mott put a rocket through an upstairs window and a second through the front door, knocking down interior walls and setting the guesthouse on fire.

Behind him, beyond the wall and out in the forest, the black Range Rovers' patrolmen twisted their M-60D machine guns around and drew down on the hovering death machine. Orange flames licked from the machine-gun muzzles, and lead began flying in earnest toward the little attack helicopter.

From behind Bolan, Grimaldi opened up with the .50-caliber XM312. The heavy machine gun had been pressed into service to replace the military's aging inventory of the M-2 .50-caliber heavy machine gun, which were roughly eighty-years old.

With advanced muzzle brakes and chambering action, the recoil and weight of the XM312 had greatly improved on the old M-2 while maintaining a respectable rate of fire at just over 400 rounds per minute. The heavy sound of a .50-caliber weapon firing remained a powerful psychological weapon in its own right.

In his driver's seat Bolan felt the recoil through the vehicle frame of the heavily modified SUV though it did nothing to slow the vehicle. He saw red tracers burn like laser bolts across his night-vision goggles and arc out across the distance before falling on target.

The .50-caliber rounds tore into the first Range Rover, which soaked up the rounds like a sponge. The weapon cycled close above Bolan's head and he heard the chunk-chunk-chunk of the weapon operating over the dull crack of the rounds firing. Out in the forest red tracer fire burrowed into the hard-shell Range Rover, some rounds skipping off at wild angles, others disappearing into the vehicle's cab.

The top gunner fired his weapon hard, the muzzle-blast taking a star-shaped burst pattern in Bolan's goggles. He saw the man suddenly convulse and heave forward only to bounce off his weapon. A red-hot tracer round burned into the gunner's back and out the front where it ricocheted wildly off the roof. One moment the gunner had a right arm and in the next moment it was gone. The man slumped across the hood with wounds large enough to be seen even across the distance and in the uncertain light.

We're in it now, Bolan thought, and pushed the accelerator to the floor.

CHAPTER FIFTEEN

Bolan saw concentrated tracer fire slip through the side of the Range Rover, and after a moment the racing vehicle suddenly veered off sharply to the right. It drifted for several dozen yards across the broken ground of the logging road, then its front end hit a narrow crevice and buried its nose in the far bank.

On the other Range Rover the topside gunner's head snapped to the side to follow the sudden erratic path of its fellow patrol vehicle. Bolan saw the wild red tracer fire and the machine gunner swiveled, searching for the source of the incoming rounds.

Beyond the M-60 gunner Bolan could see Charlie Mott's deadly Little Bird continuing its rampage as more 2.75-inch rockets from its arsenal fired off. Vehicles exploded as semi-tractors, limousines and all-terrain vehicles were struck with equal enthusiasm.

By the time the rocket fusillade had finished, multiple bonfires of burning vehicles and structures raged across the compound, all of them minuscule in comparison to the blazing inferno of the main palace. Despite the heavy damage wrought on the majority of buildings, personnel scrambled around the compound, most wielding weapons of one sort or another.

Mott's last rocket went through the front door of the guesthouse farthest down the airfield from him. It punched through the door like a breeze tossing paper and detonated inside so that thick smoke billowed out.

Without hesitation Mott switched to his 7.62 mm M-34 miniguns. The electrically powered chain guns whirred to life and a cascade of machine-gun bullets began to douse the compound, tearing into buildings and knots of struggling gunmen.

The machine-gun bursts struck the figures like chainsaw blades, hacking them to pieces and splashing guts and body parts around in sloppy, senseless patterns. As he fired, Mott worked the Little Bird, drifting out toward the edge of his effective range to avoid any intensity of return fire likely to bring down his lightly armored helicopter.

Bolan cut the SUV hard, running up off the desert and onto a track used by Bout's Range Rovers. The front wheel of the big SUV struck a head-size boulder in the dark and the steering wheel lurched hard in Bolan's grip.

The vehicle frame shuddered under the impact and the wheel shot into the air, tipping the racing vehicle onto one side. Bolan turned the wheel hard and straightened the SUV, throwing his weight hard to his right in a desperate attempt to keep the high-slung vehicle stable.

Tracer rounds cut across his front, and he realized they'd finally sped into the range of a Range Rover's M-60D. Above him Grimaldi cut loose with the heavy machine gun again. Bolan worked his brakes and slid into position onto the track, now racing toward the back gate of Bout's compound, several football fields away.

Once on the dirt road track Bolan took his right hand off the steering wheel and grabbed hold of the M-60 mounted in front of him, swiveling it around to engage the second Range Rover.

The turret gunner leaned low over his weapon, the star-pattern muzzle-blast obscuring his form in Bolan's goggles. The Range Rover spun in a tight half circle, spraying loose gravel like surf as the driver tried to meet the new threat of the SUV head-on.

Bolan saw a bullet spark off the front of his vehicle and his finger found the trigger of the M-60. The weapon roared to life and rocked in his one-handed grip.

Red tracer rounds from Grimaldi's XM312 tore into the engine hood and then the windshield of the Range Rover as the Stony Man pilot walked his fire up toward the furious machine gunner. Bolan followed Grimaldi's lead, spraying his long, ragged burst in a tight Z-pattern to keep his rounds bouncing inside the Range Rover's cab.

Grimaldi found his target. The M-60D exploded into pieces as the .50-caliber slugs buzzed into it, shattering it beyond recognition in the blink of an eye. Half a second later the machine gunner was vaporized above the sternum, reduced and shredded into bloody spray.

Bolan hit the brakes and cranked his steering wheel hard to slow his momentum. The SUV went into a power slide and stopped abruptly as the rudderless Range Rover drifted into the desert before petering out to a stop some hundred yards away. A wave of dust rolled over them as the SUV screeched to a full halt.

Working with efficient speed and ignoring the piping hot barrel of the XM312, Grimaldi secured the weapon and dropped down into the passenger seat behind the M-19 grenade launcher.

As soon as the Stony Man pilot was in place, Bolan punched the throttle again. Both men were pushed hard back into their seats by the force of the acceleration. The engine revved to a full-throated scream as Bolan roared toward the back gate of the palatial compound.

Ahead of them they saw flames climbing high into the air, and sitting amid the blank dark of the dense Eastern European forest, it seemed as if the chimneys of hell had been opened. Something exploded and a burning, unidentifiable mass shot into the air. Bolan saw tracer fire pouring out of the dark from over his head toward a section of the compound he knew was the fuel reserve farm area. The minigun burst seemed to go on forever, and then there was a whump as the reserve fuel tanks for automobiles, aircraft and semi-tractors began to blow in succession like dominos falling: two-ton exploding dominos that shot flames and jet fuel 150 feet into the sky.

The exploding fuel farm illuminated the area like a noonday sun, and as the Stony Man hit team drew closer their NVDs were overworked by the brilliant light. Almost in tandem Grimaldi and Bolan stripped off their goggles and tossed them into the seats behind them.

"Hard Light to Good Boy," Mott said, his voice alive with the energy of his adrenaline charge.

"Go ahead, Hard Light," Bolan answered.

"Alpha phase completed. I'm going to rise to observation platform as my miniguns are low. All first-strike targets engaged. All first-strike targets engaged. Over."

"Roger, Hard Light," Bolan said. "Good Boy out."

Up ahead the back gate to the compound loomed. It was a solid structure of heavy wood and reinforced wrought iron. Grimaldi grasped the dual spade grips of the Mk 19 40 mm grenade launcher and centered them on the gate.

He fired an exploratory shell from the 32-round magazine, sending a 40 mm M-430 High Explosives/Dual Purpose grenade toward the gate. The weapon fired and his round arced out over the desert, exploding into the dirt at the front of the gate, and raining dirt into the air like lava from a volcano.

Grimaldi lifted the vented muzzle on the Mk 19 and began to fire in earnest. He put the three rounds dead center on his target and blew the gate into flaming splinters. Each explosion showed as a flash of burning light spilling around clouds of dark smoke, then the gate was gone.

Grimaldi fired a second volley through the fragmented gates to soften up any potential adversaries responding from beyond the wall. The M-430 HE/DP rounds had kill zones of five yards and possessed antipersonnel capabilities out to fifteen yards.

His HE/DP rounds tore up the ground beyond the back gate, gouging deep ruts in the packed earth and spilling flames in wide arcs. Shrapnel spread out in patterns like an umbrella opening, and concussive hammers rippled out in successive, overlapping waves.

"Good Boy, this is Hard Light," Mott's voice broke over the ear jacks in the two Stony Man operators' helmets.

"Go ahead, Hard Light," Bolan answered.

"Inside the gate to your nine o'clock you have a response team oriented toward your position. I see long weapons and a RPG-7. Over."

"Roger," Bolan said. "Good Boy out."

He wrenched the wheel of the speeding SUV to the side, looped out wide to the right and then brought the nose grille back around toward the gate. Now instead of breaching the threshold straight-on through the smoking ruin of the gate, Bolan would guide the SUV through the breach at a diagonal line heading from outside right to inside left.

This would have the effect of orienting the weapons of the SUV straight onto the knot of defenders pointed out by Mott's observation platform above the fray. Bolan fought the bouncing vehicle back under control, then took up the pistol grip of the SAW machine gun angled out the front of the vehicle on its bipod through the removed windshield. Beside him Grimaldi adjusted his grip on the dual spade handles of the Mk 19 grenade launcher.

The big, heavily modified SUV ate up the ground, clawing its way forward and spewing twin rooster tails of dirt behind it. Bolan gunned the vehicle over a slight, rocky berm and muscled the vehicle into position. The angles lined up and a trajectory window appeared which Grimaldi immediately exploited.

The Mk 19 coughed a staccato pattern of high explosive death. The weapon cycled with brute economy, throwing 40 mm shells downrange with devastating effect. The relatively slow-moving projectiles shot out in front of the speeding SUV and landed hard. The explosions provided deadly, unforgiving cover as the Executioner crossed into the Bout compound.

BOLAN COULD JUST MAKE OUT the knot of armed figures in the light of the burning fires. Smoke hung as thick as London fog between the walls of the palace compound and obscured the area from the sky. Both Charlie Mott and the camera eye of the Reaper UAV could only make out the unfolding action in random, patchy glimpses.

Bolan shouted his alert to Grimaldi and triggered the vehicle-mounted SAW machine gun. The high-velocity 5.56 mm slugs lanced out before the Executioner and sliced into the knot of confused figures on flat, smooth rails of flight.

The first bullet struck the lead gunman low in the stomach where the thirty-two-foot length of the human intestine rested like a water hose packed accordion fashion on the back of a fire truck. The round struck with the force of a baseball bat and penetrated the soft flesh and viscera without slowing.

The bullet gored through the man's guts, tearing a channel large enough to stick a fist through as it cut its way out of the body, slicing through the spleen in the process. The man folded like a lawn chair, gasping at the sudden agony and a wave of bullets tore his screaming face from his body.

Grimaldi saw a black Stobart civilian work truck packed with bales of hay pull out from around the back of the undamaged stables. He shifted the blunt muzzle of the 40 mm grenade launcher to face the vehicle, its occupants hidden behind a deeply tinted windshield.

Grimaldi pulled the trigger as the work truck gunned toward him. The first 40 mm HE/DP round arched over the vehicle's roof and struck the ground well behind the vehicle, exploding in a fiery ball and rain of steel shrapnel. Grimaldi lowered his sights by half an inch and put two shots straight into the big truck.

The first round punched through the windshield and filled the cab with a sudden flash of fire that blew out the side windows and rear windshield. The second round struck the grille and detonated up against the big block engine. Instantly the engine fluids caught fire as the vehicle was driven off to one side by the force of the explosion.

The hungry flames sped along melting lines toward the gas tank and the whomp of the fifty-gallon container going up tripped hard on the heels of the first explosion. The Stobart truck lifted into the air, propelled on an orange tower of flame like a rocket leaving orbit. It spun like a burning pinwheel and then fell to the ground.

The mangled frame tumbled and bounced with Jurassic force, causing tendrils of flame to spread out across the ground in burning spines of fire. Grimaldi turned the Mk 19 on its axis and lobbed two rounds at the group of fighters Bolan was engaging with his SAW machine gun.

Bolan's fire scythed into the formation, cutting them off at the legs on one sweep of a Z-pattern burst then finishing them off with the second pass. Two grenades slammed into their midst and exploded, tossing bodies into the air like parade confetti. Bolan gunned the patrol vehicle forward, skirting a low, ornate iron fence running around the Olympic-size swimming pool.

The Executioner saw a line of burning two-story houses running between the main house and airstrip. He looked overhead but couldn't see Mott's Little Bird. He made to initiate radio contact but was suddenly taken under fire.

A stream of bullets cut toward him from a concrete pool house just behind him. The rounds struck the back of the big assault-modified SUV and hacked apart equipment boxes and shattered glass. The bullets ricocheted wildly and cut the air immediately between the two men.

"Son of a bitch!" Grimaldi shouted.

Instinctively, Bolan started to cut to his right and face the attack but realized just as quickly that such a maneuver would leave Grimaldi open to fire from that side and unable to use the grenade launcher as it was currently mounted.

Bolan slammed on the brakes, leaving the rear of the SUV oriented toward the pool house as more rounds burned around him. He bailed out of the vehicle, snatching up a combination M-4/M-203. Grimaldi threw himself sideways across the seats to avoid the angle of fire, and green tracer rounds tore apart the steering wheel inches from his head.

Bolan hit the ground, rose, and looked for a target over the knobby rear wheel of the military vehicle. Instantly bullets blew by him on all sides. He felt a slap and a sting on his right shoulder, and something punched him in the head above his ear.

He felt hot blood pour down the side of his face and soak the sleeve of his uniform blouse. He ducked, his cheek resting on the dirty tread of the thick off-road tire at the back of the SUV. He felt the rough impact as more bullets slammed home into the solid rubber. He brought his M-4/M-203 around the corner of the thick tire and angled its fire by estimation.

His finger found the metal trigger behind the shotgun breech of the attached grenade launcher and pulled it. The weapon recoiled in his hands with the solid kick of a .12-gauge shotgun. He heard the round land and explode, and risked a peek around the tire. Earth was falling in an avalanche along with pieces of a deck chair, about four feet in front of the gunman's position behind the concrete block pool house.

Bolan threw his carbine's collapsible stock to his shoulder and began pouring fire around the building, keeping the rifleman pinned down. His bullets knocked chunks off the pool house and skipped across the concrete deck encircling the pool. The carefully tended lawn began to burn.

"Get the 312 up!" Bolan shouted.

Grimaldi scrambled over the bullet-ripped SUV seats, popped up through the sunroof and brought the XM312 back on line. The black bungee tie-down shot out of the SUV like a rubber band and landed on the ground yards away. He turned the heavy machine gun in a tight traverse and unloaded on the pool house.

The weapon blew the concrete block and rebar structure into dust. The rounds smacked hard into the building, punching through the walls without slowing and baseball-size chunks of mortar disintegrated, leaving gaping holes throughout the structure. Bolan saw a figure, shirtless and barefoot, spin wildly out from the pool maintenance shed.

The man was tossed bleeding into the pool where he hung suspended in the water, floating facedown and turning the chlorinated blue darkly scarlet. Bolan rose swiftly and spoke into his throat mike.

"Hard Light, this is Good Boy," he said. "You have our twenty? Over."

"Roger. I have you by the pool but observation is spotty," Mott replied. "You want extraction? It's a hornet's nest. Over."

"Negative, Good Boy Two and I will do target site

assessment, prior to extraction. I want eyes on verification of Primary or Secondary. Over."

"Roger. I'll try to cover your six when you go in, but the smoke is bad. Over."

"Roger. Understood. Good Boy out," Bolan finished.

Grimaldi dropped out of the SUV and began quickly arming himself from several of the light weapons secured around the frame of the vehicle. In addition to his M-4 he selected a folding stock Remington 870 pump-action shotgun, a Glock 18 pistol capable of 3-round bursts and a 10 mm Glock 17, as well as the grenades, knives and equipment already secured to his web gear.

"Let's go make sure no one missed the party," Bolan said.

The Stony Man pilot nodded as he pulled a timing pencil detonator from his uniform shirt's chest pocket, activated it and then squatted by the SUV's gas tank. He reached under and inserted the pencil into the plastique charge shaped along the seam, rearming it after the long drive across the rugged mountains.

"Let's go," he said.

CHAPTER SIXTEEN

They cut across a strip of manicured lawn separating the rear pool complex from the patios and steps at the back of the now collapsed and burning house. It was becoming immediately clear as they navigated the grounds that the Keyhole satellite intelligence imagery had left them dramatically misinformed about the number of enemy combatants contained in the compound.

After the overwhelming force and violence of the initial strike, resistance should have been sporadic and ill-coordinated. Command and communications centers, staging areas and arsenals had all been struck and reduced to rubble. Despite this, there were such a large number of uninjured gunmen sweeping the complex that it was readily apparent that there had been a vastly greater number of paramilitary agents than reported.

Bolan and Grimaldi found themselves in an anthill of running, screaming men, calling out to one another in an attempt to reorganize and repel the threat. Ma-

chine-gun teams were set up rapidly and engaged Charlie Mott in standoff duals, forcing the helicopter pilot
to zip in and out of range as he took gun runs at multiple knots of fighters.

The Stony Man duo moved under fire toward the house.
They approached a long series of Italian doors issuing
smoke through the blown-out glass. They moved in a
bounding overwatch, modified to exploit speed, but basi-
cally consisting of one commando holding security while
the next leapfrogged forward to the next point of cover.

Twice their path was cut by armed men rushing to
help engage the swooping Little Bird. The first time
Grimaldi took the shirtless man down with a short burst
followed up immediately by Bolan's finishing shot to
the head. The second time a shoeless, bearded fighter
with the build of a professional bodybuilder sprinted
around a tight cluster of native Croat walnut trees with
a drum-fed AKM in his massive fists.

Both men turned and fired simultaneously from the
hip without breaking stride. The gunfire cut the giant
of a man into ribbons and knocked him back among a
nearby stand of trees.

As Bolan and Grimaldi ran, they could hear people
screaming from around the compound and once they
heard a long, ragged machine-gun burst answered immediately by Mott's M-134 minigun. Bolan cleared the
deck over a column of concrete pillars supporting a
low, wide stone rail encircling the patio. The explosive
force of the GBU-12s had cracked and pitted its surface
but failed to break the stone railing.

Bolan landed on mosaic tile, waves of heat from the burning building washing over him and casting weird shadows close in around him. He saw a flat stone bench and took up a position behind it, going down to one knee. He began scanning the long line of patio doors with his main weapon while Grimaldi bounded forward.

Grimaldi passed Bolan's hasty fighting position in a rush and put his back to a narrow strip of wall set between two ruined patio doors. He kept his weapon at port arms and turned his head toward the opening beside him. From inside the dark structure flames danced in a wild riot.

The pilot nodded sharply and Bolan rose in one swift motion, bringing the buttstock of his M-4 IM-203 to his shoulder as he breached the opening. He moved past Grimaldi, sweeping his weapon in tight, predetermined patterns as he entered the building.

Grimaldi folded in behind him, deploying his weapon to cover the areas opposite Bolan's pattern. It felt as if they had rushed headlong into a burning oven. Heavy tapestries, Persian rugs and silk curtains all burned bright and hot. Smoke clung to the ceiling and filled the room to a height of five feet, forcing the men to crouch below the noxious cover.

In a far corner the two men saw a sprawling T-shaped stair of highly polished English wood now smoldering in the heat. A wide-open floor plan accentuated groupings of expensive furniture clustered together by theme. After learning of the place both Stony Man operatives had studied the blueprints of the Bout house as closely as time had allowed. The sprawling compound and ostentatious structure had been designed by an international architectural firm out of Paris, known for the lavish estates they had built for the royalty of Sweden and Monte Carlo.

Akira Tokaido had breached the company's firewalls and snatched the blueprints of the house without leaving a whisper of a trace to witness his infiltration. Both Bolan and Grimaldi had committed the building interior to memory prior to their strike.

The bombs had rendered much of their memorization superfluous. Slowly the two men turned so that their backs were to each other, their weapon muzzles tracking through the smoke and uncertain light. Smoke choked their lungs and stung their eyes. They saw the inert shapes of several bodies cast about the room among the splinters of concussion-shattered furniture. One body lay sprawled on the smoldering staircase, hands outflung and a stream of blood pouring down the steps like water cascading over rocks.

Bolan moved slowly through the burning wreckage, approaching twisted bodies and searching the bruised and bloody faces for traces of recognition.

The Executioner had not come to know all the principals of Bout's operation in the manner by which he had pursued so many other enemy leaders, Mafia Dons, intelligence operatives and terrorist generals. There was nothing specific about this fight, it was total war, the killing of the enemy as you came upon him on the battlefield.

Now he had driven his enemy in front of him, battered him into a final, defensive stand, and Bolan risked all to deliver the knockout blow that would shatter the Russian criminal syndicate. His engagement would not be finished until he had assured that the dragon's head was cut off and cauterized.

Bolan searched the dead for Victor Bout. Around him the heat grew more intense and the smoke billowed thicker. Grimaldi moved with the same quick, methodical efficiency, checking the bodies as they vectored in toward the stairs.

Bolan sensed more than saw the motion from the top of the smoldering staircase. He barked a warning even as he pivoted at the hip and fired from the waist. His M-4 IM-203 lit up in his hands, and his bullets streamed across the room in violent shoals of lead.

The 5.56 mm rounds chewed into the staircase and snapped railings into splinters as he sprayed the second landing. One of his rounds struck the gunman high in the abdomen. The Teflon-coated high-velocity rounds speared up through the smooth muscles of diaphragm, sliced open the bottom of the lungs and cored out the left atrium of the gunman's pounding heart. Bright scarlet blood squirted like water from a faucet as the target staggered backward.

The figure, indistinct in the smoke, triggered a burst that hammered into the steps before pitching forward and striking the staircase. The faceless gunman tumbled forward, his limbs loose, his head making a distinct thumping sound as it bounced off each individual step on the way down, leaving black smears of blood on the wood as it passed.

Bolan sprang forward, heading fast for the stairs. Grimaldi spun in a tight 180-degree circle to cover their six o'clock as he edged out to follow Bolan. He saw silhouettes outside through the blown-out frames of the patio doors and he let loose with a wall of lead in a tight, figure-eight pattern.

One shadow fell sprawling across the concrete divider and the rest of the silhouettes scattered in response to Grimaldi's fusillade. The pilot danced sideways, found the bottom of the staircase and started to back up it. Above him he heard Bolan curse and then the Executioner's weapon blazed.

To Grimaldi's left a figure reeled back from a window. Another came to take its place, the star-pattern burst illuminating a manically hate-twisted face of strong Slavic features. The Stony Man pilot put a 3-round burst into his head from across the burning room and the man fell away.

"Let's roll!" Bolan shouted.

He let loose with a long burst of harassing fire aimed at the line of French doors facing out to the rear patios and lawns as Grimaldi spun on his heel and pounded up the steps past Bolan. Outside, behind the cover of the concrete-pillared railing, an enemy combatant popped up from his crouch, the distinctive outline of a RPG-7 perched on his shoulder.

Down on one knee, Bolan fired an instinctive burst but the shoulder-mounted tube spit flame in a plume from the rear of the weapon, and the rocket shot out and into the already devastated house. Bolan turned and dived up the stairs as the rocket crossed the big room below him and struck the staircase.

The warhead detonated on impact, and Bolan shuddered under the force and heat but the angle of the RPG had been off. The construction of the staircase itself channeled most of the blast force downward and away from where Bolan lay sprawled. Enough force surged upward to send him reeling even as he huddled against the blast. He tucked into a protective ball and absorbed the blunt waves.

Bolan lifted his head and saw Grimaldi standing above him, his feet spread wide for support and firing in short bursts of savage, accurate fire. Bolan lifted his M-4 and the assault carbine came apart in his hands. He flung the broken pieces away from him and felt his wrist burn and his hand go slick with spilling blood as the stitches from his garrote wound came apart under the abuse.

He ignored the hot, sticky feeling of the blood and cleared his Beretta 93-R from its underarm sling. He pushed himself up and turned over as Grimaldi began to engage more targets. As he twisted, he saw something move from the hallway just past the open landing behind the Stony Man pilot.

Bolan extended his arm and stroked the pistol's trigger. A 3-round 9 mm Parabellum burst struck the creeping enemy in a tight triangle-grouping high in the chest, just below the throat.

The killer's breastbone cracked under the pressure and either insertion point of the sternocleidomastoid neck muscles were sheared loose from the collarbones. The back of the target's neck burst outward in a spray of crimson and pink as the 9 mm rounds burrowed their way clear.

"Go! Go!" Grimaldi shouted.

He swept his M-4 back and forth in covering fire as Bolan scrambled past him to claim the high ground. The Executioner pushed himself off the stairs and onto the second floor. Stepping over the bloody corpse of his target, he turned and began to aim and fire the Beretta in tight bursts.

Under his covering fire Grimaldi wheeled on his heel and bounded up the stairs past Bolan. At the top of the landing he threw himself down and took aim through the staircase railing to engage targets below him in the open great room.

From superior position the two Stony Man warriors rained death on their enemies.

"HOLD THE STAIRS!" Bolan growled, rising to his feet. "I'll check the site for our target."

"Copy," Grimaldi acknowledged as he coolly worked the trigger on his M-4.

Bolan moved quickly down the hallway. Smoke burned his throat and irritated his eyes, obscuring his vision as he hunted. He worked quickly but cautiously, checking behind doors as he moved down the hall. Flames kept the corridor oven-hot, and the hair and clothes on still, broken bodies smoldered as Bolan hunted to verify the dead.

In several places he found that the collapse of the two floors above had penetrated onto the second story, cracking open the bedroom ceilings and dumping broken furniture and flaming debris like rockslides. Bolan scrambled over mounds of rubble and skirted charred holes dropping away beneath his feet.

Behind him Bolan heard Grimaldi's smooth trigger work keeping the enemy at bay. He refused to waste energy on being angry but deep inside he was frustrated at his own intelligence failure that had missed such a huge number of combatants in the compound. He couldn't afford to let it cloud his attention now.

He came upon a decimated body. The face looked like it had been taken apart by a tire iron and was puffy, bruised and covered in blood but Bolan was still able to identify the man as a triad street soldier. He mentally crossed the man off his list.

He turned the corner in the L-shaped hallway and saw the corridor blocked. An avalanche of ceiling beams, flooring, ruined furniture and body parts had dropped through the third floor and completely obstructed the hall. Flames ran in fingers off the cave-in spreading heat and destruction with rapid ferocity.

A bit of debris fell through the roof and Bolan looked up, stepping forward to get a better look. Dangling from the hole was a mahogany-colored Savali Pristine briefcase made from dyed crocodile hide, a prized status symbol in EU boardrooms. The case hung from a pair of blue steel handcuffs attached to a blood-smeared arm.

"Well, look at that," he murmured.

Bolan raised his arm and touched the bottom of the crocodile hide case, then stood on his toes and grasped it with a firmer hold. Realizing he was going to have to yank the whole body down to get the case, Bolan pulled hard.

There was a brief moment of resistance, then the case came loose in his hand so suddenly he was over-balanced and went stumbling back. His heel caught on a length of wood and he almost fell. He back-pedaled like a pass receiver, then cut to the side and came up against the wall.

He looked down at the case in his hand. The case was still attached to the blood-smeared wrist by the dark metal handcuffs. A man's arm hung from the dangling chain. It ended in a ragged tear at the elbow. Bloody muscle and tendon hung in scraps from the open wound.

Bolan looked up through the hole and saw only more flames. He felt a grudging acceptance that it was unlikely anyone in the floors above could have survived the twin bomb blasts. He dropped his gory artifact onto the hot ground and knelt on one knee, pinning the disembodied forearm to the ground with his leg.

He drew his boot knife and went to work freeing the arm from the handcuff.

Bolan clutched the Salvi briefcase under one arm and rose, using the back of his web harness to secure the potential find, and continued on.

He backed up to the edge of the corner and pulled a grenade from his web gear suspenders. The AN-M14 TH3 incendiary hand grenade weighed as much as two cans of beer and had a lethal radius of over more than twenty meters that spread its burning damage out to thirty-six meters; in the hallway its destruction would be concentrated, spreading fire and contributing greatly to the overall structural instability of the building.

Bolan yanked the pin on the grenade and let the arming spoon fly. He lobbed the compact canister underhand and watched it bounce down the short stretch of hall before ducking around the corner. The delay fuse was four seconds, which gave him plenty of time to gain safety.

Both he and Grimaldi carried the incendiary grenades. They were heavier than some other, more modern hand grenade versions, but their power was undisputed and they made a nice compromise to larger but more powerful satchel charges.

Bolan moved in a fast crouch toward the once ornate landing where Grimaldi fired down from his defensive vantage point to cover Bolan's search and destroy mission. Bolan spoke into his throat mike.

"Good Boy to Hard Light, I have a structural blockage. Our operation is finished. Site destruction verified to acceptable factor of certainty. Over."

"Hard Light to Good Boy, we have a sitrep," Mott said. Bolan could hear the beating of the helicopter's rotors and the muffled sound of minigun bursts. "Someone just used a cellular signal we're locked in to back at the Farm. They tell me it's Pandey. He's in a guesthouse on the edge of the compound."

"Roger," Bolan answered. "Good Boy out."

CHAPTER SEVENTEEN

Moving fast, Bolan and Grimaldi cleared the main building and crossed the stretch of burning back lawn. The area had seen considerable attention from Mott's strafing runs.

The lush, closely cut grass of the landscaped yard ended at a two-foot-high retaining wall, separating lawn from the security wall in the back. Huge pockmarks had been ripped out of the earth, and fires had sprung up in patches of spilled fuel. Bodies had been tossed into loose piles all around the area, but most of the still active resistance had left the area to converge on the main house of the compound.

Crab walking, Bolan kept as low a profile as possible until he had reached the cover of a pruned and sculpted pine tree and large and mutilated oleander bush near the left-hand side of the fence. A severed head looked at him.

As Grimaldi covered their six, Bolan controlled his

breathing, forced it to slow. He could see the backyard very clearly in all the ambient light the house was throwing through the shattered picture windows set into the back of the building. To the right of his position, across the lawn, was the Olympic-size swimming pool, complete with both slide and diving board, now showing a bloody red. Beyond the ruined pool house were the garage and kennels.

Behind him, Bolan heard the sounds of raging fires and shouting men. The chemical stench reached his nostrils. The same breeze driving the smell of destruction to him would be picking up his scent and wafting it across the yard toward the dog runs behind the modest stables. Bolan detected no movement from the well-lit and heavily damaged house, but incongruously the sound of the stereo playing reached his ears gently, over the sounds of immediate apocalypse.

"Let's make our approach," Bolan whispered. Grimaldi nodded.

As Bolan climbed out from the shelter of the wall, two Doberman Pinschers, scrambled out from beside the house. Both dogs kept their noses in the air, searching out the story borne to them on the soft mountain breeze. They whined and growled, terrified but confused and obviously primed for the attack in such a catastrophic situation.

They growled low in their chests, and the sound was like the engines of racing bikes idling at the line. The lead dog swung his head in Bolan's direction and snarled. Its mate growled in answer and began trotting toward the deep shadows of the devastated shrubbery landscaped along the far wall of Bout's guesthouse.

Bolan cut loose with the Beretta, and the dog went down. The round entered just under his ear, severing the spine and dropped the dog instantly. Its mate barked once in surprise and turned toward his fallen brother. Bolan's next shot took him through lung and heart, entering just behind the right foreleg. The black dog folded instantly.

Bolan was on his feet and moving, Grimaldi behind him, crossing the lawn in a fast jog. He did not relish killing the animals and in a sense he hated to do it. He hated the idea of losing Bout even more.

Halfway across the lawn Bolan passed through an arc of light thrown out by a floodlight set high up on the side of the guesthouse that had miraculously escaped destruction. He hurried through a flower bed, hurtled a low hedge and landed on a back patio, Grimaldi two steps behind him. Weaving his way past overturned and scorched metal-framed lawn furniture, Bolan gained the back of the guesthouse just under a second-story deck perforated with bullet holes. He moved quickly to the left corner.

Slowing his pace, Bolan set his back against the wall once flush on the side of the building. About ten yards down, toward the front, stood a secondary door.

Beretta held close to his temple, Bolan slid up next to the door.

He quickly inserted his lock-pick gun and compressed the lever trigger. He heard the subtle scrapping of metal on metal as the prongs manipulated the pins of the door lock. The bolt clicked home and the doorknob turned under his hand.

Steeling himself, the Executioner entered.

As Grimaldi covered the outside, Bolan moved through the door in a sudden, fluid movement, pulling it quickly shut behind him and stepping to one side as he entered the guesthouse. His weapon was out, leading the way, tracking for targets. The big room was dark, a jumble of hulking, shadow cloaked shapes. Dropping to one knee, weapon held ready, Bolan waited for his eyes to adjust after having his night vision blown by the house lights outside.

"Cover the door so we don't get any surprises," he whispered to Grimaldi, who nodded his reply.

Quickly, Bolan's pupils expanded and he began picking out details. He was in a games room. To one side there were two air hockey tables and a massive, even ostentatious home entertainment system. Various electronic games and expensive, comfortable furniture were scattered around. Across the massive room from the outside door a short flight of stairs led to the main floor of the guesthouse.

Bolan stood, shifting his knapsack off his back as he did so. With it in hand he crossed the room to the stairs. He could hear music from the stereo system playing upstairs clearly. He was banking on it to cover any normal noise he made while moving. At this point he had to assume that anyone left in the place was wounded or a noncombatant. Most of the gunmen had converged on the main house. He knew it was only a matter of minutes before they organized themselves into an attack force and tracked him.

To his possible detriment, however, the sound of the stereo helped increase his chances of being surprised going through egress transition points in the structure—doorways, stairs, halls and arches. This slowed him just when he most felt the need to be hasty.

Reaching the stairs, Bolan looked up. The door to the next level was tightly closed, a bar of light showing through at the bottom. Bolan mounted the steps and knelt in front of the door. A light sheen of perspiration coated his forehead, part concentration, part apprehension. The time he spent implementing his close-quarter observation equipment was time when he was at his most vulnerable. He set down the Beretta.

Bolan removed a fiber optic camera tactical video system from his pack. The borescope had been preassembled, but Bolan still needed both hands to position the surveillance device. He slid the cable under the doorway, then turned on the handheld video display screen. An image of the room on the other side of the door popped up. Bolan smoothly panned the fiber cam across the room.

The great room stretched from the front to the back of the house, encompassing a wet bar along one wall over to a sunken leisure area containing costly pieces of furniture and objets d'art. The floor was dark hardwood, and a spiral staircase ran downward from the second level next to the bar. The room appeared empty.

A tall man matching Pandey's picture stepped around a corner on the same wall as Bolan's door, coming around the end of the wet bar with a drink in his hand. Pandey sure didn't look like a man run to ground, in danger for his life. He looked pretty at ease in his surroundings.

Bolan set his mouth in a hard, straight line. This confirmed suspicions that had caused him to enter the compound on a hard probe in the first place. Pandey was obviously hand-in-glove with Bout—despite the seemingly mysterious events surrounding his disappearance from Split. Mr. Pandey was about to get a visit from someone who was there to "rescue" him.

Through the borescope, Bolan watched Pandey walk across the area and step down into the entranceway. The front door opened and a woman walked into the informal entertaining area, Pandey trailed her, standing close at her side. She was tall, beautiful, with white-blond hair and a curvy figure. Bolan frowned. They crossed to the bar and Pandey watched as the woman poured herself a drink. The woman moved with a great amount of poise for the current situation. There was a wild card in play.

Bolan quickly broke down his surveillance device and secured it in his backpack. Steeling himself, Bolan retrieved his Beretta and picked up a stun grenade. Slowly he released his breath, like a pressure valve bleeding steam. He focused, mentally imagined each step he was about to execute as clearly and precisely as he could picture. He was like a dancer choreographing a particularly difficult routine. Each step had to be perfect.

Bolan snatched the pin from the flash-bang grenade and let the lever spring free. There was a metallic boing as the coil spring holding the weapon parts together disengaged. Bolan swung open the door and stepped into the room.

Pandey stood on one side of the bar, his face registering only shock as he froze in midsentence. The blond woman was spinning, her hand diving toward the small of her back under a designer-cut leather jacket.

Bolan lobbed the primed grenade in a gentle underhand, aiming for it to roll across the well-polished top of the wet bar. Pandey's mouth worked like a fish yanked clear of the water and tossed into the bottom of a boat. Bolan stepped back around the protective corner of the door. He drew a stun gun and snapped it on. With his right hand Bolan raised his Beretta.

The bang was brutally loud and the flash blinding. The unattended stereo system abruptly shut down. Bolan stepped back into the main room from around the corner, 93-R held ready, stun gun at his hip. He leaped forward and the stun gun came out from some hidden place like the fangs of a cobra as he struck. The woman backpedaled in the face of the sudden, incapacitating flash-bang, her arms held up like a person expecting the impact of a car wreck. Pandey collapsed backward, sagging against the counter behind him.

Bolan took two steps and went airborne. He landed on the bar and his momentum carried him sliding down its length. He whipped his stun gun around and caught the blonde in her ribs. The electrical charge locked the woman up and then swept her to the ground, her eyes rolling to show only the whites. She made crude, inarticulate sounds deep in her throat.

As she went down, Bolan spun. He cleared the bar, rolling off the edge, and came down next to Pandey. The Indian scientist cringed in front of him, raising his hands and cowering like a child. Bolan snarled and moved forward, a weapon held up in each hand.

"Move!" he barked.

Bolan took half a step forward and shoved the man around the corner of the bar. He thumbed off the stun gun's power and clipped it back onto his belt. Following the slow-moving Pandey, Bolan shoved him again. This time the man fell to the floor next to the incapacitated woman.

"How we doing?" Grimaldi's voice cut across the uplink.

"Just fine. Let me know if the natives start wandering in this direction," Bolan replied.

Pandey looked up, terrified. He saw Bolan with weapon ready, looming above them, a grim manifestation of justice.

More quickly than Bolan would have thought possible, the woman began to recover. He stepped past the cowering, ineffectual Pandey and over to the woman. Leaning down, he thrust the muzzle of his 93-R into her forehead.

"Am I going to have to shoot you?"

"What?" She was still shaking off the effects of her stunning. "Who—"

"I *said*, am I gonna have to shoot you?" Bolan let the volume and cadence of his voice climb.

"No." Her voice was surprisingly calm.

Already she was suppressing her fear and disorientation. Her eyes sized Bolan up like a pit bull calculating how much play it had left in its chain. Bolan shifted his 93-R and unclipped his stun gun. One-handed, he clicked it on. The device began to hum and crackle with energy. The predatory look was pushed out of the woman's eyes.

"Okay, both of you get up. Pandey, I'm keeping my gun on you. Understand? You try anything, I shoot you. She tries anything, I shoot you. No matter how this plays out, you get shot, understand?"

The man nodded, pale, as he climbed to his feet.

"I can't hear you!" Bolan barked, never taking his eyes off the rising woman.

"Yes! Yes. You will kill us, I understand," Pandey answered.

"Good, now both of you get over against the wall next to the couch. We have a ticking clock."

With a sniper's eye, Bolan watched them, one frightened, one hating, take a position on the wall next to the couch. He replaced his stun gun, but kept a wide, glass-topped coffee table between himself and the pair.

"Nice place, Pandey," Bolan said, putting a big boot on the table. "Apparently circumventing international law on bioweapons pays well. Is that couch real Italian leather?"

"Yes," the woman answered.

She did not seem put off balance by the pedestrian nature of Bolan's question. He sized her up. She was a looker and if you let those looks lull, Bolan realized, she'd kill you without remorse.

"Name," he demanded.

"Katrina," she answered without hesitation.

"I don't believe you," Bolan said. "But it doesn't matter for now." He paused. "Katrina. And your English is excellent."

She lifted her eyebrows. "Thanks."

"You're messing up, cowboy," Pandey said. "You're American. Who are you, why are you doing this to me? I am not under your jurisdiction."

"Jurisdiction?" Bolan countered. "From what I've been able to tell, this is all Victor Bout's jurisdiction. He doesn't stand on formalities, and neither do I."

Pandey's eyes were livid points of hate as he looked Bolan up and down.

"Buddy, I'm going to have the Human Rights Watch so far up your ass that you—"

Bolan lifted the Beretta smoothly. He pulled the trigger twice, shifted the muzzle and fired twice more. In the confined space it echoed like a cannon. Pandey shrieked as two rounds tore into the wall between his head and the woman's. Katrina flinched as the wall cracked open and plaster flew to the side of her as Bolan pinioned Pandey between his rounds.

"It's not that kind of party," Bolan said. "I'm so far off the books I'm illiterate. You understand what I'm telling you? I'm just like cloning a bioweapon. Whether I'm technically right or not is immaterial when the bodies start showing up."

Pandey stood stiffly, his face flushed. He breathed in hard snorts, his nostrils flaring with the effort and his mouth set in a hard, thin line. He kept his eyes on the floor, refusing to look up at Bolan. Beside him Katrina stood very still. She wasn't afraid to look at Bolan, and the look she gave him was calculating.

Pandey shot a protective glance toward Katrina, but the woman was watching Bolan with cool inscrutability. Bolan met her gaze. He didn't break it as he reached around and unlimbered his sat phone. He manipulated the instrument and put it to his ear.

"Bring it home, Hard Light," Bolan said.

He cut the connection and reharnessed the sat phone.

"Congratulations," Bolan said to Pandey. "The United States government is prepared to offer you protection."

CHAPTER EIGHTEEN

"What!" Pandey made to step forward in sudden, incredulous outrage.

Bolan reached over and smacked the heel of his palm into the scientist's forehead, shoving him back against the wall.

"You aren't in a position to negotiate anything, understand? You failed. You didn't get away with it. You've got a lot to answer for to your country and the world. It'd be easier to kill you. Don't provoke me."

"You want me, as well?" Katrina sounded surprised, which pleased Bolan.

"Yeah." Bolan nodded. "You're somebody. I just don't know who yet." He turned away and spoke into his throat mike. "If it still looks clear, I need you up here."

"Copy. All clear for the moment. En route," Grimaldi replied.

"You did all of this to get Pandey?" The woman waved her arms around.

Bolan met her eye and locked into her gaze tightly. "Don't flatter yourself. You and your boyfriend are the booby prize. A helicopter is coming now. You will be getting on that helicopter."

"I see."

"This is outrageous!" Pandey was fairly screaming. "This is extortion, kidnapping!" Pandey grew increasingly frantic as he became increasingly secondary. "We have the right to negotiations—"

Bolan plucked the stun gun off his belt and turned it on again. "Are you going to keep talking?" he asked.

Pandey choked his words off. His face was flaming red with his indignation. Bolan looked at him, disgusted with what he saw. A man given responsibility by his nation and who had thrown that duty away over an infatuation for a woman and a hunger for wealth.

A lifetime of obsession with having the right suit, the right hair gel, the right "look" had emasculated him to the point that concepts such as patriotism and sacrifice had become lost to "grander" concerns that were nothing more than excuses for self-gratification.

"Where is the clone tech you sold Bout?" Bolan asked.

"I don't know. He purchased it. I instructed some technicians he had in the best way to use it. I was waiting for my final payment."

"You work for Bout," he said to Katrina. "It was your job to spin Pandey. You're the missing prostitute that disappeared at Pandey's room in the Hoteli Croatia." It wasn't a question, not anymore.

Katrina fixed him with a level stare. "Sure. But I'm a freelancer. I worked for Bout. If you get me out safe there's information I can give for consideration. I'm valuable."

"We'll let Poppa and Momma Bird back at base decide that," Grimaldi broke in as he entered the room.

Bolan nodded in greeting, clipped the stun gun to his belt, then stepped back as Grimaldi covered the pair.

"He's right," Bolan countered dryly. "I won't be the one to decide how valuable you are. At the moment, one screwup by you leaves you dead. Keep that at the front of your mind."

Katrina shrugged. "A Federal Witness Protection Program is the only security I have of growing old anymore."

Pandey was scarlet. The veins at his temples were vivid and the cords of his neck stood out. His mouth worked futilely as his fists clenched and unclenched at his sides. Bolan had no doubt the man wanted to rip him limb from limb, but he was unconcerned.

"Your government will be happy with the terms of our trade," Katrina answered. "But only if you get out of this compound alive."

Before Bolan could say anything his sat phone chirped. He plucked it off his harness and answered it, regarding the two captives next to the couch while he listened to the voice of Charlie Mott.

"Come in from a south, southeast approach," Bolan instructed. "The lawn at the back of the guesthouse is open enough for you to land easily. There are four of us. The bird will have no problem with weight. Though it's crowded, it's an in-and-out extraction."

Pandey and Katrina couldn't hear the reply, but Bolan lowered the muzzle of his 93-R and grunted his acquiescence into the com-link before signing off and securing it.

"You ready?" he asked Pandey.

"Does it matter?"

"No. But it's good you understand. I've got a helicopter coming into the backyard right now. You want a clean pair of underwear or a photo of Mom, you're out of luck. You take what you've got."

"I've had just—" Pandey began.

From outside the front of the guesthouse came three muted pops like the sound of fireworks going off. The expensive security monitor wall unit began to blare like a submarine Klaxon.

"Cover them!" Bolan told Grimaldi as he turned toward the alarm, his eyes searching for the display screen from the CCTV feed. On the screen, Bolan saw a pair of decorative gates hanging, blown off their moorings, and black Range Rovers speeding through the breach.

"Bout," Katrina said.

"I've got to slow them down," Bolan told Grimaldi. "At least long enough for the chopper to set down and everyone get inside."

Pandey popped off the wall like a dutiful lover, prepared to fight fiercely for the woman he felt himself charged with protecting. Bolan restrained himself from shooting the man out of pure irritation. Grimaldi pushed Pandey back.

"I'll take them down to the daylight basement," Grimaldi acknowledged.

Bolan looked back at the CCTV security camera and then at his watch, rapidly counting down the minutes in his head. He looked at Katrina and then over to Pandey. He hoped the two were worth it, because it was going to be damn close. He nodded once, curtly, to Grimaldi before turning away.

"What will you do?" the pilot asked.

"I'll keep them back, slow their advance."

"I thought you despised me," Pandey said.

Bolan looked at him. "You're a means to an end, an advantage for my country, a means to defeat people who would kill innocents in my country and around the world. That's something I'll fight for. Don't confuse my sense of duty for anything else."

Katrina regarded the big man. She met his flat gaze boldly, then nodded, ignoring Pandey. She turned from him and looked at the security monitor set into the wall beside the front entrance.

"They're in the front drive," she said.

"Get downstairs," Bolan replied.

BEHIND BOLAN, through the door, Bout's team had approached close enough that the sound of squealing tires and slamming doors could be heard from the drive in front of the main doors to the guesthouse.

"Las Vegas," Katrina said.

"What?"

"Vegas," she repeated. "Las Vegas, Nevada. I've wanted to see the Strip since I was a little girl."

"I'll mention it my debriefing."

"Good," she said.

Grimaldi snorted and shoved Pandey toward the staircase. The Indian scientist moved with the woman following close behind. The pilot shot Bolan one last, questioning look.

"Go," he said. "I'll hold them up."

Bolan turned his back to Grimaldi and walked toward the elaborate sitting area where he had used his weapon to pin Pandey and Katrina to the wall next to the couch only minutes earlier. He flicked the light switch as he moved into the room to avoid silhouetting himself. He lifted the Beretta and fired three triburst into the big picture windows facing the front of Bout's property. That part of the guesthouse had been facing away from the major conflict and seemed to have escaped relatively unscathed.

There was a chorus of answering shouts and a volley of fire erupted outside, initiating a storm of lead that tore into the room. More glass from the windows shattered, falling inward and the heavy, Renaissance curtains jerked and danced as they were shredded. After his initial burst Bolan threw himself to the floor, directing his momentum over a shoulder and rolled clear of the room, keeping below the hail of gunfire. He dropped the partially spent magazine and rammed home a fresh one.

Bolan slid around the column between the sitting

room and the entrance. He looked up at the monitor and saw three Range Rovers parked in flying-V wedges to keep the heavy engine blocks between the hit squad and gunfire from the guesthouse. Operatives fired at the building from around every protective angle offered by the vehicles.

Bolan spotted Bout. The Russian oligarch was armed with a black machine pistol. The arm that Bolan had savaged during their fight was in a sling and wrapped to his torso. Bout held his weapon and gestured wildly, shouting orders at his death squad. From the rear of one of the SUVs a man ran forward, Kalashnikov assault rifle slung over his shoulder and across his back.

Bolan swore. The man went to one knee and leveled an RPG-7 at the front of the guesthouse. Rising, Bolan turned and sprinted. The 2.3 kg 84 mm warhead could penetrate twelve inches of steel armor; it would blow through even a reinforced door with ease. Bolan scrambled across the floor and leaped up into the air. He struck the top of the bar and slid across as a fireball blew the front doors off their hinges and rolled into the room like a freight train.

Shrapnel and jagged chunks of wood lanced through the air. The mirror and crystalware on the counters behind Bolan shattered instantly, and glass rained down on him like hail. Liquor bottles exploded like bombs, and alcohol poured in torrents from the shelf.

Bolan moved up to the edge of the bar, which provided him with an angle on the front door. He took the Beretta machine pistol in both hands and lined up the open sights toward the burning entranceway. His ears still rang from the explosive concussion and his face bled from a dozen minor lacerations, but his hand was steady on the trigger as Russian gunmen rushed through the front door.

Bolan aimed for the head as they charged, knowing it extremely likely that Bout or even Lau Wing Kui would have lacked the resources to provide their teams with proper armor as well as weapons. Mercy wasn't an option as the assassins came on, Bolan met lethal violence with lethal violence.

The first shooter breached the door, AKM assault rifle up and at the ready. Bolan put him down with a 3-round burst. The combatant hit the burning floor like a bag of wet cement. The man running in behind him looked down as the point man hit the floor. He looked back up, searching for a target, and Bolan blew the left side of the man's face off.

The third man in the line tripped up with the second man's falling corpse. Bolan used a burst to scythe the man to the ground and then put another into the top of his skull. Through the swirling smoke and angry screams Bolan saw a round, black metal canister arch into the room.

Bolan noted the threat instantly—RG-42 antipersonnel hand grenade with a blast radius of 22.9 meters.

The Executioner rolled off his belly and onto his hands and knees as the grenade hit the floor inside the guesthouse and bounced toward him. He dived forward, scooping up the bouncing hand grenade and wrapping his hands around the black cylinder body.

Bolan hit the floor hard, absorbing the impact with his elbows. He rolled over onto one shoulder and thrust his arm out, sending the grenade shooting away from him. It cleared the corpses in the entrance and bounced up and out the front doors. He heard a sudden outburst of curses in Russian and he buried his head in his arms just before the grenade went off.

A cloud of smoke billowed in through the doorway on the heels of the concussive force. Bolan came to his feet, picking up an AKM assault rifle belonging to one of the downed gunners. Securing his Beretta, he shuffled backward and crouched behind the bar, heading for the door to the staircase leading to the games room. Bolan caught a flash of movement and spun toward the blown-out windows of the sitting room off the main entrance.

He saw two men in khaki jackets rush up to the shattered windows, holding AKM rifles. Bolan dropped to one knee beside the bar and brought up the AKM. He beat the men to the trigger and his carbine spit flame. It recoiled solidly in his hands and shell casings arched out to spill across the floor.

Bolan put two rounds into the face of the first man, bloody holes the size of dimes appeared, slapping the man's head back. Blood sprayed in a mist behind his head and he slumped to the ground, his weapon clattering at his feet.

The Executioner shifted smoothly, like ball bearings in a sling swivel, toward the second gunman. They fired simultaneously. The muzzle-flash of the man's weapon burst into a flaming star pattern.

The 7.62 mm slugs tore into the molding of the wall just to Bolan's right. The rounds tore through the building material, tearing fist-size chunks from the wall and door frame, spilling white plumes of chalky plaster dust into the air.

Bolan's burst hit the man in a tight pattern, the bullets drilling into the receiver of the AKM and tearing it from the stunned criminal's hands. Two more rounds punched into his chest three inches above the first, staggering him.

Bolan stood, the AKM held up and ready. He triggered two rounds into the stunned gunman and took him down, blowing the back of his neck out. Bolan moved to the side and, still facing the front of the guesthouse, held the AKM up and ready in one hand. He grabbed the knob and swung the stair door open.

A gunman came around the corner of the entrance, his Kalashnikov up and firing. Bolan put a burst into his knee and thigh, knocking the screaming man to the floor. He put a double tap through the top of his head. Brain matter and bits of skull splattered outward. Bolan took a minute to pat down the corpse, and hurriedly removed two magazines of 7.62 mm ammo from its web belt.

He moved backward toward the stairs as he took fire from the open window and swiveled to meet the threat as another pair of gunmen rounded the corner from the front entrance. Bolan threw himself belly down, his legs trailing out behind him down the stairs, angling his body so he was out of sight from the shooters in the entrance.

Bolan swept his assault rifle in a wide loose arch, spraying bullets at the gunman firing through the shattered picture windows. One of the men's weapon suddenly swung toward the ceiling and Bolan caught a glimpse of him staggering backward into the dark.

The Executioner lay on the stairs, only his arms and shoulders emerging from the door to the stairwell. He rotated onto his right shoulder to get an angle of fire on the entrance and saw one of the Russian gunmen rushing forward. He shot the man's ankles, bringing him to the floor. Bolan fired another burst into the prone man, finishing him off, only to have his bolt lock open as his magazine ran dry.

Bolan tossed off his empty AKM as a second commando leaped over the body of the first and charged forward. The skeletal, folding stock of his AKS-74U pressed tight into his shoulder, the gunman fired the weapon as he bounded toward Bolan.

The big American put his hands against the floor and snapped up, clearing the edge of the doorway. Bullets tore into the floor where his head had just been. He twisted on the stairs and jumped, landing at the bottom, his legs bending to absorb the impact. He took the recoil, felt it surge back up through his heels and rolled off to the side. He turned in the direction of the side door to the lower level of the guesthouse, where he had originally infiltrated.

A burst of gunfire echoed in the stairwell and 5.45 mm rounds tore into the floor where Bolan had landed. He went up against the wall at his back and pulled the 9 mm

Glock 17 from its holster. He heard boots thundering on the stairwell and he bent, swiveled and thrust his gun arm around the corner. He triggered four shots without exposing himself.

There was a satisfying thump as the gunman pitched forward and bounced down the steps. He spilled out at the bottom of the stairs, sprawling in front of Bolan and his weapon skidded out from his hands. The Executioner triggered a round into the back of the man's head.

The world was collapsing around him in a hellish vortex.

CHAPTER NINETEEN

Another figure appeared at the top of the stairs and took a shot at Bolan.

He leaped back out of view of the stairwell, grabbing up a fallen AKS-74U by its shoulder sling. Bullets struck the corpse of the dead Russian. Bolan caught a motion from his right side in time to see a khaki-clothed figure come through the outside door.

Behind him Grimaldi was wrestling with Pandey, trying to push the man out of the guesthouse and toward the lawn.

Bolan attempted to bring the AKS to bear but didn't have time. He let it dangle from the strap and raised his 9 mm pistol as he dropped to one knee. Instead of firing from the hip, the gunner brought his AKS into play, hoping for a more accurate shot.

Bolan's shot took him in the throat. Immediately the big American spun in a tight crouch and fired blindly up the stairwell for the second time. There was an answering burst of automatic gunfire, but no sound of bodies hitting the floor.

He turned to look toward Grimaldi, but the pilot had the situation under control and was shoving both of their "guests" outside. There was no sign of Charlie Mott.

Bolan holstered his Glock pistol and unslung his conscripted AKS. He quickly ducked his head into the stairwell before thrusting his weapon around the corner to trigger a burst. Using the covering fire to keep the enemy back, Bolan snagged the dead man at the bottom of the stairs over to him by his belt.

Bolan pulled a Soviet era RGD-5 antipersonnel hand grenade from the man's web harness. Like the RG-42, it had a blast radius of 22.9 meters, a little more than seventy-five feet. He held his AKS by the grip and stuck his thumb out. He used his free hand to help hook the pin around his extended thumb. He made a tight fist around the pistol grip of the AKS and pulled with his other hand, releasing the spring on grenade.

Bolan let the spoon fly. He turned and put a warning burst down the hall fronting the games room, through the side door. He counted down three seconds, then chucked the grenade around the corner and up the stairs. He turned away from the opening as the blast was funneled by the walls up and down the staircase, spraying shrapnel in twin columns.

Ears ringing, Bolan made for the door to the guest-house. He reached it, AKS-74U held at the ready. The door hung open, broken. From outside he heard gunfire as the commando force engaged Grimaldi. A figure darted past the open door and Bolan gunned him down.

Bolan darted a careful look around the edge of the door, looking back up the gradual incline running on the side of the house toward the front of Bout's property. He saw men taking positions at the corner of the main house and he fired a burst to keep them back.

A security force gunman flopped down onto his belly and threw down a bipod-mounted RPK 7.62 mm machine gun in front of him. Bolan jerked back inside the doorway as the machine gunner opened up, sending a virtual firestorm in Bolan's direction.

Bolan's heart pounded as he moved. His perception of time seemed to slow as adrenaline speeded up his senses to preternatural levels of awareness. His mind clicked through options like a supercomputer running mathematical algorithms. His head swiveled like a gun turret, the muzzle of his weapon tracking in perfect synchronicity.

He saw no movement from the staircase, turned and looked at the glass doors to the patio on the back lawn. Shrapnel and stray rounds had broken much of the glass, leaving jagged openings. He saw the flash of muzzle fire from along the back wall where Grimaldi held his position. It was time to go.

He checked the side door to the downstairs and saw woodchips fly off in great, ragged splinters from the withering machine-gun fire. Sensing movement, he twisted toward the staircase. A khaki-clad man with a beard rushed off the stairs.

Bolan had the drop on him and gunned him down. The AKS bucked hard in the big man's hands and he stitched a line of slugs across the Russian gunman's chest. Geysers of blood erupted from the mercenary's chest and throat as the kinetic energy from Bolan's rounds drove him backward. The man's heel caught on the outflung arm of his compatriot and he tumbled over, dead before he struck the ground.

Bolan swapped out magazines, then scrambled back from the staircase, dodging tables and furniture in the ruined and shot-to-hell games room. He saw a flash from the stairs and felt the air split as rounds blew by his face. Bolan fired wildly behind him for cover as he rolled up and across the air hockey table to land on the other side. He swung back around and covered the staircase and the side door, prepared to send a volley in either direction. His finger tensed on the smooth metal curve of the trigger.

There was a lull in the firing for a moment and Bolan heard Bout yelling instructions in Russian outside the side door. Cold anger burned deep inside Bolan, his desire to kill the oligarch was nearly overwhelming. How many innocents would lose their lives through that man's actions?

A haze of smoke hung in the room and the stench of cordite was a stimulant to Bolan's hyperstimulated senses. A burst of gunfire broke out from behind him. From the sound of the weapon caliber it seemed Grimaldi had found another target of opportunity.

"Forward! Forward!" Bout barked.

Bolan stood, weapon up, and started to turn toward the blown-out windows facing the back lawn. As he rose from his crouch behind the air hockey table, Bolan saw the dark ovals flying down the stairs.

He threw himself flat as the grenades landed in succession on the ground past the corpses of dead Russians and bounced once before detonating. The twin blasts were hellishly deafening and shrapnel whizzed through the air. Bolan knew a team would be rushing down the stairs after the grenade blasts, and he fired a ragged burst up the stairwell through the billowing plumes of dirty smoke.

He heard an all too familiar clunk and turned back toward the side door as a third grenade bounced in. Again Bolan threw himself down behind the air hockey table as the grenade exploded. From the floor beyond the table he heard the sound of automatic weapons being fired from both entrance points. Behind him the plasma-screen television finally caught a stray round and exploded in a shower of sparks.

Bolan tucked himself into a ball under the lip of the heavy air hockey table. He rose up out of his crouch slightly and set his muscular shoulder against the table. As close as the fire teams were to his position, Bolan knew he'd never make it across the lawn to Grimaldi. This place was his last stand.

Bolan pushed down against the floor with his legs and heaving his back into the lift. The air hockey table was unbelievably heavy and Bolan gasped in surprise at its solid weight. He grunted savagely and pushed harder. The table crashed onto its side with a profound bang and brightly colored air hockey balls spilled out of the pockets and rolled wildly across the floor.

He shifted around to one side of his barricade. Through a break in the smoke he saw a figure emerge into the basement from the outside. A quick burst took the guy out. Bolan twisted around the edge to look at the stairwell and saw another gunman rushing down into the hellzone.

Bolan pulled the trigger on his AKS and a single round struck the charging gunman in the groin before the bolt locked open. The man screamed in agony and triggered a blast from his weapon into the ground as he fell.

Dropping the AKS, Bolan rolled back behind the shelter of the air hockey table. He gulped in gritty oxygen and pulled his 9 mm pistol clear. He heard boots pounding on the floor a heartbeat before a weapon blast and then the sound of rounds striking the upended air hockey table.

The Executioner rolled onto his stomach and looked around the opposite side of his makeshift barricade. He saw a clean-shaven man in the now too familiar khaki uniform reaching down to pull the wounded gunman to his feet. Bolan sighted down the barrel of his weapon and put the man down with a single squeeze of the trigger.

Bolan rolled across his back out of view and then spun all the way over onto his stomach, emerging out from behind the other end of the air hockey table, pistol held out in both hands.

A Russian gunman came through the outside door, weapon up and firing for cover as he made the hostile entry. His wild burst passed over Bolan's head, and he finished the man with a double tap to the forehead.

Bolan put his free hand down and got to his feet into a tight crouch behind the air hockey table. The Glock 17 was up, at the ready, muzzle held beside his face. He pivoted smoothly behind his cover back toward the staircase where he knew Bout was driving his men forward.

As Bolan spun, a hand grenade came lobbing gently over the top of the table and bounced off the ground at his feet.

Bolan didn't think as the grenade landed. He had time only to react. He dived around the edge of the overturned air hockey table, desperate to put the big structure between himself and the exploding grenade. Bolan was still in the air when the little bomb went off, and he was knocked flat by the force of the detonation.

He hit the ground hard and heard the lurching bang as the air hockey table was picked up and then dropped back down by the force of the explosion. Next to it a wide marble-and-oak pool table soaked up the grenade shrapnel, protecting Bolan even as it was ruined beyond repair. Bolan rose, feeling dizzy and slightly disoriented.

He sensed movement in the smoke and whirled to fire in that direction. He felt more than saw a man go down and then he turned and stumbled back around the overturned air hockey table, heading for the broken patio windows. He heard squelch break from the sat phone on his webbing suspender and then Charlie Mott's voice projected over the microphone.

"I'm coming in, Good Boy."

"Hard Light, this is Good Boy Two. We're ready but it's hot!" Grimaldi answered.

"This is Good Boy, Hard Light," Bolan echoed. "I'm coming out of the guesthouse now, I have a visual. Everything behind me is hostile. Copy?"

"Copy. I got eyes on Good Boy Two now, Good Boy. Over."

"I'm damn glad to hear you say that," Bolan answered, panting. "Out."

Bolan ran out of the guesthouse and looked up to see the helicopter coming down to make a landing on Bout's back lawn. Underneath the landing skids Bolan saw Pandey and Katrina rise up out of their positions to make for the hovering chopper, Grimaldi behind them.

Bolan raced for the helicopter, running bent over, head down even as he heard automatic weapons fire open up from behind him. Grimaldi spun his weapon around and raked the already brutalized guesthouse and the gunmen inside, sending bullets that tore into the house, shredding walls and blowing out windows.

On the other side of the open cargo doors the racing Bolan saw Pandey shove Katrina up into the helicopter cargo bay. Once she was inside Pandey scrambled in after her. Bolan ducked low, running at an angle to keep clear of Grimaldi's line of fire. From the side of the bullet-riddled guesthouse the Russian gunslinger with the RPK sprinted around the corner.

Bipod still extended on the squad weapon, he triggered a blast at the hovering helicopter. Sparks flashed as rounds struck the fuselage, and the man walked his rounds up the length of the armored special operations model helicopter.

As Bolan ran, Grimaldi responded to the fire by swiveling to face the new threat. His rounds clawed through the guesthouse and tore up gouts of earth before smashing into the machine gunner with savage velocity. The Russian shuddered under the impact of a dozen rounds as if he were being electrocuted. Blood and gouts of flesh were torn from his frame as he absorbed the heavy-caliber bullets.

His finger still on the trigger, the man was knocked off his feet and tossed to the ground. His last burst sent rounds skipping up into the rotor blades of the helicopter before he was knocked completely over onto his back where the big weapon fell from his lifeless fingers.

Bolan scrambled into the cargo hold of the helicopter and felt Mott compensate for the sudden weight shift as the rotor mechanisms soaked up damage from the machine-gun rounds. Bolan slid across the floor and grabbed a seat strut to hold on to. Mott looked back into the bay from his seat and smiled when he met Bolan's eyes. Bolan slipped his weapon away and gave the pilot a thumbs-up. Bolan felt the pitch of the aircraft shift as Mott prepared to pull the bird out of the hot LZ.

Bolan heard Grimaldi's weapon go silent and looked

over at the Stony Man pilot. Grimaldi's face registered shock as he took two heavy hits to his bulletproof vest and stumbled backward. Bolan lunged for the man but missed as the helicopter suddenly lurched. He heard bullets like angry hornets rip through the open door and strike the inside of the helicopter.

From his belly Bolan looked out the open helicopter door at Bout's nearly demolished house and guesthouse. He saw Bout lower the RPK machine gun he'd taken from the fallen gunman and fire single-handed, shoulder stock tucked between elbow and ribs. The oligarch's face was twisted with a savage satisfaction. Beside Bout another man in khaki was already on one knee, a RPG-7 grenade launcher snug against his shoulder.

From inside the house half a dozen automatic rifles opened up and bullets peppered the helicopter at close range. Bullets cut through the space over Bolan's head and he heard the impact as some of the rounds slammed into the back of the pilot's armored seat.

Tracers flew in an unbroken stream, arching in through the open door to strike the inside of the helicopter and rattle around inside. Pandey shoved Katrina down and lunged over her, but the blonde took two wild rounds and her brains were splashed across the Indian scientist. Bolan cursed. Too much mystery had died with that woman.

Rounds ricocheted off the armored seats and swing out panels back into the troop transport area. Pandey screamed as a white-hot round creased his leg in the outer thigh and he threw himself away from the mutilated woman as more tracer fire poured in directly over his back.

The battered helicopter finished its swing so that its nose was oriented toward the fence at the rear of Bout's property. Bolan looked back, still on his belly, and saw the man beside Bout fire his rocket-propelled grenade. It shot out in a streak like a sluggish bolt of lightning and struck the hovering helicopter in its tail rotor, shaking the whole aircraft frame hard enough to scramble eggs.

Bolan looked toward the cockpit and saw blood spurt from Mott's shoulder. The veteran pilot rocked from the impact of the round but kept fighting with the controls to keep the helicopter on course, and for a moment Bolan thought Mott was going to pull it off.

Another tracer round burned past Bolan's face and clipped the reinforced pilot's seat.

Suddenly the helicopter swung wildly around, and it was sickeningly obvious that Mott was no longer in control. Bolan felt the bottom drop away beneath him and from brutal experience he knew the helicopter was going down.

Bolan grabbed hold of the seat strut again and spread himself wide on the floor to absorb the impact. He looked over his shoulder and out the front of the helicopter through the windshield. He saw the downward pointing nose of the bird clear the top of the fence surrounding Bout's house by mere inches and then the helicopter spun wildly to the side.

Centrifugal force pinned Bolan flat. He gasped for breath as he spun. He heard Pandey scream something in his own language, then caught a glimpse of the bullet-shredded house before the fence obscured his view.

Half a heartbeat later the helicopter hit.

CHAPTER TWENTY

Bolan felt the skids strike the ground hard. The landing gear folded under the impact and the belly of the bird slammed into the ground. The sound made by the rotor blades as they tore into trees was audible. With a wrenching sound of twisting metal the already weakened rotor head mechanism, designed to come apart on impact anyway, cut loose from the mainframe of the helicopter and went spinning into the woods.

Bright flickers of yellow flame appeared from the nose of the helicopter and Charlie Mott slumped forward loosely, suspended against his seat restraints. Bolan pushed himself up and looked over at Pandey and Grimaldi. The impact had knocked the Stony Man pilot unconscious, but Bolan could detect the rise and fall of his chest as Pandey struggled beside him to rise into a sitting position.

Bolan reached out and grabbed the pilot seat, noting the huge tears where machine-gun rounds had struck.

Using the seat as a brace, Bolan pulled himself forward. Blood was pooling in Mott's lap from two bullet wounds in his right shoulder. The smell of burning rubber and mechanical fluids was sickening in the confined space of the aircraft cockpit. Bolan knew the bird could take a hard landing from as high as sixty-five feet and that the fuel system was self-sealing, so he wasn't worried about the downed helicopter bursting into flames, at least in the next couple of minutes.

Bolan thrust two fingers under Mott's chin and against his neck. He felt a pulse but it was rapid, weak and fluttering, indicating a frantically beating heart struggling to make up for a reduced blood volume. Mott was bleeding to death.

Bolan cursed, realizing the numbers were counting down on him. Even now Bout had to be organizing his forces to cross the back lawn and penetrate the wooded hills behind the compound where the helicopter had gone down. Pandey was saying something behind him but Bolan ignored the man and snatched up the helicopter's radio control.

"Stony Base, this is Striker, over." Bolan forced himself to squelch the apprehension he felt and keep the tension out of his voice.

The radio responded instantly and Carmen Delahunt's voice broke the squelch. "Striker, this is Stony Base, go ahead." Delahunt was one of the Stony Man cybernetics experts.

"We are down. Repeat, bird down. Pilot needs

medical. We have a squad of hostiles en route to our twenty, over."

There was a moment of silence. Bolan waited for what seemed entirely too long before another voice came over the radio. The voice broke an unbidden smile of recognition from Bolan. It was Stony Man mission controller Barbara Price.

"Striker, this is Stony Base actual, over," she said.

"Go ahead, Actual," Bolan replied.

"We are running up possibilities for secondary extraction."

"I understand. I'll be in contact at earliest connivance, per protocol," Bolan said.

The operational support contingent for Bolan had, by necessity, been limited. Charlie Mott. Regular intelligence and military units had been studiously avoided though there were several in the region. Now Stony Man would have to break op-sec and reach out to the special operations community. As a last-ditch fail-safe, two F-22 Raptors staged out of Incirlik air base in Turkey had been scrambled for overflight during the extraction and would provide unit closure if things got out of hand.

"Copy, Striker, good luck." Price paused. "We'll get you backup. Just stay alive."

Bolan believed her. "Can do. Striker out," he said, and let the mike drop.

His eyes trailed over the cockpit instrument panel. He made sure the bird's GPS locator was functioning. When the Raptors flew over the area their missile guidance systems would lock on to the signal and vaporize any evidence of U.S. equipment on Croatian soil. If Bolan didn't get Mott and Pandey out of there in the next several minutes, they would all be bloody particles.

Assuming Bout's hit squad didn't finish them first.

Bolan yanked a medkit off the back of the seat. He opened it and quickly riffled through the contents of the green canvas bag. He found what he was looking for and pulled it free. Putting the packet to his lips, he bit down and tore it open.

Bolan turned and began dumping coagulation powder on the unconscious Mott's wounds, halting the bleeding almost instantly. Even in the dim, uncertain light inside the crashed helicopter's cockpit, the pilot looked deathly pale. He murmured something Bolan didn't catch and then fell silent.

"Jack," Bolan shouted, "how are you doing?"

"I'm fine. I've got Pandey covered but we need to boogie. How's Charlie?" Grimaldi replied.

Bolan just shook his head.

"You've got to help me!" Pandey shouted from the back. "They've breached the fence! Katrina's hurt."

"She's not hurt, you idiot," Grimaldi replied, firing his weapon. "She's dead."

"Slow them down, Jack," Bolan called out. "Once I finish giving Charlie first aid, we'll take them out of the chopper. If Pandey blinks wrong, kill him."

"No! Damn it! Katrina is the one who's important, do you understand? That pilot knew the risks, now leave him and help me!"

Bolan twisted and whipped out his Beretta. He snatched the startled, frantic Pandey by his collar and shoved the muzzle of his weapon into the man's face hard enough to split his lip. Pandey squawked in protest. His eyes were big as he stared down at the muzzle of the pistol.

Bolan yanked the man closer, and Pandey looked up into the cold blue flint of the Executioner's eyes. Pandey saw death there, and hell. His bowels froze into an icy rictus and he froze in Bolan's grip.

"You want to save your life?" Bolan whispered. "You do exactly as I say. If you question me again, I'll kill you where you stand. Do you understand?"

Slowly, Pandey began to nod. The motion caused his teeth to click against the hard metal of the pistol muzzle and he winced in pain.

"Say it!" Bolan snarled. "Do you understand?"

"Yes, yes, I understand," Pandey babbled.

"Good, now get flat until I'm done! Down!"

Bolan shoved Pandey in the direction of the floor and turned back toward Mott. The pilot was still unconscious and needed considerably more first aid than Bolan could provide for him in the field, but his bleeding had stopped for the moment.

Bullets began to snap into the helicopter's airframe as Grimaldi continued to lay down suppressive fire. Things had gone to hell in a handbasket.

Bolan reached down and closed his hand around the handle of the 440 stainless-steel, full-tang Gerber boot knife and pulled it free of its sheath. After putting his pistol away, Bolan lifted the straps of the seat restraints up and cut Mott free of his flight harness.

Automatic weapons fire began to strike the downed aircraft's frame with greater frequency. Despite being shot down Bolan still felt fairly confident in the helicopter's armor protection from small arms. If not for the inbound Raptors, he might have tried to fight the attackers off from the downed helicopter since Bout was a rogue agent in Croatia. Instead, he had only minutes to get away from the helicopter wreck before it was sanitized by missile fire.

As rounds from machine guns and assault rifles began striking the helicopter, Grimaldi opened up in retaliation with his primary weapon.

Ignoring Pandey and the incoming rounds, Bolan kept working steadily. He pulled Mott from his seat and laid him out on his back on the floor of the helicopter. He scooted farther into the troop transport area and began working even more quickly.

He pulled out a second packet of coagulation powder and cut it open, using the tip of Grimaldi's boot knife. He sprinkled a liberal amount on Mott's bullet wounds and then quickly wrapped a 4x4 pressure dressing around both. He tied it off and looked at the fighting Grimaldi. The situation was ugly. Having Pandey had screwed up everything because the man couldn't be trusted and he was too dangerous to leave behind for Bout to exploit.

"You want morphine, Jack?" Bolan yelled.

Grimaldi shook his head as he pushed himself up

into a sitting position and looked down at his leaking leg. "I can't afford to have my alertness compromised."

"Fair enough. Let's slide out and head for the woods before Bout gets us surrounded. We have to move. There's a sanitation strike coming any minute."

"Let's do it." Grimaldi nodded and rolled over onto his hands and one knee, trailing the hurt leg straight out behind him and still firing harassing bursts.

Rounds sliced the air above their heads as they maneuvered inside of the downed helicopter. Grimaldi slipped out the side cargo door, Bolan right after him. Once his feet hit the ground Bolan turned and grabbed Mott to him.

"Let's go!" he shouted toward Pandey.

The Indian scientist lay flat on the floor of the helicopter and only the fact that his fear of Bolan was greater than that of his fear of the machine-gun fire got him to move. Pandey looked over his shoulder and saw Bolan hoist Mott over his shoulder. He saw Grimaldi level a smoking muzzle on him.

Pandey immediately spun away from the machine-gun fire and slid across the floor of the cargo bay and out of the open door. He raced away from the downed helicopter. Bolan was just ahead of him, muscling through the underbrush with Mott on his shoulder.

Bolan saw Pandey race past him, reach the temporary shelter of a fallen log and slide behind it a little over a football field away. The Indian scientist turned and looked back, obviously checking to see if he was still being covered by Grimaldi. The pilot pulled even with the shuffling Bolan, his weapon still trained on Pandey.

"We got to hurry!" he shouted. "When the sanitation strike hits, it's going to be big."

Bolan nodded and charged forward through the underbrush. He struggled along, working hard until he reached the log. He used his free hand to keep his balance as he slid over the top of the downed tree with Mott still on his shoulder.

Behind them Bout urged his men forward in the face of the silenced return fire and the Russian gunners responded. A hand grenade exploded by the nose of the helicopter, and a three-man fire team charged the cargo bay from the tail of the helicopter. Their weapons raked the aircraft with fire as they assaulted the Little Bird.

Bolan spun and pulled his pistol. He rested his arm on the trunk of the fallen tree to steady his aim. Pandey leaped across the top of the log behind and landed heavily on the other side, cowering. Bolan saw the first of the Russian mercenaries clear the door of the downed helicopter. Bout, still packing the RPK one-handed, shouted something out in an angry voice and more khaki-garbed men emerged from the wood line.

Bolan calculated the distance to the downed helicopter from their position among the rocks behind the fallen tree. He realized that even an optimistic calculation put the ragtag band of wounded operatives much too close to the wreckage.

Bolan got to his feet and grabbed Mott by the back of his flight suit collar.

"Come one, we're too close!" he shouted at Pandey. "Help me, we've got to get away!"

Pandey didn't question Bolan's orders. He turned and draped Mott's arm around his neck. Bolan began to move rapidly over the broken ground, guiding Mott down a short incline and into a brush-choked ravine. Grimaldi laid down covering fire, stopped to change magazines then continued covering them. Bolan was panting as he struggled to put a fold in the topography between themselves and what he knew was coming.

He never heard the Raptors but seconds later, the bomb struck.

THE CONCUSSIVE FORCE of the GBU-32 JDAM 450 kilogram bombs was devastating. It shook the earth like the wrath of God. A gigantic flash of flame materialized, turning night into day and the ground under Bolan's feet shook hard enough to knock him down. Dirt and rocks rained down around them. As he fell, Bolan tried to throw himself over the helpless Mott and protect him from falling debris.

For a flashing second all the oxygen in the area was sucked up by the explosion and Bolan gasped to breathe. Spots appeared in front of his eyes and then in an instant it was over. Waves of heat rolled past him, leaving him cold in the sudden aftermath of their passing. Bolan huddled over Mott, with the pilot's head in his arms.

When the detritus stopped falling Bolan risked a look. He lifted his head in time to see the fireball from the explosion roll up into the sky and then dissipate. A column of black smoke, deeper than the night, roiled up from the burning oil slick that was all that remained of the downed extraction helicopter.

Bolan pushed himself to his feet and looked at the flame center. There was a huge crater where the wreckage had been. He knew the Croat government in Split would strongly suspect that this had to be American work, but it was unlikely they would ever be able to prove it, should they choose to bring the complaint before the UN Security Council. Deniability was the key to any black op gone wrong. It had served as a funeral pyre for the mystery woman Katrina.

Bolan heard Pandey groan and he looked over in time to see the Indian scientist pick himself up onto his hands and knees from where he had been thrown by the force of the massive explosion. Grimaldi lifted his head, still clutching his weapon. He looked shaken, pale with pain from his wounds, but still together, still under control. The pilot forced Pandey to his feet as the man turned to survey the damage.

"Shiva," Pandey muttered.

The way the man said it made Bolan think that it might, truly, have been a prayer. Bolan saw no one moving, heard no screams. He had every reason to believe the JDAM had vaporized not only the Russian mercs, but their paymaster, Bout, as well. He didn't intend to leave it to speculation, however, no matter how overwhelming the chances.

Bolan turned toward Grimaldi. "You okay?"

He nodded. "I'm fine. Let's just get Charlie safe."

"Good. We've got to get moving. That will bring

every army and special police unit in the region in a hurry. We have to be long gone by the time they get here."

"Agreed," Pandey said, attempting to insert himself into the conversation. "I will laugh when they arrest you."

Bolan ignored him. "The road is only about a hundred fifty yards down from here, obviously our SUV is back at the raid. Assuming someone didn't trip the Semtex surprise."

"It would be easier to take one of Bout's," Grimaldi suggested.

"Right." Bolan nodded. "I'm going to attempt to verify that Bout is dead, if possible. Pandey will come with me. See if you can get one of those Range Rovers down to where I can link up on the road. With Charlie so bad off, I don't see what else we can do but split up. It's not the best plan, Jack, but I don't see any alternative. Without a vehicle, Charlie's dead."

Grimaldi nodded. "I'll—"

"I'm not staying here alone with you!" Pandey shouted, interrupting. "You just had a bomb dropped on me!"

Bolan was on him before the man could blink, punching the scientist in the face.

The Indian scientist went sprawling, his arms flapping wildly. He was knocked straight over onto his back and Bolan heard the man's breath jerked from him on impact with the unforgiving ground. Pandey moaned, confused and disoriented from the blow.

Bolan moved forward and stood over the man. He put one big boot across the struggling man's throat. His face was granite-hard as he pressed down, abruptly cutting of the man's ability to breathe.

"You're a real slow learner, Pandey. Next time I won't be as gentle."

Pandey grasped Bolan's foot with both his hands and tried to wrestle it free. It was a futile attempt. Bolan pressed down with the full weight of his two-hundred-plus pounds.

The scientist gasped and spittle flew from his mouth as his face turned red.

Under Bolan's heel Pandey ceased struggling. The Executioner abruptly stepped off the man's throat and Pandey sucked in a huge breath of air, gasping, and his hands flew to his throat. He sputtered and coughed as he tried to rise to a sitting position.

Bolan looked over at the watching Grimaldi.

"Go ahead—I can handle them both. We've got to have a vehicle. I'll get them down to the road we inserted on and wait for you there."

Grimaldi nodded. He knew that even if, by strange chance any criminal gunmen had survived the final bomb strike on the downed helicopter his was still the less arduous task. His face was grim as he set off through the woods.

Bolan watched the man go, knowing he was their last best chance for survival at the moment.

CHAPTER TWENTY-ONE

"Get up," Bolan snapped, watching Pandey as the man struggled to his feet.

Bolan looked at the man, saw the fear in his eyes.

"What's your plan?" Pandey asked.

"I need to see if I can ID Bout's body. You check my friend, do what you can. After I radio back damage assessment we'll start down the hill toward the road. And, Pandey." Bolan paused.

"What?" The man's voice was sullen.

"There's nowhere for you to run. You can't get one hundred yards in this terrain before I'd catch you. Understand?"

Pandey nodded and looked away. "I understand."

"Good. I'm going to scout the bomb site."

"And then?"

"We head for the Croatian coast. I have contacts who will make sure we get out."

He moved away from the unhappy man without the

slightest remorse. Under normal circumstances he would have knocked a black market bioweapons profiteer to the ground and cuffed him, and that would have been the least of his reactions.

The last thing he wanted to do was to trust Pandey, but it was a small trust dictated by the situation and common sense. He just didn't have much of a choice. Bolan looked over at Mott as he walked toward the blast area. The pilot looked bad, his wounds were grave and he needed medical attention ASAP. On his own Bolan knew he could escape and evade to safety. Watching Pandey, his chances shrank drastically. Lugging a wounded comrade, those chances became almost nonexistent.

Bolan had every faith that Hal Brognola and Barbara Price would move heaven and earth to help him—they'd proved that often enough in the past. But he also doubted seriously that that help would arrive in time to save Charlie Mott.

He quickly surveyed the scene and found no trace of the men next to the helicopter when the JDAM had landed. He moved past the crater where the helicopter had been and closer to where Bout's estate met the wood line. Here he spotted three corpses still relatively intact. He picked up and shouldered an AKS-74U that appeared, somewhat miraculously, none too worse for the wear.

Bolan looked up. The fence at the back of the compound had been blown down. Grimaldi was crossing the lawn and went up the right side of the still smoking house toward the garage amid bonfires of burning debris. If Bout had left a security detail with the cars, then Grimaldi was in very real danger. But they had little other choice and the pilot knew that.

Bolan turned and looked around him. He spotted a Soviet RPK machine gun, broken like a matchstick. He walked over to the ruined weapon and looked around. Just down the hill from the weapon he saw the corpse of a big man. Bolan walked toward the body.

He took in the charred business suit stretched over a 250-pound frame. There were the melted remnants of a sling and bandages on the corpse. Bolan knelt and picked up the slack weight of the head by a bloody tangle of black hair.

The left side of the face was charred black. Where the man's beard had been was only raw, singed flesh. The right side of the face was a bloody fissure. Bolan dropped the head unceremoniously. He reached over and picked up a beefy fingered hand covered in coarse black hair. It was not Bout.

Bolan stood and attempted to make contact using his sat phone.

"Striker to Stony Base."

Hal Brognola's gruff voice answered. "Go ahead, Striker."

"AO sanitized."

"That's a good copy." Brognola paused. "Striker, we had a frag-op from your region."

"Go ahead."

"A mutual friend of ours has been in contact with Mountain Peak."

Bolan nodded. From preinsertion briefings he knew Brognola was speaking about the commandos of the 7th Special Operations Squadron deployed with the Air Force command to the UN mission in the region. The unit specialized in the recovery of personnel or sensitive equipment from hostile and rugged geography. It meant gunships and men to man the triggers were rolling.

"Go ahead, Stony Base."

"All right, Striker, listen up. We've got Echelon Encryption but I still don't want to take chances on this frequency. I say this once over the radio and you get it all the first time and hope we're not compromised. Okay?"

"Understood," Bolan acknowledged.

"You have a vehicle?"

"Yeah." I hope, he added.

"Get off that mountain. There is a stretch of highway to the east of your position. It's flat, about twenty klicks out, makes a LZ big enough for what we need. Can you make it?"

"Sure," Bolan said. Do I have a choice? Bolan wondered.

"There's a Chinook and a Little Bird and crews on loan from NATO mission. It's rotors up to your twenty now, over. I'll coordinate communications from my location. You want to get home, you get there, Striker." Brognola paused, as if he wanted to say more, but then checked himself. "You got that, Striker?"

"Roger."

"Stony Base out."

Bolan looked back toward Bout's estate. He heard no

gunfire or angry shouts. He turned and quickly traversed up the hill back to where Pandey was hiding with Mott in the ravine.

The Indian scientist was kneeling beside the wounded pilot, adjusting bandages around his wounds. He looked up sharply at Bolan's approach, his eyes wide then relaxing visibly when he recognized Bolan and finished tying off Mott's bandages.

"Bout?" he asked.

"Missing," Bolan answered. "How is he?" he asked, indicating Mott.

"Your friend's lost a lot of blood. I don't think a lung was nicked, but I'm afraid of internal septic infection. He's starting to feel feverish. We have to get the bullets out."

Bolan knelt beside him and looked down at the pilot. How many times had Charlie been there to pull his ass out of the fire? How many times had the man served as backup in some violent backwater during a Stony Man operation? Nothing compared to the sort of service Jack Grimaldi had offered to be sure, but significant. The man was owed every allegiance by Bolan. He had to do everything he could to save him.

"Your friend will die without immediate help. Have you thought about giving up?"

"Don't hold your breath, Doctor. There's been a change in the plan," Bolan replied.

IT WAS A ROUGH JOURNEY down the mountain and despite Bolan's best efforts Mott's wounds broke open again. The pilot was burning with fever now, and by the time Bolan lowered him to the ground next to the logging road, his breathing was horribly rapid and shallow.

Grimaldi had already arrived with one of Bout's Range Rovers. He had parked the vehicle off the secondary road leading up to Bout's isolated estate and then hidden himself in the brush overlooking the bend in the road. As soon as Bolan and Pandey appeared, Grimaldi rushed from hiding to check his fellow pilot. He had bandaged his wound but red had already seeped through to the outside.

Bolan shrugged out of his jacket and draped it over the wounded pilot. He used a rock to elevate Mott's feet. Grimaldi knelt beside Mott to arrange his bandages after the scramble down to the road. Bolan rose, walked over to the rear of the Range Rover and opened up the back. He looked inside, made his determination.

"Come on, Pandey. Help me get him into the back of this vehicle. Time is running out."

From down the valley the sound of sirens could be heard. Bolan looked at Grimaldi.

"From the sirens, I think those are fire response vehicles."

"There will be internal security forces, as well," Grimaldi replied.

"Right, we have to get on the road."

Pandey and Bolan put the unconscious Mott in the rear of the Range Rover on top of the folded seats. Bolan forced himself not to dwell on how close the pilot had to be to death. Mott's life was in his hands and now depended upon Bolan playing every move exactly right.

"You drive," Bolan told Grimaldi. "Get us down on the highway. Extraction is waiting."

"That's good to hear." He spared a glance back toward the unconscious Mott. "For a lot of reasons."

Bolan just nodded and traded his captured AKS for an M-4 carbine lying in the stolen SUV. There was nothing more to say.

THEY HAD BEEN on the road for less than a mile. Two vehicles fell in behind them and gunfire opened up. Grimaldi floored the gas pedal and Pandey began muttering in his own language. Tracer fire streamed by on either side as the hostile vehicles rushed in close.

Bolan knew that if he didn't find a way to knock the pursuers off course, they were doomed. Again.

He made his decision.

"Pop the hatch, Jack," he ordered.

Bolan crawled between the two front seats and into the back of the SUV, folding one of the seats down to sprawl out in the back. He forcibly shoved Pandey down and out of the way, all the while knowing there was nothing he could do to help better protect Mott. All he could do, the best thing he could do, was to kill the enemy.

"What are you doing!" Pandey shrieked.

"Shut up!" Bolan snapped. "Do what the hell I say and stay down!"

In the front of the vehicle Grimaldi swore, then

reached down and yanked on the plastic lever controlling the catch-release. The rear hatch popped open and swung up, revealing the racing road just beneath the bumper and the two vehicles following close behind.

Bolan was tossed to one side as the SUV dipped into a rut and bounced out on the other side. He bumped in to Mott and flinched in sympathy. He grunted under the impact but managed to maneuver his M-4 carbine into position. The hydraulic support struts caught, locking the hatch open.

A sudden brilliant star-pattern burst erupted from the darkness next to the windshield of the first chase vehicle. Bolan heard the unmistakable sound of 9 mm rounds being burned off. The SUV lurched hard to the side as Grimaldi wrestled it around a corner.

Bolan used his thumb to click the fire selector switch on his carbine to the 3-round-burst position. He spread his legs wide in the rear compartment to equalize his balance, overlapping Mott's leg as he did so, and dug in with his elbows to steady his weapon. The buttstock slapped into his cheek and opened a small cut as their SUV drove over a jutting rock, shuddering the vehicle on its frame.

Ignoring the stinging wound, Bolan crammed the stock back into the pocket of his shoulder. The headlights of the first vehicle appeared around the tree-choked corner of the road and Bolan caught a brief flash of a human figure hanging outside the passenger window of a battered white Stobart truck.

He squeezed his trigger.

The carbine rocked smoothly into the tight seal of his shoulder and three smoking brass cartridges arched out of the ejection port and tumbled across the back of the SUV before bouncing out onto the dirt road. Bolan felt the vehicle shift beneath him as Grimaldi took another corner, and he braced himself harder.

He lowered the muzzle of the M-4, aiming for the area between the front bumper and the bottom of the windshield. He squeezed his trigger again, felt the muzzle climb slightly with the burping recoil and saw the left headlight on the Stobart truck wink out as one of the 5.56 mm Teflon-coated rounds struck home.

The submachine gunner on the truck's passenger side returned fire with Bolan, burst for burst, but the effect of speed and road conditions on the two men's aim made the duel nearly futile for several exchanges.

Then Bolan found his rhythm.

He rode out another jarring pothole and adjusted his fire. Suddenly their Range Rover hit a patch of washboard gravel, actually smoothing out the ride because of the vehicle's dangerous level of speed. He felt the rocking lurches of the road give way to an almost pleasantly even vibration as the SUV rolled across the washboard, and he squeezed the trigger on his M-4.

He put two 3-round bursts into the front windshield of the Stobart truck, shattering it. The vehicle swerved hard to the right and the front tire rolled up an embankment. The driver was flung across the steering wheel in a bloody mess, and Bolan could discern the man's dead bodyweight locking the vehicle onto its course.

The truck rolled up onto its side as it half climbed the embankment then slammed into the gnarled and twisted trunk of a squat evergreen. The hood crumpled under the impact, then the kinetic energy of the forward-moving truck was redirected and the vehicle rolled over. For one incredulous moment the truck remained upright, balanced precariously on the outer edges of two tires. Then centrifugal force pushed everything into fast forward and the truck flipped. It struck the broken road hard, the cab smashing flat with a horrific crunch followed immediately with the brutal thunderclap of metal on metal as the second chase vehicle slammed into the first.

The overturned truck spun away from the contact like a child's top while the second vehicle lost control and careened off into the heavy underbrush beside the road. Bolan scrambled up, grabbed hold of the open rear hatch from the inside and yanked it closed.

"Jesus, you killed them all!" Pandey shouted as Bolan shoved himself back into the front seat.

"I doubt it," Bolan muttered. "And stop shouting."

"We good, Sarge?" Grimaldi asked.

"Don't know. Depends on if that was the last of Bout's men or if he's got more in the wings coming. All we can do is drive," Bolan said, buckling his seat belt. He placed the M-4 carbine muzzle down between his legs.

Bolan turned his attention toward the road. A thick wall of forest raised up black-shadowed walls on either side of the corridor formed by the logging road. Vines and branches and rotted logs had fallen across the single lane, forcing Grimaldi to swerve the vehicle around the obstacles while navigating potholes, rain-wash trenches and protruding rocks. The vehicle's suspension was taking a brutal beating.

"We still on course for the RZ?" he asked.

"Off road, back down to regional highway then the road into valley. Ten, maybe fifteen minutes."

"You think we'll avoid pursuit that way?"

"Possibly. I'm laying bets on it. Government has troops in the area to combat who might respond to reports of fighting. We've got to try something."

"Got that right."

They came around the corner fast. Headlights filled the windshield as another vehicle raced up the narrow road toward them. Bolan cursed as Grimaldi yanked the wheel hard to one side, swerving the SUV to avoid the onrushing vehicle. The abused Range Rover lurched to the left, and there was a horrendous screech as the metal of the two vehicles' sides skidded off each other. A shower of sparks formed a rooster tail in the driver's window, and Bolan had a quick impression of a battered Jeep filled with figures.

It seemed obvious that their luck had not held.

CHAPTER TWENTY-TWO

A second vehicle followed closely behind the first, and Bolan caught a glimpse of a third set of headlights beyond that one, as well. Then the front of their SUV bucked up hard into the air and came down, leaving the windshield filled with the leaves and branches of mountain foliage.

Grimaldi tried to turn the Range Rover out of the forest and onto the logging road, but suddenly the massive trunk of a forest tree appeared in front of the racing, out-of-control SUV. Bolan threw his arms up instinctively.

The bang of the impact was followed hard by the violent reversal of the vehicle occupants' momentum. As the hood crumpled and the fender was bent inward, Bolan was thrown hard against his seat belt. He felt something smack his face, then heard the pop of the air-bags deploying.

He was blinded by the emergency cushion and could see nothing of what was happening but felt the SUV begin to roll. His world suddenly inverted and he was thrown against his door. Then just as suddenly he slid up in his restraint to bang his head on the roof as the Range Rover completed its roll and landed on its blown-out tires. The airbags settled, quickly deflated, and Bolan sprang into action.

"Are you all right?" he asked Grimaldi.

"Yeah. Christ my leg is killing me—check on Charlie," the pilot answered, his voice tight with pain.

Bolan snapped the release on his seat belt and reached for his door handle. The inside lock popped up as he manipulated the device, but the door refused to budge. There was no sound from Pandey.

"Are you all right?" Bolan shouted at the Indian scientist.

"Yes, I'm fine."

Bolan threw his shoulder up against the inside of the passenger door, attempting to dislodge the damaged frame.

"Can you get out?" he asked.

"No, my door is jammed!" Frustration was thick in Grimaldi's voice.

Bolan leaned back and pivoted in his seat. He pulled both knees up to his chin and kicked outward. The soles of his boots struck the door just to the right of the handle. With a screech of protesting metal the stubborn door finally opened. Bolan snatched up his M-4 and scrambled out.

"Come on!" he snapped, securing the AKS-74U for good measure.

He looked over the caved-in hood of their SUV and saw a short convoy of three vehicles stopped in the middle of the logging road on the other side of the thick brush from his wreck. A long column of mashed foliage revealed the track the out-of-control SUV had taken.

Two European men dressed in upscale civilian clothes and packing AKM assault rifles appeared. Bolan moved toward the rear of his vehicle as one of the men raised his assault rifle to fire. The Executioner drew a snap-bead and put the man down.

Automatic weapons fire struck the ruined Range Rover, and Bolan saw Grimaldi crawl out of their wrecked SUV. The soldier pivoted his barrel across the collapsed roof and fired a second time, putting the other gunman down, as well.

Angry shouts rang out, and weapons up and down the length of the convoy erupted into action. A hailstorm of lead cut through the forest, ripping the flora apart, shredding bark and leaves and riddling the light skin of the expensive SUV.

Pinned down, Bolan struggled to act.

He realized that Pandey and obviously Mott were incapable of maneuvering under fire. He would have to draw the enemy's attention away from the wreckage and toward himself.

Bolan threw himself down next to Grimaldi in the cover of their crumpled SUV. The Stony Man pilot was burning through rounds, trying to drive the attackers back. Bullets blew out the remaining glass from the

overturned vehicle in a spray of shards and pinged as
they ricocheted off the wrecked SUV structure. Bullets
burned through the air all around them, whistled and
snapped as they cut into the undergrowth. Geysers of
dirt burst up, spilling rich black forest soil over the two
crouched combatants.

Bolan shoved his mouth down toward the Stony Man
pilot's ear. He had to shout to be heard in the din of battle. The situation was bad, and Bolan knew there was
no getting around that fact.

"I've got to draw their fire!" he yelled.

Twelve yards ahead of them an old forest giant had
been battered down in some gale from off the Adriatic
years before. Its trunk would form the closest true bul-
wark against the withering fire tearing up the topography around them and provide him with a fighting
position to try to turn the momentum of the conflict.

He shifted his weight off his body and immediately
started scrambling forward, his belly in tight with the
ground and his head down. Bolan began to scratch forward, dragging his M-4 by the shoulder sling so that the
muzzle was kept up out of the dirt by the back of his
hand.

Bolan reached the log and made to slither over it,
but another burst tore splinters of wood from the dead
tree directly beside his and he was forced back. Grit-
ting his teeth, Bolan charged forward, coming up to his
hands and knees and ramming his shoulder through a
screen of branches, sending him tumbling over the top
of the tree.

He dived forward and landed on a shoulder, then levered his rifle barrel over the edge of the tree trunk and tore loose with a long burst of answering fire. He pulled his weapon down then rolled across his back to take up a position at the end of the log where a tangled mass of old roots had been torn up from the earth. He used the broken cover to quickly survey the scene.

The militia gunmen from the convoy had advanced and fallen against the road bank, using it like a berm to gain cover as they fired, ineffectively dividing their attention between Grimaldi's and Bolan's positions. On the left side two of the braver Russian mobsters had begun to creep forward under the covering fire of their teammates, intent on carrying the battle to Bolan.

Bolan pivoted his carbine and began spraying the abandoned lead Jeep. Three times he poured tight bursts into the vehicle until he managed to ignite the gas tank. The already damaged vehicle exploded into flame with a powerful whoosh, and heat rolled off it like a sun going nova. Black smoke rolled off the bonfire of gas, rubber and oil. It caught in the low-hanging branches of the trees around the battle and began to choke that section of thick forest with dense smoke.

Bolan rolled back around and crawled across the ground next to the end of the tree. He pushed himself forward to speed his flight into the forest with an aim to cut off the flanking Russians. He turned to cover his retreat and caught a flash of Grimaldi holding back more attackers. A Russian gunman raced forward, weapon at the ready. The man's eyes were squinted hard against the choking smoke, and Bolan used the advantage to put a single 5.56 mm round through his throat.

The man tumbled forward and sprawled on the ground. A second gunman leaped over the body of his comrade, weapon chattering in his fists as he fired from the hip. Bolan triggered a 3-round burst that put the man down two steps from the corpse of his syndicate ally.

Behind him, across the road, Grimaldi lurched to his feet and stumbled around the cover of a thick forest tree, swatting low-hanging branches from his way as Bolan burned off the rest of his magazine in covering fire along his rear path. Grimaldi slid into the better position and turned his own weapon loose, crossing tracer fire arcs with the mobsters.

The Stony Man pilot hollered something in a furious voice, and Bolan turned in time to see Pandey running from their wrecked SUV.

Across the stretch of woods from the pilot the bolt on Bolan's M-4 locked open as he fired his last round and ejected the empty magazine as he turned and sprinted for cover. More fire answered his and bullets tore a deadly swath through the nighttime forest to every side of him.

Bolan slid around the cover of a tree and slammed a fresh magazine home. His finger tapped the carriage release on his carbine and the bolt slid forward, chambering a round. He was coated in sweat. He went to one knee and twisted back around the edge of the forest tree.

Figures moved in the smoke and foliage and triggered snap bursts in their direction without striking a target. He heard an all-too-familiar shrieking sound and instinctively ducked behind the tree.

A second later the 84 mm warhead of a RPG-7 struck off to his left and exploded with savage, devastating force. Bolan felt the concussion shock waves roll into him even through the sturdy protection of the massive tree trunk. Shrapnel burst out through the forest and Bolan heard Pandey scream from somewhere behind him.

Bolan rose and whirled, his ears still ringing from the explosion, and sprinted away from the battle. He stormed through the undergrowth, searching frantically. He saw the huddled man lying on the ground and went to one knee beside him.

"You stupid son of a bitch," Bolan snarled. "I told you not to run."

The Indian scientist made no sound.

He rolled him over and saw his shirt splattered with blood and a long gash open across his forehead, turning his face into a mask of blood. His breathing was rapid and shallow, and his eyes flickered beneath his lids. He moaned in pain as Bolan lifted him and threw him over his shoulder in a fireman's carry.

He rose, hefting the man's tall form easily, and began to run. Behind him gunshots rang out, but the bullets flew wider and wider as Bolan ducked around and through trees, heavy brush and bamboo stands.

He knew from the reconnaissance maps he had looked over prior to the run on Bout's compound that a system of canals met a river tributary running out of the mountains very near his location. He was unsure of how far Grimaldi had driven in their chaotic, nighttime hell ride, but he estimated the bridge for that river could be no more than a few miles down the road from their present position.

Breathing heavily against the strain and adrenaline bleed-off, he began to make his way back toward the road. Roots and vines tugged at his feet, threatening to trip him up at every step and twist his ankle. Branches slapped at his legs, and angry shouts chased him as he fled. He had no time to check Pandey's wounds and the tall, skinny man had ceased to groan so that Bolan now feared he had dropped into shock.

He knew pragmatism insisted he leave the man. If push came to shove and it came down to Pandey or Mott or Grimaldi, then he would do so. Ultimately it was Pandey's mercenary decisions that had led him to this place, but Bolan felt responsible for his predicament. He also knew there was no way in hell he would abandon a helpless comrade to the wolves of modern terror. If he were forced to choose, he'd dump the traitorous bio-weapons merchant. Bolan gritted his teeth against the strain and ran on.

He cut out of the brush minutes later and hit the road well below the location of the initial contact site with the battered white Stobart truck. He gritted his teeth and jogged out onto the road. It was simply too much work to break trail through the forest with the man on his back. For his admittedly dicey plan to work he would need to make it to the bridge over the tributary relatively quickly and as fresh as possible.

He began to move quickly down the road, leaving the angry shouts of his pursuers behind him along with their damaged vehicles. He crossed the road to the other side and began making his way back toward the stalled convoy that had transported the men now engaged in hunting him.

He could easily pick out the sounds of Grimaldi holding them off and knew he had to hurry. A clock was ticking. A death squad had been assembled by corrupt forces to silence the truth, and Bolan had been charged with that defense. He was in a race against time opposed by one band of killers in his quest to stop the proliferation of weapons of mass destruction.

He pushed through the forest on the far side of the road, moving quickly back the way he'd come until he caught sight of the vehicle convoy. He slowed his approach, choosing his steps more carefully. The reflection of the burning Jeep caused flame to light and shadow to flicker and dance across the vehicles.

Bolan paused and scanned the scene. The remaining convoy vehicles, two battered Stobart SUVs, had been left with their engines running to facilitate movement under fire. Two AKM-armed men in black and olive-drab clothes and headbands had been left behind to secure the vehicles.

Up toward the front a knot of fighters was trying to maneuver in closer to Grimaldi's position, but the Stony Man pilot was proving too tenacious for the men, at least for the moment.

Both men stood at either end of the convoy out in the middle of the road. The hectic action in front of them in the forest kept drawing their attention away from their posts. Bolan gauged the distance, frowning. When he moved, there would be no time for hesitation. Other members of the mobster's convoy were calling out from inside the forest, close at hand. Bolan was running a gambit based on seconds and heartbeats of time, not minutes.

He made his decision.

He looped the end of his rifle sling around the shoulder of his gun arm. Grabbing the M-4 carbine by its pistol grip, he was able to steady his muzzle one-handed by thrusting his weapon against the pull of the sling braced against his shoulder. At this range it would be enough.

Bolan gritted his teeth and shifted the limp form of Pandey across his other shoulder into a more comfortable position. He jogged forward out of the brush and onto the road about five yards from the tailgate of the last SUV in the line.

He took four steps forward before the sentry closer to him turned. Bolan flexed the muscles of his forearm and triggered his weapon. The M-4 bucked in his hand with the recoil of his 3-round burst. The 5.56 mm rounds caught the spinning militiaman high in the chest just to the left of the sternum.

The man staggered backward at each impact of the high-velocity rounds, and gouts of red-black blood splashed out from his shirt as he went down. Bolan adjusted his aim, bringing the M-4 to bear one-handed as the second sentry turned in alarm at the ambush. He saw the man snarl in fear and outrage as he lifted his Kalashnikov and a burning cigarette tumbled from his mouth as he fought to bring the AKM around in time.

Bolan slowed him with a 3-round burst to the gut that folded him over and drove him back before finishing him off with a second lead trilogy through the forehead and frontal lobe of his brain. The man spun outward, his arms flailing, and the AKM tumbled to the ground and bounced before the slack corpse of the gunman pinned it to the dirt. Almost immediately a questioning cry was raised by the trailing members of the hunter-killer team deployed near Bolan's crashed vehicle.

Bolan wasted no time. Letting the M-4 dangle from the sling, he jerked open the door on the Stobart SUV and ducked inside. He unceremoniously thrust the unconscious Pandey onto the front seat and up against the passenger door. A quick examination told Bolan that Pandey had a minor head wound and most likely had fainted from shock.

The glass in the window of the driver's door beside Bolan's head suddenly shattered as bullets slammed into it. He dropped and spun, swinging the M-4 up by its pistol grip like an Old West gunfighter. He narrowed his eyes against the glare of the burning forest and saw a figure at the top of the berm above the roadside.

He triggered a blast from the hip across the fifty yards and punched the man back into the underbrush. Wasting no time, he jumped behind the wheel of the

SUV and slammed the door shut. Leaving his carbine across his lap, he threw the vehicle into reverse and gunned it, twisting in the seat to look out the back window.

He heard Pandey moan on the seat beside him as he began to regain consciousness, but he couldn't risk looking down. Still driving in reverse, he navigated the primitive road as more bullets began to strike the vehicle frame and punch holes through the windows.

There was no time or space to perform a bootlegger maneuver on the narrow track and Bolan simply drove balls-to-the-wall in reverse. The windshield caught a round and spiderwebbed, but the intensity of fire coming from the forest had begun to slack off and he knew the Russian crew was making for its vehicles now, leaving him desperately wishing he'd had time to disable the other SUV before making his escape.

Suddenly a screaming gunman raced into the middle of the road and took up a position in Bolan's path. Kalashnikov rounds punched through the rear windshield and burned through the space around Bolan's head. He floored the gas pedal on the already erratically bouncing Stobart SUV and hurtled toward the threat.

CHAPTER TWENTY-THREE

Green tracer fire arced through the cab of the SUV and rounds thudded into the seat. Pandey screamed at Bolan's side as the plastic screen over the gas gauge and speedometer shattered. A 7.62 mm round struck the steering wheel, and for a wild second Bolan thought it was going to come apart in his very hands.

Then the speeding SUV struck the fanatic. There was an audible crunch as metal made contact with flesh and pulverized it. Blood splashed onto the back of the SUV. The body was knocked back and driven into the rutted, hard-packed ground of the road where it slid along before the rear wheels caught up to it and bounced across it.

Bolan felt the vehicle shudder as he rolled over the man, and he adjusted the wheel so that he was able to catch the downed fighter with the front tires, as well. Then he was past the corpse and around a bend in the logging road.

He continued to drive in reverse, frantically hunting for a place where the road widened sufficiently to turn the SUV around, but as dark forest sped by no opportunity presented itself. He was drawing closer to where Jack Grimaldi was holding off the other group, but unless he could discover a way to maneuver the vehicle into position, his gambit was fatally flawed anyway.

He had another problem, as well. In reverse he was unable to use his headlights and so was unable to circumnavigate some of the more egregious ruts and potholes. The SUV was taking a brutal beating, and both he and the wounded Pandey was being knocked around mercilessly. If he was putting out this much effort, he damn well wanted the rogue scientist handed over for interrogation—not dead on arrival.

The man was moaning softly, but when Bolan risked a glance to look at him he was surprised by how alert he seemed.

"How do you feel?" he demanded. "How badly are you hurt?"

"I feel bad, dizzy and my arm and back hurt badly. But I'm okay."

"Good, because we're in a damn tight spot."

Pandey struggled to sit up. He lifted his arm and pointed out the spiderwebbed front windshield back down the road from where they had fled.

"Here they come!" he cried.

Bolan whipped his head around and saw more headlights appear out of the darkness, bearing down on them at suicidal speeds.

He snarled something Pandey didn't catch and continued to drive. The rpm gauge raced toward the red, and the vehicle was shaking apart from the brutal beating it was taking on the rough road. Pandey fought his way into a sitting position and snapped his seat belt into place. Bolan pushed the gas pedal into the floor of the SUV.

It was then that the grenades began to rain down.

BOLAN WAS BLINDED by sudden flashes of light, then the deafening sound of explosions hammered into him. He heard glass shatter as shrapnel punched through it, and suddenly the steering wheel was wrenched from his grip. He felt the SUV float into the air and suddenly tilt. He rolled, weightless, for a long moment, then the vehicle crashed back to the ground and he was jarred hard against his seat harness.

He heard metal shriek in protest as the roof of the SUV crumpled and felt the frame slam into his head. He hung upside down from his seat belt and his M-4 flew up from his lap and smashed his nose. He felt the oily slickness of his salty blood running down the back of his throat as it spilled across his face.

He felt the inverted SUV sliding forward, hurtling across the broken road, and dirt flew through the shattered windshield to spray into him. He fumbled with the latch release on his seat belt and found it, dropping straight down onto the crumbled hood. He felt the vehicle pitch up abruptly, and he was thrown across the screaming Pandey.

The sliding vehicle slammed hard into something immovable and Bolan was catapulted forward again. He caught his hip on the steering wheel and shouted in surprise at the hurt. He buckled around the wheel, then dropped against his seat in a crumpled heap.

He was disoriented from the wreck and his head was spinning from the blasts and crash. He could feel the sticky mask of blood on his face and he gasped for breath. He felt around for his assault rifle and couldn't find it. He pulled the Glock clear of the sling beneath his arm and struggled to get oriented properly inside the caved-in roof of the SUV.

Machine-gun fire raked the bottom of the vehicle. Bullets burned through the frame and tore the covers off the seats, exploding stuffing in the air. Bolan was clipped above the elbow and felt a hammer blow on the heel of his boot. Pandey screamed again louder, more animal-like this time, and Bolan twisted to look as the man tried shoving himself forward through the blown-out windshield. Bolan made no move to stop him.

He waited until Pandey was clear, then followed. He rolled out onto the ground and smelled gasoline fumes so strong it made his already spinning head swim. He staggered forward from the wreck and saw the body of the vehicle wrapped around a forest tree like a bow on a birthday present. He saw forest all around him, but his hearing had been too abused for him to pick out any sounds. He turned to look back down the road, but his vision was blocked by the ruin of the SUV. He saw green tracer fire scorch the night like laser beams on all sides of him, snapping branches, shaking bushes and blowing bark off the trees.

He saw Pandey stumble, and he put a hand under his arm and shoved him forward. Bullets kicked up leaves and dirt like miniature volcanoes, so Bolan moved in closer to support the man as they scrambled for the dense forest and the cover it offered.

"Go!" he shouted.

He reached out a hand to give his support again and the SUV exploded behind him.

Bolan was picked up by the concussive force and hurtled like a rag doll through the air. He felt waves of heat rolling into him like boiling surf and his breath was smashed from his body. He somersaulted in a crude spin and struck the ground on his feet. He was pitched forward and his head hit the ground and bounced back crudely.

It was a miracle he was still conscious and as he shook the impact daze from his head he was startled to realize he still held his pistol. He blinked, almost amazed, then looked up as a Range Rover slid up and skidded to a stop. Two men popped out the front doors.

Bolan dropped them both with single shots.

He ran forward and jerked up the fallen Pandey from the ground. Time had slowed until the air around him felt thick as soup. He should be dead. He wasn't dead. He reached the Range Rover and forced Pandey into the front seat. He saw a muzzle-flash off to his left and he turned, firing purely on instinct. The muzzle-flash winked out and he slammed Pandey's door.

He made his way to the open driver door. He looked up the road and saw the hobbling Jack Grimaldi put a final burst into a mobster sprawled across the road.

He felt like he wanted to crawl into a bed and sleep for a thousand years. He climbed into the Range Rover and drove instead.

GRIMALDI RESTARTED the Range Rover as Pandey climbed into the back to help support Mott. The Indian scientist seemed to have grasped that Bout's men were killing indiscriminately, and he was as anxious as the rest of them to make his escape. After putting Mott in the back of the new vehicle, Bolan went around the rear of the Range Rover heading for the passenger side door. In the distance the sound of the sirens Grimaldi had identified as fire emergency vehicles grew more prominent as they raced up the hill toward the estate.

Bolan stopped, the Glock in his hands. He cocked his head into the wind, squinted in concentration. The sound came to him like a rumor on the wind, with the cacophony of approaching sirens it was hard to pick out a single sound.

He walked forward to a berm on the side of the road and saw that behind the line of bushes the terrain dropped away in a sudden valley.

"Let's go!" a nervous Pandey called from the back of the Range Rover.

Bolan frowned, ignoring the frightened man. He could almost pick it out now. Then the sound solidified enough for him to identify its origins and Bolan began moving fast.

He raced to the front of the Range Rover and looked out over the valley leading to the rise. The unmistakable thudding of helicopter blades was easily discerned now. Instantly, Bolan knew the sound didn't belong to the big Honeywell T55-714 turboshaft engines of a U.S. Air Force CH-47D Chinook rescue helicopter.

The approaching craft was much smaller, with lighter engines, but it was coming up the mountain draw hell-bent-for-leather. Bolan turned and sprinted back toward the waiting Range Rover, jerking open the passenger door. He slid into the seat and slammed the door shut behind him.

"Go!" he shouted.

Grimaldi didn't hesitate. He slammed his foot on the accelerator and the vehicle sprayed gravel as it tore out onto the mountain road. The front tires of the all-terrain vehicle hit the pavement and the traction bit hard, increasing the Range Rover's speed.

Even as Grimaldi maneuvered the Range Rover onto the mountain road, the helicopter flew up over the downhill side of the road and pinned the vehicle in its spotlight. Bolan looked out through the windshield, trying to determine the threat he faced.

The Falconi 5 Sikorsky light observation helicopter spun in front of the Range Rover as the vehicle careened down the winding mountain road. Bolan powered down his window as Grimaldi put the Range Rover square over the center line to give himself more maneuverability.

Bolan half crawled out the open window to bring his

weapon into play just as the road dropped sharply around a tight corner. Grimaldi made the wheels scream in protest as he took the corner too tight for the boxy vehicle's suspension. Bolan could actually feel the tires on his side of the vehicle come loose from the asphalt paving.

As that happened, the helicopter dropped sharply to keep the racing vehicle in a tight overwatch position. In that moment, as the chopper banked, Bolan got a clear picture of his pursuer.

Bout had returned.

The Sikorsky's doors had been removed prior to take off and the traitorous Russian oligarch leaned half out of his passenger seat with one foot propped on the landing skid. Bout had attached a RPK to a bungee cord from the top of the helicopter door and he manipulated it with one hand while bracing himself with the other. Behind him, as anonymous as a storm trooper in his flight suit and helmet, the pilot handled the little helicopter with cool skill.

"Get the floodlight!" Grimaldi shouted as he jerked the Range Rover around another corner. "It's blinding me!"

Bolan thrust the top half of his body out the passenger window and aimed quickly at the bobbing helicopter. His blast went wild, and Bout triggered a burst in response that knocked up sparks on the road but failed to connect.

The helicopter suddenly shot straight up for a moment and let the racing Range Rover pass underneath it. Bolan looked ahead and saw the flashing light bars of the approaching emergency response vehicles. He slid back into the vehicle's cab and snatched up Grimaldi's M-4.

In a moment of incongruous surrealism Grimaldi blew past two regional fire trucks and an ambulance doing twice their speed, his foot never straying from the accelerator toward the brake. His window was down and his hair flew like a tattered banner behind him. His knuckles were white on the steering wheel as he drove the vehicle expertly, but his face was a serene mask.

Fifty yards later they took a corner wide and almost crashed head-on with a Croatian police Jeep. Grimaldi whipped the car to the side at the last minute, rocking the occupants with the sudden motion. The police Jeep jerked toward the other side as well, and the two vehicles knocked their driver's side view mirrors off in a metal on metal clap.

Grimaldi snarled curses but refused to slow by even a small margin. Bolan turned to stare out the back of the Range Rover, trying to determine how the police car was going to respond to the near miss. He saw brake lights flash red and cursed himself in exasperation. On the road behind them the police vehicle spun and pointed its nose back down the mountain toward them before starting pursuit.

Bolan didn't hesitate. It was not a time for half measures. He could either escape to save Charlie Mott's life or he could choose not to engage the Croat Frontier Police agents. He could not do both. He grabbed hold of the handle on the cab roof and sat up on the edge of the door through the open window.

As he brought the weapon up, Bolan snapped open the M-4's folding stock and shouldered the weapon. Behind the police Jeep Bolan saw the civilian model Sikorsky helicopter swing wide over the steep valley and begin to bear down on them.

Bolan looked down the open battlefield sights and triggered a long, ragged burst toward the front of the chasing police vehicle. His rounds skipped off the pavement, striking sparks. Tracers poured like lava from the muzzle of his chattering weapon. Smoking shell casings bounced off the roof of the Range Rover and spun out into the night.

The first of Bolan's slugs tore into the front grille of the police cruiser and burrowed into the engine block. The vehicle's hood snapped open and popped straight up as the lock mechanism burst apart. The stream of rushing air grabbed the front hood and flipped it back into the car's windshield.

The driver locked the brakes of his vehicle and went into a sloppy power slide. More rounds struck the front of the vehicle and clawed the engine into scrap metal. Like a tornado, the Sikorsky zoomed in over the stalled police vehicle and charged down on the fleeing Range Rover. The single Cyclops eye of the forward-mounted spotlight blazed out, blinding Bolan.

He saw a flash of yellow fire above and to the right of the spotlight and tracer rounds began spitting out toward Bolan. Grimaldi locked the brakes hard and took yet another corner in the endless succession of turns, momentarily blocking the helicopter from sight.

Bolan anticipated the helicopter's flight path and shifted in his seat so that his weapon was pointed straight across the roof of the Range Rover. Inside the vehicle Grimaldi's hand reached out and snatched Bolan by the belt to help keep him from tumbling out. Bolan realized Grimaldi was driving with every ounce of skill he used to fly.

Forced to take the turn in the road wide, just as Bolan had predicted, the Sikorsky swung around into view again. Bout and Bolan triggered simultaneous blasts. The Executioner, with a sniper's skill, blew out the floodlight on the helicopter undercarriage. Bout's blast raked the side of the vehicle from front to back just above the wheel wells.

The civilian vehicle was jostled by the impact from the high-caliber slugs but Grimaldi kept the Range Rover steady. Bolan realized the freelance operative had to have his vehicle outfitted with at least some armor upgrade in order for the rounds not to have penetrated into the passenger areas of the vehicle.

Despite that, Bolan knew the Range Rover could not long take such damage unanswered. Sooner, rather than later, the SUV would falter under the assault. Bolan lifted the M-4 and sighted in on Bout. He fired, but the weapon didn't have the range. The bullets traveled in an arch from his weapon but fell underneath the circling helicopter. He twisted again and fired another burst, throwing his rounds wide as Grimaldi powered through yet another corner. The landscape they raced past was a blur to Bolan, and his face and arms were numb from the cold air buffeting him.

The Sikorsky rushed forward and Bolan fired, lifting his weapon in a smooth, continuous angle as the helicopter passed over him. Bout had the RPK wide open, making no attempt to control his bursts. Rounds fell around the swerving Range Rover in a deadly hail of lead. Two stray rounds struck the hood of the vehicle and punched through. One skipped off the radiator and white plumes of steam began spilling out.

Bolan traced a line of slugs off the Sikorsky's passenger side skid and across the belly of the aircraft. The chopper's undercarriage was perforated by half a dozen bullets but the Sikorsky seemed to easily soak up the damage as it again leapfrogged out over the Range Rover. Bolan twisted, following the helicopter with his weapon blazing.

CHAPTER TWENTY-FOUR

Bolan's M-4 went empty and he punched the magazine release button as he slid back down into the Range Rover. Once inside Bolan realized that a 7.62 mm round had punched through the windshield on his side and buried itself in the dash. A long crack ran out from the bullet hole and reached over to splinter the windshield in front of Grimaldi.

"We're almost off the mountain," Grimaldi gritted out.

Now that Bolan was back inside, Grimaldi steered with both hands on the wheel. Again and again Bolan felt the detached, floating sensation as the tires of the Range Rover lost grip on the pavement as he cornered too sharply. Somehow Grimaldi always managed to keep the vehicle from flipping.

"Give me another weapon!" Bolan shouted back at the huddled Pandey.

"From where!" the man screamed back, obviously terrified.

"Look," Bolan snarled. "We threw enough in here. Hurry, damn it!"

Laying half sprawled over the still comatose Charlie Mott, Pandey scrambled around on the floor before coming up with an extra MP-5 Grimaldi had thrown in when taking the wheel. Bolan snatched the weapon up and prepped it for firing.

Bolan looked at the submachine in disgust. It was a pitiful defense against even such a light helicopter and it was no match whatsoever for Bout's RPK machine gun. The capability of Bout to stand off beyond the bullets' range and return fire with his heavier caliber was obvious. Bolan wished he'd had more time to loot the corpses of the Russian oligarch's men for their Kalashnikovs. The only modicum of hope Bolan held out was that Bout would need to draw closer to compensate for Grimaldi's insanely erratic driving.

"You think that's going to do any good?" Grimaldi asked, his voice grim.

"I'm thinking I might just chuck rocks at them when they get closer."

"Well, you're going to get your chance," Pandey said, thrusting his head up between the seat like a precious child pushing himself in between his parents. "Here they come!"

"Christ!" Bolan snarled.

The Range Rover was out of the twisting decline of the mountain road and on the valley straitaway now. Grimaldi had the speedometer up over 150 km per hour and wind buffeted the vehicle savagely. From in front of them the Sikorsky spun hard like a child's top, put its nose down and came flying straight toward them.

"What does he want!" Pandey screamed in frustration. "He knows he's done!"

"He wants to make sure no good deed goes unpunished," Grimaldi replied.

Bolan didn't answer. He thrust the MP-5 out the passenger window and opened fire. The Sikorsky swung toward them like a metallic bird of prey. Grimaldi swerved the Range Rover like a drunk as he handled the racing vehicle, but he was trapped within the confines of the road. Nothing but dark, Croatian forests, thick with trees, waited on either side of the road as they raced onto the valley floor.

Bout was remorseless. He hung half out of the helicopter pod, his foot on the skid, and fired the RPK in a long burst. He pivoted the bucking weapon back and forth with one hand on the end of the bungee cord, just like the scout observers had done in the early days of the Vietnam War. His mission was attrition and he was a hunter-killer team unto himself.

Bolan aimed his weapon straight toward the bubbled front of the speeding helicopter. He triggered the submachine gun and fought to keep the jumping, twisting chattergun on target. Bullets from the Soviet RPK ate up fist-size chunks of the road.

Grimaldi jerked the Range Rover from one side and then snapped it back to the other. He was snarling in an unending stream of curses as he drove, and his leg wound had begun to seep more blood. In the back, Pandey just screamed.

More bullets ripped through the engine hood of the Range Rover. They clawed their way up and blew out the windshield. Propelled by the wind shear of Grimaldi's nearly 100 mph speed, glass blew into the cab, forcing Bolan to throw up his arm as a shield.

The Sikorsky roared by overhead. Bolan twisted as it passed, still stubbornly returning fire with the MP-5. Machine-gun bullets punched through the Range Rover's unarmored roof, whining loudly in their ears and striking hard inside the cab of the vehicle.

Grimaldi cried out as another 7.62 mm round hit his leg. The new wound was barely an inch below the prior one, and blood spouted hot and sticky across Bolan. The emergency brake set between the passenger and driver's seat exploded, sending fragments of the hand break into Bolan's thigh and side.

Hanging outside the window, Bolan kept the MP-5 roaring. He poured 9 mm rounds into the low-flying helicopter as it passed directly overhead. He saw sparks fly as bullets struck metal, and he nodded with grim satisfaction when glass shattered under the impact of the soft-nosed slugs even as he grunted in pain at the sudden force of bullet and plastic handle fragments striking his leg. He emptied his magazine as the Sikorsky swung out and around.

Bolan slid back into the Range Rover, realizing the a burst of Bout's fire had penetrated the passenger areas of the vehicle behind him, as well. He saw Grimaldi with blood pouring from a fresh wound in his upper leg.

He looked farther back and felt his throat constrict in savage frustration.

The back of the Range Rover was splashed with blood. The unconscious Mott had been struck in the right thigh and arm. His clothes were soaked with blood. Bolan twisted farther to feel for a pulse in the pilot's neck and saw Pandey.

The Indian scientist had taken multiple rounds through the torso. Bout's machine-gun blast had torn him apart, shredding the muscles and bones of his upper rib cage. The man's eyes stared back at Bolan, wide and sightless. His mouth hung slack in death, and his chest looked like ground hamburger. A small sigh escaped his open mouth as his lungs collapsed and he pitched forward.

Seething, Bolan moved into the rear and shoved the dead man aside. He thrust his fingers onto the side of Mott's neck. He sagged with relief as his fingertips found a pulse, weak and fluttering, but still present.

"Come on, Charlie, hang in there," Bolan muttered.

Blood leaked from the new wound in the pilot's arm, and Bolan pulled the shredded collar of his flight suit to one side to get a better look. Bolan's adrenaline was pumping so hard he almost laughed out loud in relief when he saw the horrid funnel of ruined flesh gouged out of Mott's upper arm. The bullet had grazed his friend but not lodged.

Bolan stuck his finger into the bleeding hole to stem the tide.

"They're coming back!" Grimaldi warned.

"Drive!" Bolan shouted. "Just drive!"

He ducked and looked out the window. He saw the

Sikorsky pacing them, saw the helicopter swing into a parallel course with the speeding Range Rover, flying fast at treetop level. He could see Bout raising the RPK, knew there was nothing he could do to keep the man from raking the car with bullets.

Bout fired and Grimaldi slammed on the brakes. Unprepared for the maneuver, Bolan was thrown forward, his arms flying. He struck the top of the cab and bounced down to hit the dash hard. The wind was knocked from him and he turned, sliding down into his seat.

Out to the side the Sikorsky shot past their position and Bout's deadly blast missed them by a wide mark. The helicopter swooped forward, traveling at just under 150 miles per hour, and began to sweep back toward their position.

Grimaldi threw open his door and turned toward Bolan. The Executioner thought he looked half crazed in the light from the dome, blood splashed across his stark, cold features. He smiled at the surreal feel of it all; they'd been in situations like this before.

"We've got to get into the trees!"

"Go!" Bolan ordered him, knowing there was no way the man would leave but also knowing there was no need for everyone to die.

Without looking back, Grimaldi jumped from the driver's seat. His wounded leg crumpled as his feet hit the ground and he fell, clutching the open door to stay erect. Bolan opened his door and jumped out of the vehicle. He winced as pain lanced up from the fresh wound in his thigh, but he did not falter.

Limping badly, Grimaldi made his way toward the dark line of trees beside the highway. Out beyond the limits of the Range Rover's headlights Bolan heard the change in pitch as the Sikorsky came around and began its approach. Dimly, from somewhere far back in his awareness, the wounded Bolan heard the RPK open up again.

Bolan slammed open the rear passenger door. He reached in and grabbed Pandey by the shirt. He closed his hand into a fist around the twist of cloth and jerked the body back and out through the open door, dumping it on the ground. Mott's M-9 automatic pistol tumbled out of Pandey's cold, limp hand and clattered onto the ground. The scientist had been desperate enough to steal it when unobserved but had never found the courage to use it, either to murder Bolan and Grimaldi or to help defend them. Bolan had no respect for the dead man and was only sorry he hadn't lived to provide them with intelligence.

The roar of the rushing helicopter was deafening as it bore down on Bolan. The sound of bullets eating into the asphalt rang in his ears. The big American grabbed the unconscious Mott and heaved with all his might. The pilot slid into Bolan's arms and he tried to pull him farther out, to get a better grip and drag him toward the safety of the roadside. Something happened and Mott's body wouldn't budge, caught somehow half in and half out of the vehicle.

Bolan could hear Grimaldi screaming something at him, then his voice was drowned out in engine roar and rotor wash. Bolan turned toward the helicopter, forced to let the severely wounded Mott dangle out of the vehicle's open door. He bent and scooped up Mott's fallen M-9 pistol. As he rose, Bolan cleared his own Glock 17 handgun, as well.

Bolan thrust both pistols in front of him and stepped up to the open car door and in front of the helpless Mott as Bout bore down on them. Bullets tore through the stalled Range Rover and struck the road all around Bolan. He snarled like a cornered wolf and began blasting away with both pistols.

The heavy 7.62 mm ComBloc rounds whipped through the air around him. They shattered windows in the Range Rover and gouged up chunks of road pavement. They smacked into the body of Pandey and drilled through the roof of the Range Rover. The armor Bout had reinforced the doors of his vehicles with soaked up rounds, slowing them or causing them to deflect from the dangling Charlie Mott and offering a modicum of protection for Bolan as he fired his pistols. Blasting away Bolan didn't have time to appreciate the irony.

Rounds shattered the reinforced window of the open rear passenger door, spraying Bolan with glass shards. He kept pulling the triggers on his pistols. Machine gun rounds plucked at his clothes, creased his ear on one side of his head and parted his hair on the other. He kept pulling the triggers on his pistols. Bolan sent round after round at the charging helicopter, trying to shake the steady hand of the pilot, determined to go down fighting.

The M-9's smaller magazine ran dry and Bolan dropped it, taking his Glock 17 in both hands. Shell casings from Bout's RPK rained down around Bolan like steel hail for one intense, brief moment and Bolan lifted his 9 mm straight up over his head and pulled the trigger until the bolt slammed open, locking.

Then the Sikorsky helicopter was past. Bolan dropped the empty pistol and turned back toward Mott. Flames flared up from the hood of the Range Rover's engine compartment. Leaking oil and engine fluids dribbled onto the ground, spreading flame underneath the vehicle.

Bolan looked to see where Mott was tangled up and saw he was snagged on the seat belt bracket. Bolan pulled his Gerber fighting knife free as the flames from the engine fire roared up. Shadows from the flames wavered and danced in the night air and across his face. Bolan quickly cut Mott's clothes clear and pulled the wounded man out of the devastated vehicle.

Grimaldi suddenly appeared out of the night at Bolan's side, helping him take Mott's weight despite his own wounds. Steam rose into the cold night air around them from the growing pool of Pandey's steadily spilling blood and their own breath.

"That was the stupidest thing I've ever seen," Grimaldi said with a grin.

"Stick around," Bolan replied. "Night's young. You'll get your turn."

Bolan heard the Sikorsky coming back for them. He threw a look over his shoulder and gauged the distance to the dubious safety of the tree line. He looked toward the helicopter and knew they would never make it. Bout could see them, unarmed and helpless, and Bolan knew the son of a bitch was loving it.

"Just run," Bolan told his old friend. "There's no point in you dying, just run." He knew the sentiment was wasted on the veteran pilot.

"What? Miss all the fun? Shut up and pull, Sarge."

Bolan heaved at Mott's limp body with all his strength, rushing toward the edge of the road as the Sikorsky came down on them for a final run. Bolan backpedaled until his heels crunched on the gravel of the roadside and he knew he'd crossed the road. Then the helicopter was on them.

The soldier twisted and heaved Mott into the ditch at the road's edge with Grimaldi's help. The helicopter was directly overhead and the rotor wash was beating into them like hurricane winds as bullets cut through the air. Grimaldi looked up at the hovering machine, and Bolan shoved him down on Mott before collapsing on top of them both in the ditch, shielding them with his body. Above him, Bout triggered the RPK in another long burst.

Bullets poured down around them and Bolan squinted as flying dirt and asphalt chips stung his face. He heard the whip and crack of rounds zipping past him and the soft heavy thud as they struck the forest floor around him. Suddenly the gunfire stopped. Bolan heard the roar of massive Honeywell engines drown out the smaller Sikorsky. He heard the powerful burp of miniguns going off and felt rotor wash beating down on him in typhoon winds twice as strong as those of the Russian light helicopter.

Looking up, he saw the gigantic hulk of a U.S. Air Force CH-47F hovering over the area, its rear cargo ramp lowering. Bolan craned his neck but couldn't see Bout's Sikorsky. The big cargo helicopter touched down and men in OD green flight suits ran out holding M-4 carbines, commandos of the 7th Special Operations Squadron. Behind them came two more men bearing a stretcher and medic bags.

Bolan rolled over and let Grimaldi up. With the unconscious but still breathing Charlie Mott lying between them, they looked at each other. Grimaldi reached out a hand toward a puddle of shiny black fluid on the road, he stuck his finger in and held it up.

"You shot something loose, fuel line, maybe the pump," the pilot said.

Bolan squinted his eyes. "He'll have to set back down."

Grimaldi nodded. "And where else has he got but the estate? A place where he has vehicles still readily available. It can't be far...not with the bird about to go down."

"He'll set down and head for the coast."

Grimaldi was nodding with renewed energy as they stood. Around them the combat medics of the pararescue team were loading Mott onto a stretcher and starting IVs. "Barb and Bear are locked into everything Bout uses to communicate. I saw it myself when I was running the relay equipment back in Split."

"We'll never get mobile in time. We'll have to have a bird," Bolan argued. "Only way it'll work."

Grimaldi's rugged face split into a grin. He pointed at one of the 7th Special Operations Squadron commandos. "We'll just use one of theirs."

Bolan grinned back. "Let's call Hal."

CHAPTER TWENTY-FIVE

They were flying fast.

Grimaldi flew the helicopter low, following the highway as it hugged the river. He ran with blacked-out lights, using night-vision goggles to operate the controls as they shadowed the racing ZIL limousine below them. The clock was counting down, and if Bout got away this time, it would be over. The weaponized cloning technology would be unleashed on the world markets and one firestorm would become a dozen, or a hundred.

Their injuries—mostly flesh wounds—had been cleaned and dressed in the back of the big transport helicopter while medics had worked feverishly over Charlie Mott. Bolan had used the time and his enhanced cell phone to explain the situation to Barbara Price, who had promptly pulled her Hal Brognola card.

While the Stony Man cyberteam had used the boosted gear positioned in Grimaldi and Mott's electronic forward operating base to vector in on Bout, a directive from the Oval Office was making its way with the accuracy and speed of a laser into the ear of the Air Force unit commander and by the time the Chinook has set down there was a Little Bird helicopter ready and waiting for the two men.

While Price fed them information Bolan and Grimaldi had wasted no time in outfitting themselves from the armory of the 7th Special Operations Squadron and getting into the night air above Croatia.

Below them the river took a sharp turn and suddenly the road met a steel girder bridge. Without signaling, the ZIL cut off the highway in front of the structure and onto a dirt access road that ran underneath the iron span. Grimaldi flared the helicopter out over the dark expanse of the old growth forest, and next to him Bolan lifted his detached Starlite sniper scope and began searching the area.

Bout was running for the border and seemed to have led them into a place where the Executioner could easily and finally end the wild chase, but stopping now to admire the beauty of a moonlit river made no sense. Apprehension began to grow in Bolan's stomach. Something was wrong.

"We have movement on the river," Grimaldi said suddenly. Brilliant shafts of light suddenly cut through Bolan's scope, causing it to flare out in a whitish glare before the dampeners could mute the effect. "They're running full lights and moving fast against the current," Grimaldi continued. "I've never seen a watercraft like that—"

Bolan turned away from his sniper scope and back toward the front of the helicopter. From a curve in the river he saw a blazing island of light skimming across the surface of the water. Despite himself Bolan was surprised by what he saw and the severity of the implications.

The former GRU colonel had arrived to rendezvous with a SK5 Air Cushion vehicle. It ran to fifteen tons in weight and required a crew of four to operate, using a helicopter engine to drive a propeller that sat behind the gun platform perched atop an inflatable air bladder. The vehicle skipped across the surface of the river like a flat stone under the protection of two .50-caliber gun emplacements and a central-mounted 40 mm grenade launcher.

"We're out gunned," Bolan said. His voice sounded flat to his own ears.

"I've got the rocket pod," Grimaldi countered. "It won't take every one of them if the damn boat's been outfitted with reactive armor—but it should slow them down."

Bolan nodded, then said, "Let's stick to the plan."

THE SK5 SKIRTED UP the remnants of an ancient bridge and powered down, pushing water in a huge wave ahead of it. The military hovercraft bobbed for a moment in the wake, then men in black knit caps and dark, heavy clothing began scrambling across the front of the powerful watercraft, securing mooring lines while the muzzles of the vessel's organic weaponry oriented toward forest beyond the road as the limo pulled to a stop on the dirt road.

As Victor Bout stepped from the car Bolan noticed a small radar dish rotating in sluggish repetition on top of the wheelhouse's superstructure. The dish suddenly slowed, then stopped and began to bounce back and forth like a bobble-head doll on a dashboard.

Instantly a pinging sound began to emit from one of Grimaldi's sensors. "Crap!" the pilot snarled. "We're being painted. They know we're here."

Bolan fitted his night scope onto the Picatinny rail set atop the sniper rifle with deft movements, clicking it into place. He reached down and slid open the helicopter door on the retrofitted tracks as Grimaldi swung the helicopter out over the trees and around the bridge. Below them Bout had broken into a run toward the hovercraft, the briefcase with the cloned bioweapon sample in his hand.

The deckhands had immediately reversed their activities and unhooked their mooring lines while two of them scrambled across the metal deck toward weapon pods. The military hovercraft was a squat, ugly and utilitarian-looking monster with armor planking, powerful engines and bristling with the barrels of deadly weapons.

Grimaldi popped the helicopter straight up, clawing for altitude as twin .50-caliber machine guns opened up and red laser bolts of tracers cut through the night following the sweeping arc of a floodlight set atop the flying bridge.

Bolan squeezed off a round too soon as his platform jerked underneath him, and a heavy-caliber slug burned past the racing Bout's head and splintered an old rotted pylon. The Russian oligarch lunged toward the gangplank on the bank, shoving his bodyguard and driver out of his way.

The floodlight cut through the dark like a knife, trailing the twisting helicopter back and forth as Grimaldi attempted to dodge machine-gun fire and get into position to place his 6.8-inch rockets on target. Bolan thrust a foot out onto the landing skid and held on to the handle over his seat with his free hand.

He saw the front toe of the landing skid suddenly dent and crumple as a wild machine-gun bullet cut across it. He felt the vibration from the impact travel up his boot like a hammer blow. Grimaldi worked his flight pedals expertly and the tail rotor swung into position like a weathervane in a high wind.

There was a pause, then three rockets flew out of the pod beneath the nose and dropped toward the hovercraft below as it reversed away from the bank, sending waves of water spilling out around it.

The first rocket struck the old pier. There was a brilliant blinding flash and an explosion easily heard over the frantic working of the helicopter engine. Black smoke roiled up and water splashed higher than the hovercraft's bridge. The scene was obscured, and the next rockets flew like arrows into the writhing smoke.

Two more quick, hot flashes followed by the thumps of the impact detonations reached the Stony Man warriors. Grimaldi cut the helicopter up around the smoke screen and they saw the hovercraft surge down the river.

Victor Bout scrambled over the deck and into the safety of the hull cabin. Chunks of smoking armor were missing on the skirting of the SK5, but other than that the vehicle was unharmed and it began to skim down the river as its engines picked up speed.

Grimaldi slammed his fist into the control panel. "Goddamn it! They've got reactive armor," he cursed.

"We've got one shot," Bolan said, his tone grim. "Get in close and try to fire on the weapon positions. If we can knock those out, then we can get close enough for me to board and take the crew out."

"Oh, that's a great plan!" Grimaldi shouted over the racing helicopter engine and its pounding rotors.

"We've got nothing else!" Bolan replied, and the Stony Man pilot knew he was right.

The helicopter plunged downward, racing to catch up with the fleeing hovercraft. Below them the SK5's 40 mm grenade launcher began to open up. Sky bursts of black smoke and razor-sharp shrapnel punctuated by the deep bloops of the firing started to hammer the night sky. Their hellride began in earnest.

Grimaldi swung the chopper out wide then brought it sharply back in toward the river, cutting his altitude as he did so. The 40 mm explosion boomed out close enough for the concussion to rock the helicopter like punches, causing it to shudder under the impact and rocking the two men hard in their seats. Machine-gun fire crisscrossed the sky around them in curving arcs, forcing Grimaldi to fly too erratically for Bolan to bring his sniper rifle into play.

Up ahead they could see another ubiquitous series of river bends approaching, and Grimaldi cut the helicopter away from the river and across the intervening finger of land. He flared the rotors hard, turning the helicopter almost on its side as he changed direction.

He cut the nose around as they shot past the speeding hovercraft and dropped down between the trees on the edge of the river. He worked his yoke and lifted the tail, putting the nose down and surging forward just feet above the water.

Beside him Bolan leveled his rifle against the frame of the door and drew a bead through the crosshairs of his scope. His finger rested lightly on the curve of his trigger as he held the rifle level. Up ahead of them the SK5 burned around the turn in the river, kicking spray up behind it in rooster tails of surf.

"Gotcha," Bolan whispered.

He squeezed the trigger on his rifle just as Grimaldi's thumb found the fire select switch on his yoke.

CHAPTER TWENTY-SIX

Bolan's round sliced across the distance and he watched
the Plexiglas windshield shatter under his 7 mm round.
From fifty yards away the final three 6.8-inch rockets in
the weapon pod under the nose of the helicopter shot out,
contrails flaring through the night. The rockets were merciless and shot across the distance, striking the port machine-gun placement and 40 mm grenade launcher in a
brutal one-two fashion while the third hit the armor plat-
ing and was blown apart by the hovercraft's reactive
armor.

Bright orange fireballs rolled off the hovercraft and
out across the water as the SK5 suddenly turned and
began racing, apparently out of control, toward the steep
and rocky left bank of the wide river. Bodies and weapon
parts pinwheeled from the superstructure and fell into
the river.

The single remaining machine-gun emplacement
swiveled on the turret track, but Grimaldi had cut hard

in the opposite direction and now the vehicle's flying bridge was between them.

"Good job!" Bolan shouted. "Put me down on top."

As Grimaldi swung the agile helicopter around, Bolan placed his sniper rifle behind him and secured his Beretta 93-R. In the crammed space and close quarters on board the hovercraft the machine pistol would serve him in much better stead than a longer weapon.

Below them the careening hovercraft suddenly arrested its headlong race toward a collision with the riverbank and started back for the open water in the middle of the river. Grimaldi flew down toward the skimming watercraft, his face set in the same grim mask held by Bolan.

The Executioner pushed himself out onto the helicopter's landing skid. The wind off the river struck him and tore at his clothes, while below him the hovercraft grew in size as Grimaldi descended. The roof was a metal field of sensors, floodlights and conduit housings. Up close the impressive size of the SK5 struck him, it was like a small house on an inflatable platform.

Bolan pushed off the skid and let go. He hit the roof of the flying bridge wheelhouse and rolled, coming up with his Beretta ready for action. The hovercraft's big engines were screaming as it skimmed across the water at blinding speed.

The craft was racing so fast the frame was shaking beneath Bolan's feet as he struggled upward. He turned and made for the ladder at the rear of the roof in time to see a black-clad figure with a submachine gun crawling up the rungs. The mustached, Slavic-faced gunman snarled at Bolan and fought to bring his stuttergun into play.

Bolan beat the man to the draw, raising the Beretta in a single fluid motion and squeezing off a 3-round burst from the hip. Across the twelve-foot distance the effect of the Parabellum slugs was dramatic. The gunman's head snapped backward and the back of his skull erupted outward.

A shower of sparks exploded next to him and there was the ballistic whine of lead off steel as weapons fire burst from the lower skirt of the SK5. Bolan threw himself belly down. He saw a gunner coming up out of the machine-gun turret, a Russian M-4 submachine gun in his hand. The weapon belched again, and Bolan flinched back from the edge. He brought the muzzle of his pistol around and dropped the man, splattering blood across the deck like dark drops of rain.

Bolan got up on one knee and grasped the metal crossbars of the deck ladder with one hand. He scooted across the surface and flipped over the edge. His boots caught on the rung and he thundered down. As he was climbing, he saw the metal hatchway to the bridge swing open and someone emerge.

Reacting on instinct, Bolan let himself fall back to the end of his long-armed grip and swung his leg back and then forward. The toe of his boot met the man's face just as the Russian emerged from the doorway. There was a hard crunch as his jaw fractured and the man sailed back inside the hovercraft bridge cabin. Bolan hopped down, bringing his pistol to bear. He fired a 3-round burst through the open door to suppress any return fire and plunged through the entrance.

Behind him flames suddenly leaped in a fierce wall of brutal heat and he turned toward the new stimulus, perplexed as to its source. One of the rockets from Grimaldi's second barrage had ripped into a section near the port machine-gun turret where a previous round had stripped the reactive armor away. Metal had been torn and twisted like cloth, revealing the fuel pump and lines for the massive Herber-Volk propulsion system.

A sheet of flames had sprung up, blazing white as the highly combustible fuel burned at incredible temperatures. Bolan was close enough to the sudden, searing heat that the fine hair along the back of his hands singed and his skin stung with the intensity of the blaze. He realized the hovercraft was going to blow, and he had only moments to ensure the cloned bioweapons went up with it.

He swung back around as a second man charged through the doorway, Skorpion v.75 machine pistol chattering and bucking in his grip. Bolan felt the lead stingers cut past his face, and he fired the Beretta from his waist. The man folded over, caught low in the gut by his burst, and Bolan stroked the trigger again, drilling him through the crown of his head.

As the guy fell, Bolan lunged forward and leaped the leaking corpse into the room. The bulkhead of the bridge had blocked the wind, but the windshield shattered by his sniper round let a seeming hurricane of streaming wind into the compartment, forcing him to squint. He sensed movement in the spacious bridge and fired. A bearded man in a slouch hat went down, a Tokarev pistol falling from limp fingers.

Then Victor Bout shot Bolan.

The man's pistol roared, and Bolan felt the sting in his shoulder and an impact like a hammer blow. He staggered and a second round gouged out a path along his scalp just above his ear. His head snapped as if he'd been struck with a baseball bat.

Suddenly the burning fuel reached the injector in front of the main tanks and it exploded, causing the racing vehicle to lurch heavily to the starboard. Bout was thrown off balance and bounced off the steel bulkhead. He spun, and Bolan fired twice across the scant distance that separated them.

The bullets made flat, wet smacking sounds as they ripped into the oligarch's flesh, and crimson splashed from his wounds. The man's mouth worked and more blood poured across his lips and over his beard, staining his pale flesh and dark hair scarlet.

His finger spasmed around his trigger and at point-blank range his round struck Bolan dead-center of his combat vest. The big American grunted like a gut-punched boxer and doubled over. He squeezed the trigger on his Beretta for a third time and the gun shimmied in his hand.

The Parabellum rounds clawed into Bout, knocking him back. Gasping for breath, Bolan lifted himself up and fired again, pumping more bullets into the

Russian at intimate range. Bout gasped and more blood dribbled from his gaping mouth. His hand released his pistol and clawed ineffectually at Bolan's coat. The man crumpled at the knees and fell face-first to the deck.

Bolan watched him crumple, his eyes following him down. He spotted the sample case and reacted instantly as a wall of flame thrust through the open door. He kneed the dying Bout to one side and scooped up the case. Without remorse he spun and lunged toward the shattered window. Outside the hovercraft was careening toward the right bank of the river. At his back the flames were blistering in their intensity, and he felt the cloth of his clothes begin to smolder.

He was forced to drop the Beretta as he scratched for purchase on the navigational console. He hopped across the radio and radar displace and cut his knee open on broken glass. He lunged into the face of the wind and saw the rocky wall of the riverbank rushing toward him. He tore at the edge of the jagged windshield, scrambling for a grip and pushed himself up.

The explosion came rushing up behind him like a freight train rolling down the track. It punched him out the hole in the window and sent him spinning head over heels out across the armor skirting of the hovercraft.

Bolan hit the water at a hard angle and nearly blacked out at the impact. He felt the concussion of the exploding hovercraft as it raced away from him. The fireball shot white and blue flames into the sky, and pieces of burning metal began to rain down around him. Spilling fuel rolled across the river surface, making it burn like a hellish illustration from Dante's Inferno.

Suddenly, Bolan felt wind beating down and saw the water pushed out into a hollowed concave pool around him. He looked up, kicking hard to stay afloat, and saw Grimaldi lowering the helicopter down in a hover over his head.

He kicked hard and lunged up, getting his arm around the skid. Looking out, Grimaldi made sure Bolan had a good grip before gently pulling up and snatching him from the burning water before the flames could reach him.

The Stony Man pilot gently banked the helicopter toward the dirt road running alongside the river to set down. Bolan coughed and winced as his bruised flesh under his ballistic vest screamed in protest. He thought ribs might be broken, and there was the bitter taste of blood in his mouth where he'd accidentally bitten into his tongue somewhere along the line.

He looked over toward the fully engulfed wreck of the hovercraft where it had run aground burning like a Viking funeral pyre. The Croat run was finished.

TAKE 'EM FREE

2 action-packed novels plus a mystery bonus

NO RISK
NO OBLIGATION TO BUY

James Axler
Outlanders®

JANUS TRAP

Earth's last line of defense is invaded by a revitalized and reconfigured foe....

The Original Tribe, technological shamans with their own agenda of domination, challenged Cerberus once before and lost. Now their greatest assassin, Broken Ghost, has trapped the original Cerberus warriors in a matrix of unreality and altering protocols. As Broken Ghost destabilizes Earth's great defense force from within, the true warriors struggle to regain a foothold back to the only reality that offers survival....

Available August wherever books are sold.